Risky Business

'It's a well-known syndrome,' said Rebecca to her friend, Annie, 'that independent feisty women often long to be dominated, shamed even, as a release from the pressures of work.'

'But wouldn't you fancy it?' said Annie. 'Imagine a crowd of power-suited men, all gorgeous, all gathered around you in a secluded expensive house, all with their cocks out and playing with themselves. I'd like to go around each man in turn and tease them until they were panting with lust. Then I'd make them lick each other while I watched, purring like a contented cat.'

'I bet you would,' said Rebecca. It was three weeks since she'd had sex with Liam and her hunger for him was a constant torment. She used to share Annie's men-in-suits fantasy but things had changed since she'd met Liam. Now she had her own, very different fantasies, and her appetite for non-stop partying was vanishing as quickly as the champagne in her bloodstream. She'd found something much, much better.

Risky Business
Lisette Allen

Black Lace books contain sexual fantasies.
In real life, always practise safe sex.

This edition published in 2005 by
Black Lace
Thames Wharf Studios
Rainville Road
London W6 9HA

Originally published 1998

Printed and bound in Great Britain by Clays Ltd, St Ives PLC

ISBN 0 352 33280 8

The Random House Group Limited supports The Forest Stewardship
Council (FSC®), the leading international forest certification organisation.
Our books carrying the FSC label are printed on FSC® certified paper.
FSC is the only forest certification scheme endorsed by the leading
environmental organisations, including Greenpeace. Our
paper procurement policy can be found at
www.randomhouse.co.uk/environment

Chapter One

'Oh, well done, Rebecca.' The girl with the coppery mane of hair and big amber eyes leant her forehead reproachfully on the leather steering wheel as her expensive sports car stalled yet again. She straightened up and turned the ignition key sharply, then tried once more to wedge the open-topped car into the tiny parking space alongside the busy Islington pub. The sultry heat of the June evening seemed to envelop her, making her skimpy dress cling uncomfortably to her warm skin. A bunch of drinkers, mostly male, were lounging at the tables just outside the pub, making the most of the lingering sunshine. They turned to nudge one another and laughed openly at her efforts.

Rebecca wrestled anew with the short thick gear lever, trying not to hear their appreciative comments about her technique. At last, she managed to get the thing into reverse and squeeze it into the gap alongside the pavement, just a few yards from her amused spectators. Damn them, she thought. Ignoring them, she leant back, pushing her sleek hair away from her face, and made an effort to appear nonchalant.

It was almost ten o'clock, and she was terribly late for

1

the party, for Max. 'You must be there, Rebecca,' Max had told her down the phone last night. 'And wear something stunning. Look expensive. This guy is important to me, right? I need to make a good impression.'

Rebecca needed to make a good impression too, on Max. That was why she was so late. She'd suffered the usual last-minute panic over what to wear and, by the time she'd pulled up in the elegant north London street to which Max had given her such careful directions, the kerb outside the house had been lined with expensive cars, and the only space left had been outside the flower-festooned pub a little way down the road. So, getting hotter and wearier, Rebecca had manoeuvred her way into it.

Her eye-catching car was still attracting hot looks from the assorted male drinkers gathered outside the pub. She wondered fleetingly if it would still be there when she came back for it; and then she remembered that it was hardly hers anyway. She'd lost track of how many repayments she'd missed. Her bank manager had given up writing and had now resorted to ringing her, his voice growing increasingly stern. 'We seem to have a cash-flow problem here, Miss Lansdowne.'

Rebecca, resisting the temptation to reply, as her friend Annie would have done, 'Oh, dear. Have you really?' kept thinking up desperate excuses to put off the inevitable meeting with him. He wouldn't, she knew, be fobbed off for much longer.

But tonight, Thursday night, she'd forced herself into optimism, because the party beckoned. Time for fun, Rebecca, she told herself resolutely. Time to forget the awful last two months, during which her cosy and affluent world had fallen shatteringly apart. Time to prise Max away from his rich business associates, so that she could talk properly to him – that was, if she could keep her hands off his tantalising body for long enough to engage him in some serious conversation.

2

Conversation was something she and Max tended to neglect. They were usually too busy contemplating another frenzied sex session to waste much time on talking.

She felt hotter than ever at the thought, and her breasts tingled pleasurably in anticipation. She was wearing a dress she'd pinched from her friend Annie's chaotic but enticing wardrobe, since her own favourite clothes were at the dry cleaners'. She only just fitted into the tight little sheath of black silk that Annie had left dangling temptingly on its satin hanger. Rebecca was undoubtedly slim, thanks to a constant battle with the calories; but Annie, an ethereal, waiflike blonde whose delicate exterior hid a most determined appetite for fleshly pleasures, was barely a size ten, so the sleeveless number with its row of tiny silk-covered buttons down the front hugged Rebecca like a corset.

Rebecca was worried that Max, ever the perfectionist, might point out how it over-emphasised her feminine curves. But the dress certainly met with approval in this north London street. The flashily dressed Islington lads outside the pub, their keen eyes glittering with thoughts of sex instead of beer, had gathered closer, drinks in hand, to leer at her with open relish. And she knew why.

It was because she had to get out of the car.

The car was low. Her heels were high, for Max's benefit – Max loved her in sharp stilettos because they indicated, he said, a readiness for sex – and her skimpy dress was short and tight. Her long legs were covered with sheer smoky-dark stockings, and the lacy tops were barely covered by her hemline.

Resolutely, Rebecca pressed the button to close the hood. She felt a momentary pang of loss as she realised just how much she was going to miss this car. Then she ran her fingers through her hair, and checked her dark bronze lipstick and charcoal mascara hastily in the mirror. Taking a deep breath, she thrust the door open.

The air of expectation on the hot dusty street was almost palpable. Defiantly, she swung her legs out on to the pavement, then straightened up as quickly as she could, hurriedly pulling down her dress. All around her, the silence seemed absolute, except for the distant throb of music from inside the pub.

And she knew, she was sure, that the watching men had glimpsed a bare expanse of suntanned thigh above her lacy stocking-tops.

The silence broke suddenly. The colour rushed to her face as she heard lecherous whistles of approval, and an ironic outburst of clapping. Someone called out, 'Nice one, darling!' and she whipped her head round as soon as she'd pressed the remote-control lock, to glare at them with all the scorn she felt. They were ignorant, stupid.

But then one of the men, whom she'd not noticed before because he was leaning back in his chair a little way from the others with his hands clasped lazily behind his head, gave her a slow, secret grin; and Rebecca almost fell back against the car door.

He was gorgeous. Utterly, heart-poundingly gorgeous. He had tousled sun-streaked hair that was swept back casually from his face, and a narrow, wicked smile that was so openly erotic, she became hotter than ever. She had the sudden sensation that his glorious blue eyes, sleepy though they seemed, could see all of her, from the tips of her rosy nipples down to her mound beneath the skimpy black panties that were all she wore under the tight sheath of her dress. Prickly beads of moisture trickled beneath her breasts, between her buttocks, down to the satiny folds of her sex. Her eyes roved, horrified at her own fascination, over the blatant virility of the man's body.

He obviously wasn't with the others because, instead

4

of wearing sharply fashionable clothes like them, he was dressed simply, almost scruffily, in an open-necked white shirt and faded jeans. His muscular thighs were spread casually apart, emphasising a potent-looking mound at his groin that made her think instantly, help-lessly, of bed.

And he knew it, damn him. She tore herself away from his grin, her cheeks colouring, her head held high, and hurried to cross the road in her ridiculously strappy shoes. She was followed by a collective ripple of laugh-ter from her hormone-charged male audience. Oafs, she thought angrily. Idiots.

But she couldn't forget the face of the quiet one. The one who'd been watching her with smiling, narrowed blue eyes. Oh, God, he'd set her pulse racing sweetly, tormentingly.

She'd been aroused all evening in anticipation of meeting Max at the party. She'd soaked herself in an exquisitely scented bath, caressing her own nipples with dreamy restlessness. Afterwards, the first thing she'd put on had been the chunky gold bracelet Max had given her last Christmas. It made her feel like a slave, his slave. Then she'd pampered her skin with the lus-ciously perfumed body lotion she'd treated herself to, in defiance of her bank manager, and let her fingers touch softly between her thighs, aware that a tiny lascivious pulse was already thrumming at her loins.

Oh, yes, she'd been hot for Max all evening. And yet it was the fair-haired man outside the pub, with his tough, blatantly physical body and his sleepy smile, who had sent all her hormones into overdrive. In fact, Max was pushed from her mind completely as she found herself fantasising wildly that the stranger was coming after her, catching up with her with long pur-poseful strides as she tottered along on these ridicu-lously flimsy heels in what she hoped was the right direction. What would he do then? She caught her breath. He would swing her round, his strong fingers digging hard into her quivering buttocks. Then he would kiss her, his tongue probing deep, while he ground his blatant erection against her silk-clad stomach, just to let her know exactly what he intended.

Rebecca almost tripped over an uneven paving stone. Steady, she told herself warningly. You're late already. Concentrate. What had Max told her about the house? 'You can't miss it, Rebecca. Find the King's Head in Calham Street, and the house is further along on the opposite side of the road, a little beyond the row of white terraces. It's set back behind a high wall, rather imposing. We're talking serious money here, Rebecca.'

Max always talked serious money. He was a banker: rich, smooth and eligible. She'd been seeing him for almost eight months now, and the thought of his perfectly proportioned, exercise-honed body never ceased to send shivers of sensuous delight racing down her spine. Yet even as she slowly wandered past the elegantly stuccoed terraces Max had described, it was still the image of the fair-haired man smiling that slow, insolent smile that kept stimulating the aching little pulse of torment at her groin.

She must be going mad, she told herself a little weakly. It was all Annie's fault, and of course the fault of the game.

Rebecca and Annie had a secret game, a challenge. No matter how broke they were, they put ten pounds each, every week, into a kitsch blue sugar bowl in the kitchen of the little Kensington house they shared; and the one who could recount a really stunning erotic fantasy claimed the money. Annie had been the last one to win it, just over a fortnight ago, as they shared a bottle of wine Annie had pinched from the restaurant where she worked.

'Think of a gorgeous man working on a building site,' Annie had said dreamily, 'just like the one on the advert – you know? Well, in my fantasy, it's a glorious sunny afternoon, and everyone's lounging about, too hot to work. So, I go up to this man and put my hand on his bare arm, which is warm from the sun, and thick with muscles. I ask him, beg him, to fuck me there and then.'

'In front of everyone?' breathed Rebecca.

'Oh, yes!' Annie's face was serenely angelic. 'Don't you see, that's half the fun? I sidle up to him, and whisper in his ear. And all the other workmen would stop what they were doing, and passers-by gather round us to watch, as I kneel submissively at his feet. I undo his jeans and caress his thick, pulsing cock with my fingers and tongue – it's huge, so huge I can barely take it in my mouth.'

'How long?' interrupted Rebecca intently.

'Oh, eight, nine inches, at least.' Restrained, for Annie. 'And then,' the blonde girl went on eagerly, 'just when he's on the point of exploding, with all those people watching, I push him to his knees, and pull my skirt right up, above my hips. Then I lower myself astride him, and feel his lovely thick dick pounding into my juices, while everyone watches, breathless with jealousy . . .'

'You win,' Rebecca had said, pushing the sugar bowl towards her.

Annie nearly always won their fantasy pot. She had three key words relating to her ideal man's anatomy – long, thick and strong – and, once those basic requisites were satisfied, she told Rebecca seriously, anything – literally anything – could act as a stimulant to her wild imaginings. Rebecca just wished that her beautiful yet somehow vulnerable friend could find some man who would fulfil her dreams, instead of the selfish scumbags she usually seemed to end up with.

Rebecca had a strong suspicion that Max wanted to sleep with Annie. She'd once told him about their game, and now he questioned her about it persistently, lingering especially over Annie's more exotic stories. Max liked talking dirty: it got him hugely aroused.

She shivered just thinking about his lean body, his lovely penis, and reminded herself that she was going to see him very soon at the party. She also reminded herself, reluctantly, that she must try to stay cool and calm for as long as possible, because she had rather a lot to talk to Max about. In fact, she had rather a lot to ask him. The conversation, she feared, would be somewhat one-sided, because she needed to ask him for money.

Her heart beat fast with apprehension. She recognised the high brick wall Max had described, behind which stood the imposing house where the party was being held. This guy must be rich – in fact, hadn't Max told her so earlier? Climbing the stone steps that led to the forbidding gate, she tried rather desperately to remember what Max had told her about their host when they had met briefly for lunch, a couple of days ago. 'He's one of the success stories of the decade,' Max had said. 'Started off as a City whizz-kid, then saw how the market was going, and turned his attention towards environmental credibility – after all, that's where the strong money's going now. People are looking for ethical soundness in their investments. He launched his own development company earlier this year, to concentrate on enterprise projects that positively help the environment, and it's been a phenomenal success. Of course, Hugh can be relied on to keep his finger firmly on the pulse of all the latest growth areas. This party is a kind of thank-you for the people who've supported him.'

Rebecca was unimpressed. 'So the place will be full of people talking business. You really think I'll enjoy it, Max?'

He pulled her close, and let his mouth trail down her cheekbone. 'I'm sure you'll enjoy it,' he murmured. 'This

8

guy has a reputation for hard play as well as hard work. This party will be something to remember, believe me.'

The big gates set into the high wall were shut, and there was an entryphone. Rebecca hesitated, wishing Max could have brought her, but he'd said he would be pushed for time, and would have to come here straight from the office. Behind the wall, the sumptuous four-storeyed house twinkled with lights, and the air throbbed with some subtle jazz melody. It was still oppressively hot, and the lingering sunset was turning the white façade of the house into softest pink. Rebecca looked slowly back down the street. She could still see the pub in the distance, with the crowds round its pavement tables thinning out now. But she imagined that the man with blue eyes was still watching her, and she shivered suddenly, rebuking herself for her stupid fantasy.

Time to go inside. She was late enough already. Hoping fervently that Max was already here, because she wasn't sure that she would know anyone else, she pressed the entryphone button and suddenly realised that she couldn't even remember the name of the man whose house this was.

'Yes?' The voice crackling down the entryphone sounded forbidding. Security, of course: he must have his staff on the alert all the time at a place like this, even when there was a party. Especially, perhaps, when there was a party.

'I'm Rebecca,' she said desperately. 'Rebecca Lansdowne. I'm with Max Forrester.' She smoothed Annie's sleek black dress down over her hips, wishing she'd resisted diving into the box of Belgian chocolates that Annie had left lying temptingly in the sitting room. Silence. Then, to her huge relief, she heard the lock clicking, and the big gates swung open. She walked slowly up the wide steps as they closed again behind her, and caught her breath in wonder.

The front garden of the stuccoed house had been

turned into a miniature lamplit world of enchantment, filled with terracotta tubs of exotic flowers and glossy potted palms. A fountain shimmered delicately in the centre of a tiny pool, and throngs of fashionably dressed guests circulated languidly, sipping at the glasses of champagne and iced vodka that were being handed round by uniformed waiters. And there, thank God, were some people Rebecca knew: a magazine editor, and another friend who worked in a fashionable West End gallery.

Rebecca moved towards them with a smile on her face, feeling instantly at home in the privileged circle she'd been used to all her life. As people opened up to take her in their midst, it was as if nothing, nothing at all, had changed.

But the trouble was that everything had changed. She suddenly remembered the bank manager's stern voice on her phone that morning, and her legs felt weak. After a few moments with her friends, she began, somewhat apprehensively, to fight her way inside to find Max. Oh, please, Max, she prayed. Please understand.

Back down the road where her car was parked, the sun glinted with fading glory on the gaudy signs and bright petunia-filled windowboxes of the King's Head. The customers outside the pub had moved on, heading for the nightclubs and wine bars of Soho or Covent Garden. Only the man with the tousled blond hair and scruffy jeans was still sitting at one of the tables, on his own.

He drained the remnants of the half-pint of lager that had lasted him all evening, then got up slowly. He'd meant to move earlier, but the arrival of the girl in the sports car had delayed him a little, because of the diversion she'd caused: a diversion he himself had not been immune to. She'd looked cool and classy in that little black dress, with her sleek coppery hair and her exquisitely made-up face. Some rich man's plaything, no doubt. He'd met her kind before.

Letting a lazy smile play around his strongly chiselled mouth, he imagined kissing her until she was hot and feverish, her immaculate hair all rumpled, her mouth swollen. He would take her somewhere quiet, perhaps round the back of the pub, where the gathering darkness already cast long shadows. There he would gently ease her tight black dress up over her hips; and then he would free his erect penis from his jeans, and press her against the sun-warmed wall, feeling her sweet silky flesh as he slowly ravished her. She would utter little gasping cries of pleasure, quivering against him, clinging to his strong shoulders as he gazed down into her dazed, avid face. He would take his time as he brought her to the edge of ecstasy and beyond. He would tantalise her, tell her exactly what he had in mind for her; and she would love every moment. He knew, because he'd had plenty of experience of women of her kind: rich, spoilt, and utterly bored, whether they knew it or not, with the effete attentions of men of their own class.

Her eyes were amber, he'd noticed, a feline orangey-gold. They would blaze with fire as the convulsions of sex shook her body.

He grinned at his own imaginings self-mockingly. Sex was just a complication at the moment. He had other, far more important, things on his mind. Slowly he picked up his black leather jacket from the back of his chair, slinging it over his shoulder. Then he took one last look down the lamplit street where the girl had gone. So she was going to the party, too.

He still had a hint of a smile on his face as he made his way inside the smoky pub, walking with a distinctive loping stride that had female eyes watching him from every corner of the room. He paused on his way to the bar, his gaze resting on a girl who was sitting at

11

a table by herself, smoking nervously as she watched him. Her face was wide-eyed, vulnerable, framed by cropped dark hair that gleamed like velvet in the soft light of the bar. Several silver rings and studs ornamented her earlobes, and her mouth was painted a vivid red. Her skinny white lace top clung to her small conical breasts, hinting at a glimpse of prominent dark nipple. She wore jeans and thick-soled boots. One leg was hooked over the other, and she swung her foot with rhythmic impatience as she dragged on her cigarette.

The man came over to her. He said, 'I've told you, Cass. You shouldn't be here. I'll handle this by myself.'

Ignoring his mild rebuke, she said impatiently, 'You should be in there by now, Liam. We're running out of time.'

Liam said softly, 'I've been watching the house since eight. It's only just starting to fill up properly.' He spoke with a distinctive south London drawl.

The girl's eyes were haunted. 'If you leave it too long, you won't stand a chance. How will you know where to find what you want?'

'I know where to find it. I had information, remember? And by the time I get inside, they'll all be suitably distracted by the various entertainments on offer.'

'Out of their minds, you mean,' she snapped.

'Well, yes.' He smiled faintly. 'This host's not running a kids' tea party, you know.'

She shivered, hunching up her thin shoulders. 'I hate him. I hate them, all of them, all the stupid, rich, rapacious people he surrounds himself with.'

Liam put his strong brown hand over her small white one. 'He won't be so damned arrogant by this time tomorrow, Cass,' he said. 'You go back now, will you? No point in you waiting, too. I could be hours yet.'

She nodded abruptly, setting her silver earrings jangling, and stabbed out her half-finished cigarette. Her

12

huge kohl-rimmed eyes seemed dark and burning. 'OK, Liam,' she said at last. 'You know what's best.'

He was surprised and relieved that she gave in so quickly. Then she hesitated and said, 'You'll walk me down the street? Just to the corner, so I can see the tube station? I don't like it around here. It's not my sort of place.'

'I don't believe you're scared. Not you.'

'I'm not scared,' she said stiffly. 'I just feel alienated amongst all the rich bastards who live round here. Please. Come with me, just a little way.'

He looked at his watch. 'OK, but I can't be long.'

He should have guessed. It was dark outside when they got away from the bright doorway of the pub; and almost immediately she started drawing him into the warm sepia shadows of the little yard at the side of the building, where some narrow stone steps led down to the cellar. Wrapping her thin arms hungrily round his neck, she pulled his head down so she could kiss him. 'Oh, God, Liam. I want you to fuck me, so much. Please fuck me.'

His eyes were hard, icy splinters of blue. His hands remained at his sides. He said, 'Cass, I've told you. It's over.'

'I'm not asking for an engagement ring, for Christ's sake,' she muttered. 'I just want – this.'

She'd pulled up her stretch lace top to reveal her small jutting breasts with their stiffly aroused nipples. Her hands moved swiftly to his loins, struggling with the buttons of his jeans in the darkness; and Liam's shadowed face tightened imperceptibly as his penis, already stirring with life, grew swiftly into full erection. Cass fondled it hungrily, stroking its long silky thickness as it jutted from his groin, crooning to herself. Then she hitched herself quickly back on one of the wooden tables that had been dragged round there for the night. She pulled down her tight jeans to reveal naked loins;

13

then she spread her slim legs wide and started to play with herself, letting her finger slide fervently up and down beneath the thick bush of her dark pubic hair.

'Do it to me, Liam,' she muttered. 'You're ready, aren't you? You want me . . .'

The folds of her sex were wetly pink as she caressed herself, her eyes fastened desperately on his throbbing penis.

'It's fairly obvious,' he said quietly, 'that I want somebody.' But still he didn't move.

She leant forward with a little cry of longing and closed her mouth round his manhood, moistening its rigid length with her saliva. Then, sitting upright again, she gripped his narrow buttocks and guided him towards the apex of her thighs, taking his penis between her fingers and rubbing its velvety head longingly against her parted sex.

With a sigh of mingled resignation and surging desire, he drove himself deeply, strongly into her lush depths, and she clasped him to her, moaning and rubbing her nipples against his warm chest. 'Oh, God, Liam. Your cock is so strong, so lovely. Drive it into me, harder. Please.'

Her pale face was stark with ecstasy, her body trembling with liquid pleasure as Liam slowly and powerfully took her, his lengthy penis driving slickly between her splayed legs. She lifted her hips to him, whimpering with delight as her fierce orgasm flooded through her; and he drove harder, faster, spending himself with grinding thrusts that made the girl cry his name aloud.

Afterwards, when she had covered herself again, he looked down into her passion-hazed green eyes and said gently, 'I told you some time ago, Cass. It's over between the two of us.'

'Of course,' she said, moistening her swollen mouth with the tip of her pointed tongue. 'I'll find my own way back now, Liam. And you'll have to be making your move soon, won't you? Good luck. I'll see you later.'

She went quickly, heading for the tube station without a backward glance. Liam, frowning, went to sit once more outside the pub with a small scotch in his hand, taking care to place himself in the pool of darkness just beyond the light from the pub's windows. He gazed down the street, in the opposite direction Cass had taken, looking towards the big floodlit house where the girl in the sports car had gone, where the party was. Every window was lit up now, even at the very top of the house. Music thumped heavily down the street. Cars and taxis were pulling up in a steady stream outside the gate, blocking the road; laughing people were piling out, clambering up the steps from the pavement, clutching bottles of champagne and balancing against inebriated partners. He saw that the gate was, for the time being, wide open.

Time for him to move.

Rebecca had never felt less partyish in her life. She was with Max in a tiny bedroom at the very top of the house. Music drifted up faintly from downstairs, along with shrieks of merriment; but the atmosphere up here was at least ten degrees frostier. Max was lying on the big bed, naked except for a white linen sheet drawn across his loins. Rebecca was curled up at the other end of the bed watching him, her amber eyes lambent in the dark. She was dressed, but rumpled and tense.

'Sorry, Rebecca. For the last time, I just can't do it,' said Max matter-of-factly.

Rebecca felt a bitter stab of disappointment; resentment, too. 'Christ, Max. It's a business proposition, not a payout I'm asking for,' she said lightly. 'Buy the lease of our house off our grasping landlord, and Annie and I will pay you the rent. At least,' she added hastily, 'we will as soon as things settle down.'

15

'As soon as things settle down?' he queried with some acerbity, propping himself up on one elbow against the crisp white pillows. 'Rebecca. In case you've forgotten, your rich daddy's disappeared into the wide blue yonder, leaving a colossal amount of debts. How on earth are things going to settle down? Your family money's gone; your nice little monthly allowances to pay for the flat and the Porsche and the Harvey Nichols account have vanished into thin air. Your parents' house in Gloucestershire is on the market and, to make matters worse, the whole sordid affair has been scattered by gleeful journalists all over the tabloids. Sorry, darling. I can't fill a bottomless hole.'

'Look, Max,' said Rebecca desperately, 'I'm not expecting you to take on the whole family disaster. OK, so my father's done a runner with his secretary – sorry, PA – and left his business and personal finances in a hell of a mess. I acknowledge that. I just thought, seeing as we've been together for quite a while now, that you might be able to help out a little by purchasing the house.'

Max said, 'Perhaps you should try getting a job. Shouldn't be too difficult, with all your connections.'

'I've no qualifications, Max. And my connections, as you put it, tend to have melted away with the trouble my father's got himself into. Look, surely buying a lease in Kensington Place would be a good investment? You said last month that mews cottages like ours were all the rage. You're hardly going to lose money, are you?'

He looked thoughtful. 'It would certainly be interesting, acting as landlord to you and the raunchy Annie. I could claim my rent in unusual ways. I've always fancied you and Annie in bed together, playing with each other and a huge rubber vibrator. Shall I tell you what else I'd like? I might even win your fantasy competition.'

'Bastard,' said Rebecca shortly, nibbling at one long

16

red-painted nail. She was tense with disappointment, because he wasn't going to help her, and now she wished she hadn't asked him. Also, she was desperate for sex.

They'd scurried, laughing, up to this little bedroom soon after she arrived. Max had been watching for her just inside the front door, and he'd greeted her eagerly as she fought her way through the mass of guests towards him, drawing her into his arms and murmuring, 'Darling. I thought you weren't going to make it.' She'd felt all the usual tuggings of desire as she gazed up at him, loving the way his thick dark hair fell enticingly over his chiselled public-school features. They'd chatted lightly, having to shout above the din, and had a glass of iced champagne each, and kissed and danced a little as the music thumped out. But then Max had held her closely against his hard narrow body, running his well-manicured hands up and down her black silk sheath, muttering, 'God, you turn me on,' and Rebecca had felt the firmness of his erection pressing against her loins.

'I thought you wanted to network?' she'd murmured.

'I've networked.' He'd grinned. 'The host, Hugh Raoni, is a client of our bank – one of our most successful clients, in fact. I introduced him about half an hour ago to two beautiful but brainless nymphos from our accounts department. He's disappeared with them, for the time being anyway, and I imagine he's doing just the kind of things I want to do with you . . .' His tongue had stroked her sensitive earlobe, and Rebecca had been all but overwhelmed by the painful throb of physical need.

'Max. Please, let's go upstairs,' she'd whispered.

He'd elbowed his way through the crowds to the stairs, with Rebecca following closely, her lips swollen from his kiss, her nipples hard and aching. Once, Max had been stopped by a woman who began to talk to

17

him in a low voice, an immaculately-groomed blonde woman whom Rebecca had recognised as Janey Franklin, one of Max's high-flying banker colleagues. She'd heard that Janey Franklin was a man-eater. Rebecca had pushed her way closer to Max and caught his arm possessively, noticing how Janey was giving her a strange, almost mocking look. 'Come on, Max,' Rebecca had said flatly. 'Let's move on.'

He'd bent to kiss her, with Janey looking on, and Rebecca had felt her unease disappear. Max was a randy bastard, she knew, and she didn't think for one moment that he'd been entirely faithful to her all these months; but all the same, she was gloriously, hopelessly addicted to being seen around with him, to being in bed with him.

Giggling together, they'd found this dark, deserted little room at the top of the house, and bolted the door. Rebecca had slithered out of her dress, and had been just about to pull off her tiny panties. They had been wickedly tight against the pouting flesh of her heated sex, and her juices had been running in anticipation when Max, who'd already draped his expensive clothes with typical precision over the back of a chair, had stopped her.

'Stay like that,' he'd muttered hoarsely. 'And kiss me. Please.'

So he'd lain back on the bed, and Rebecca had climbed astride him, kneeling with her bottom to his face, so he could finger her panties as they rode high in her silky cleft, and caress the creamy flesh of her thighs just above her black stocking tops. Rebecca, shuddering with her own desire, had flicked out her tongue to lick at his taut belly, travelling along the line of soft black hairs that arrowed down to his groin until she reached his waving cock. She had taken the dusky shaft eagerly in her mouth and pleasured him until she'd felt him jerk and tighten beneath her.

'Oh, God, I'm nearly there,' he had called. 'Keep going, angel. I'm nearly there.'

Rebecca wished she was. Her panties were soaking with lust, and the silky fabric chafed painfully at her swollen clitoris. Max was certainly beautiful; he had a lovely long silky cock, and she adored playing with it, but he was basically lazy. It was always her making all the effort, while he just lay back and took what he arrogantly assumed was his due.

She tried desperately to clamp her yearning vulva against Max's caressing hand, so she could rub herself against him, like an animal on heat; but he ignored the hint, and instead he used both his hands to clutch fiercely at her bottom, and scratch with his finger at the outline of her anus through the silk of her panties, until she was aching with frustration. Then he went very still before starting to thrust his rigid penis hard into Rebecca's mouth. Then at last he was finished, and Rebecca lay back, hot, tense, unsatisfied.

She should have asked him before. Should have asked the bastard earlier about the house, with his cock hovering between her lips, and his balls tightening in readiness.

Too late now. She wasn't going to get any money, and she wasn't even going to get an orgasm, by the looks of it.

Well, she wasn't going to plead, for either item. 'I don't think Annie or myself would be into the idea of fucking our landlord for the rent,' she said rather slowly, pulling her unbuttoned dress closer across her breasts and crossing her arms in the darkness. 'Forget it, Max. I'm sorry I ever asked.' She could hear people on the stairs outside, stifling giggles, trying their locked door, desperate to find somewhere private. Max was watching her narrowly.

'Perhaps it's as well you did ask,' he said eventually. 'You see, I've been meaning to say this for a while. In

19

fact, ever since you told me that business about your father. Look, Rebecca, perhaps we should call it a day, you and I. Your father, all this mess he's left behind – I mean, it's not going to do my standing any good, is it? I have my reputation, my position in the firm to think of.'

She gazed at him in disbelief as the clichés poured from his beautiful sensually curved mouth. 'Max. Are you there, Max? It's me, Rebecca. I'm not my father. I hardly ever used to see my father, for heaven's sake – he was never at home! How can being seen with me affect you so badly? Who do you work with who's so damned holy they can turn and point the finger at my father? What about the man who owns this house, this Hugh Raoni, the one you're so anxious to impress, who's already got himself fixed up with two blonde tarts for the night? Surely you can't be worried about *his* opinion, Max?'

Max leant back against the pillows. He'd raised one knee, so the sheet had fallen back from his hips and his long muscular legs. His sleek greyhound body was still tanned from the holiday they'd spent earlier that year at a friend's house in the Caribbean. Oh, God, thought Rebecca with a pang, she could still remember rubbing the suntan oil along his flat belly as they lay together on the silvery wave-lapped beach; could remember, so vividly, slipping her fingers under his swimming briefs and rubbing gently at his sizzling erection . . .

They'd had sex then, lying facing one another on the beach mat, a towel draped across their hips their only privacy. Rebecca had been so wet, so ready for him, that she'd come almost as soon as his penis had penetrated her.

She dragged herself back to the rather less palatable present. To make matters worse, his cock was stirring again now, thickening with blatant life as Max, the bastard, continued to stare with lazy interest at her naked breasts. Rebecca felt her vagina clench hungrily. How she longed to crouch over him, to pin him down with her body, to spread her thighs and guide his stiffening cock into her slippery silken sex. But she didn't move.

Max was running his hand through his exquisitely cut locks of dark hair. 'Look, Rebecca,' he was drawling, 'let's be mature about this, shall we? Hugh Raoni's a law unto himself; he works hard and plays hard. Ten minutes after shagging, he'll be out there driving another business deal. I've enormous respect for him, and I really have to take on board the fact that he suggested that you and I have a cooling-off period –'

Rebecca went very still. 'Hugh Raoni told you to finish with me? Why? What business is it of his?'

'I told him who I was bringing to this party, and naturally he recognised your name, put two and two together, and realised it's your father who's been at the centre of such a lot of financial scandal lately. He told me it wouldn't do my career much good, being seen around with you, and of course he's right. I do understand your disappointment about us. But really, as I say, I've got my position to consider.'

Rebecca drew back slowly. 'You've got someone else. Haven't you?'

He didn't even flinch. 'Why,' he said. 'How perceptive of you. As a matter of fact, I have.'

'Janey Franklin,' said Rebecca.

He had the grace to look a little embarrassed at the swiftness of her guess. 'Well, yes. It's an open-ended thing, of course, but the truth is that Janey and I are great in bed together.'

'She's great in bed because she's had so much practice, according to what I've heard.'

'Jealous, Rebecca? At least she knows how to keep a man guessing. The trouble with you is that you're too eager, too greedy for sex. You need to develop a little more subtlety . . .'

Rebecca felt the hot waves of anger engulf her. 'You bastard,' she muttered, 'you bastard,' and she picked up his neatly folded, expensive clothes and flung them at him, one by one, in a quiet, rhythmic frenzy.

He held his hands out to protect himself. 'Cool it, Rebecca, can't you? This is another of your problems. Sometimes you're so lacking in sophistication.'

'Am I really?' She broke off to catch her breath, her amber eyes ablaze with rage, her hair a fiery halo in the glow of the streetlamp outside the window. 'Anything else, Max? So I'm too eager for sex, and I lack sophistication. You tell me I need to lose weight, and you're not too happy with my face, either, judging by the way you'd rather make love to my arse. Well, let me tell you this. It seems to me that the only thing I lack is a brain, going out with you for so long,' and with that, she fastened up the buttons of her dress, and struggled into her ridiculous strappy shoes.

'You'll get another asthma attack,' he said calmly from the bed, 'if you carry on getting so uptight.'

'Oh, no,' she breathed. 'You're not worth that, Max.' And she stormed out of the room, slamming the door behind her.

It was close on midnight, and the house was packed to the limits with people talking, laughing, dancing. Half-full glasses of champagne, plates of nibbled-at canapés, discarded handbags and expensive jackets littered every available surface. Cigarette smoke hung in the air, mingling with the latest designer perfumes. And a number of guests had seized on the vast anonymity of the luxurious house to engage in more furtive activity, like Rebecca and Max. All the bedrooms had quickly been occupied, and in the dark recesses of an upper landing the shadows heaved as a couple twined together.

Rebecca paused on the galleried landing and thought, briefly, of finding her host and telling him just what she thought of him. How dare he tell Max that she wasn't suitable for him any more, just because of her father? Hugh Raoni must be a conceited, arse-licking scumbag, just like Max Forrester. Then she reflected sadly that, even if she did confront the mega-rich Raoni, he would just laugh at her. After all, he could afford to laugh at the whole world since his company had been launched to such acclaim on the stock market. Hadn't Max told her that was what this party was all about? 'Hugh has his finger firmly on the pulse of all the latest growth areas . . .'

Hugh Raoni would steer well clear, then, of the notorious shrinkage areas surrounding her aching heart and her black-hole bank balance. She gazed down rather hopelessly at the crowded reception hall below, where people were dancing. She was naggingly aware that her only priority now was to find a loo, so she could relieve her uncomfortably full bladder before she slunk off home.

Then something strange happened. She thought, just for a moment, that she glimpsed among the swirling crowds below the figure of the man who'd been outside the pub, the blond man in scruffy jeans. Her heart stopped, and she leant over the banister rail that stretched the length of the galleried landing, striving desperately for a glimpse of his lean, lust-inducing face again.

No sign. The party guests shifted and moved in a frenetic haze of laughter, dance and gossip. Of course he wasn't there. He couldn't be. She was just stupidly, childishly obsessed with the man outside the pub, that was the trouble, and the sooner she forgot about him the better. It seemed as if tonight men and sex were disaster areas for her, and she would be as well cutting her losses and making back for the relative safety of the little house she shared with Annie.

First, though, the loo. She found an unlocked bathroom on the second-floor landing, and thrust open the gaping door. Then she stopped in disbelief. A woman was already occupying the darkened room; she wasn't on the toilet, but on her feet, and she was leaning breathlessly back against the oak-panelled wall as a man humped her energetically.

The woman was Janey Franklin.

Neither of them saw Rebecca. Both of them were still dressed, but Janey's skirt was up round her waist, and the man's trousers were round his knees. He was small, squat, and balding; but his penis, which protruded rather grotesquely from beneath his loose shirt, was quite startlingly long and thick. His hands grasped Janey's, holding them back against the wall on either side of her body, while his reddened cock pounded in and out between the softly swollen lips of Janey's sex. His face was red, too, and glazed with effort; Rebecca recognised him now as some minor newspaper columnist. Janey whimpered and moaned as he withdrew, his penis shiny with her juices, and Rebecca watched, openmouthed, as Janey grabbed his white buttocks and pulled him into her again, grinding herself against him. The man kissed her hard, muttering, 'Oh, God, Janey.' His hands fought for access to her heavy breasts, pulling her ivory silk blouse apart, twisting and teasing at her long coral nipples where they thrust out over the halfcups of her lacy bra.

Janey was flushed, in the throes of orgasm, as the man's stalwart cock thrust in and out of her quivering flesh. And still, neither of them had noticed Rebecca.

Rebecca moved silently backwards, her hand poised on the heavy oak-panelled door. Then she said, in a clear, cheerful voice, 'Hi, Janey. Max is looking for you. I'll just go and tell him you're in here, shall I?'

She just had time to see Janey's face jerking towards her with an expression of horror. Then Rebecca fled, feeling a little better, but not much. In fact, by the time she'd found an empty loo at the back of the house, and had fought her way out through the front door into the warm Islington night, her heart was aching with mortification and hurt pride.

What a snake Max was. He was a useless lay anyway, she told herself angrily as she set out towards her car. Just wait till the energetic Janey Franklin found out exactly how much of her precious, highly-paid time she would have to spend on pampering Max's stupid vanity, and his egocentric cock.

But she was going to miss him.

Her strappy shoes were growing uncomfortable. The pub where her car was parked, down at the end of the street, suddenly seemed a long way away. A sickly moon hovered above the dull glow of the streetlamps, and the hypnotic thump of party music followed her mockingly down the road.

Although it was nearly midnight, it was still suffocatingly hot. Rebecca forced herself to breathe slowly and deeply, remembering Max's cheap jibe about her asthma. She hardly ever got an attack these days, but even so she was always wary of the warning signs. At least the heat meant it didn't matter that she was only dressed in this thin sleeveless sheath of a dress. But the shoes were a disaster.

In a moment of impulse, Rebecca pulled them off and tramped on down the warm dusty pavement in her stockinged feet, feeling the thigh-high ladders zinging enthusiastically at every step. A young couple walking arm-in-arm down the other side of the street turned to stare at her scantily-clad figure with open-mouthed curiosity. Rebecca glared back at them and hurried on. Oh, to get snugly behind the wheel of her beloved car; to head for home, and share a huge glass of soothing white wine with the sympathetic Annie, and tell her friend all about what a snake Max was, an utter, lousy snake.

She reached the pub at last. It was all shuttered up and dark, with the chairs and tables dragged round the back. Rebecca headed towards her car like a ship-wrecked sailor making for dry land. She thought she heard the far-off sound of raised voices, somewhere back along the street she'd just walked down; but by then she'd unlocked her car, and was inside, sinking with relish into the firm leather upholstery. With a sigh of relief, she slung her ridiculous shoes and tiny designer bag into the back, and turned the ignition with a loving caress. The engine purred into powerful life.

Then things happened quickly. Just as she was about to ease the car away, she heard the sound of someone running hard along the pavement behind her. The next thing she knew, the passenger door had been wrenched open, and a man was leaping in: a man with tousled, sun-bleached hair, wearing faded denims and a scruffy leather jacket. As the amber streetlights cast vivid shadows across his face, Rebecca stared at him in disbelief.

He was the man who'd been lounging outside this very pub, hours ago in the warm evening sunshine, smiling sleepily at her with his gorgeous navy-blue eyes and setting her pulses racing with erotic conjecture. He was the man she thought she'd seen at the party, only to dismiss her observation as some fantastic mirage.

One thing was certain. He wasn't smiling now. As he slammed the passenger door shut, he turned to confront her, and Rebecca saw that those eyes that had been like chips of dark-blue sky were now as chilling as freshly sharpened knives. His strong hands were purposefully clasped round a mahogany leather document case, which he rested tensely on his muscular thighs.

'Drive,' he said harshly to Rebecca. 'For God's sake, put this thing into gear and get moving.'

His voice was flat, hard: unmistakably south London. She moistened painfully dry lips. 'What's happening? What do you want?'

She suddenly heard more pounding footsteps in the distance, coming towards them; she thought she heard someone shouting.

The man gripped the steering wheel. 'I've just told you. Get the hell out of here, will you? Drive. Now.'

Chapter Two

Somehow Rebecca got the car moving. Her legs were shaking on the pedals, and her hands, with their frivolously red-painted nails, seemed to be fighting with the steering wheel. There were people after him, people chasing him. Were they people from the party? Why? What had he done?

She let the car slide to a halt as they came to a road junction. Her heart pounded with tension. The man grated out, 'Straight on, then right at the next turning. Take the centre lane. Next right, now. Now, I said, damn you.'

She knew he might be armed. His aggressive thigh, tightly clad in well-worn denim, intruded constantly into the corner of her vision as she drove, reminding her of his implacable, silently threatening masculinity. When she was forced to stop the car at traffic lights, her movements were jerky, and she stalled the engine.

'Start it again,' he said. 'Quickly.'

Her fingers fumbled numbly for the key; the oppressive silence inside the car seemed to force her into speech. 'You were at that party, weren't you?' she whispered.

He was silent for a moment. Then, when he spoke, she wished he hadn't. He said, 'Look. If you ask me questions, and I answer them, then I won't be able to let you go. Do you understand?'

She felt sick with fear; the ignition key was frozen in her hand. 'Then let me go now, before I find out anything else. I won't tell anyone about what's happened. I promise I won't.'

He laughed at that. 'What,' he mocked, 'and let you run to the police, and get them straight on my tail? I'm afraid not, sweetheart. Get the car moving again, will you?'

The lights had changed to green without her noticing; a driver had pulled up behind them, and was hooting angrily. Rebecca drove jerkily away from the lights, openly shivering now in her little black dress. The heavy gold bracelet Max had given her felt like a manacle around her wrist. She drove with agonised concentration, trying her hardest to follow the man's curt instructions, because for the moment she didn't know what else she could do. She'd lost her bearings long ago; the man was ordering her through narrow dark streets she didn't recognise at all. But she guessed, with some kind of wild intuition, that they were heading south towards the river.

Once, while passing through a busier area, they had to stop beside an all-night grocery store, to give way to traffic. Rebecca gazed at the open doors behind which people – ordinary, everyday people – were doing their shopping in a state of tedious normality. Oh, God, she thought, would they help her? If she called out, tried to run from the car, would any of them help her?

The man's voice broke chillingly into her thoughts. 'You won't try to do anything stupid, will you?' he said.

Rebecca caught her breath as her turn came to ease the car forward into the late-night traffic. 'Any suggestions?' she said sharply. 'Jumping out and running, perhaps?'

He probably had a knife, or even a gun. She'd already confronted, and accepted, that possibility. And he didn't even reply to her challenge because, just as she was concentrating on joining the fast-moving stream of traffic, he was twisting round sharply to look behind him; not the first time he'd done that, she realised. And then he snapped out, 'They're still after us.'

The police? Hope flared wildly in Rebecca's heart: an unspoken hope that was instantly crushed as he went on, 'Not the police. Oh, no. Nothing as simple as that. And I thought we'd lost them . . . So it's time for you to show me what this expensive little car can do. Take the next right, after that church. Quickly, damn you.'

Rebecca's heart hammered so madly she thought it would burst. He was turning round again in his seat to scan the street behind them. She thought she heard the faint squeal of tyres; and then a pair of fast-approaching headlights on full beam dazzled her rear view mirror.

'Left,' he ordered, 'now,' and his hands were wrenching the wheel in her grip, taking the car hurtling round a corner. Then he snapped off the car's lights, so she was driving by streetlight alone, past silent factories and car yards, and rows of small terraced houses where people slept behind closed curtains. Again and again he directed her left, or right, tersely urging her to keep up the speed as the low-slung car twisted and turned down seemingly impenetrable lanes and alleys. A dream, a nightmare. In spite of herself, Rebecca felt the adrenalin fizzing through her veins.

He reached out to put on the headlights again. 'You can slow down a little. I think we've lost them.'

Dear God. He sounded as if he was expecting her to be pleased. Rebecca was driving now with a huge effort, every gear change requiring enormous concentration.

She realised suddenly that she couldn't carry on like this for much longer.

The street signs she glimpsed told her they were heading east, along the line of the river. She felt as if she could almost sense the wide, silent expanse of the Thames. She kept expecting to see the dark water; but in the end it was a dead end, a cul-de-sac that he guided her into, lined with builders' skips and piles of bricks. He touched the wheel almost gently. 'We're here,' he said. 'Time to get out.'

She pulled in by the pavement. Then she turned the engine off and sat there, her hands still clasping the wheel, her head bowed. He climbed out with the brief-case in one hand and walked round to open her door, taking her by the arm. 'I said, time to get out. I'm afraid that includes you.'

She pushed at his hand in revulsion. 'You're hurting me,' she said, her eyes filling suddenly with tears of despair. 'You're hurting me.'

'I'm sorry. But those guys who were following us back there would have hurt you a lot more.'

'You expect me to believe that?' she said scornfully.

She scrambled out of the car, shrugging off his offer of help, and stood there in the warm night air, bare-footed, her arms folded defensively across her chest. She felt fear tightening her spine anew as his dark blue gaze ran slowly from her head to her toe, taking in her dishevelled hair, her skimpy thigh-high dress and lad-dered black stockings.

'Believe what you like,' he said. 'It doesn't really make a lot of difference, does it?'

Rebecca shivered. So there really had been people after them, hurtling through the darkened back streets of London at breakneck speed. What had he done at that party? What had he taken, who had he offended? Oh, God, this was a nightmare – worse than a nightmare.

Her captor had gone to the nearest front door, and was knocking at it softly but insistently. Rebecca, looking around her, saw that she was in a street of freshly refurbished warehouses, no doubt in the process of some fashionable conversion into apartments, especially if they were in the vicinity of the river. The builders hadn't finished. Dusty cement-mixers were surrounded by piles of plastic-covered breeze blocks, and some parts of the street were cordoned off. She thought briefly of running, of screaming for help; but it didn't look as if there was anyone here to listen to her.

Yet the man was still knocking at the door, as if he expected a reply. And at last, very cautiously, it opened.

A man stood in the softly lit doorway, clad in T-shirt and jeans. He had a gentle face and long wavy brown hair. 'Liam,' he said, his face lighting up. 'We thought perhaps you weren't going to make it.'

'For a while, so did I,' replied Rebecca's captor curtly. 'Look, Stevie, get this car into the garage, will you? And make sure you lock up.'

The man's eyes widened as he took in the car. 'Nice motor,' he said. Then he saw Rebecca, standing there a little behind Liam, and his eyes widened still further.

Liam said, 'Just take it, Stevie, will you?'

Rebecca stepped forward in protest. 'My car. My handbag, my shoes – I need my shoes . . .' But Liam was hustling her inside, and when he'd shut the door firmly behind them, he turned to look at her stockinged feet with scorn.

'Those shoes were no good for anything anyway. Except perhaps the bedroom,' he said, in that slow voice that licked so brutally at her senses.

Rebecca felt the hot colour staining her cheeks. 'Don't even dare to think about it,' she breathed.

He laughed, but his blue eyes were cold. 'Don't get excited,' he said. 'I couldn't fancy you at the moment if you were in high heels, a leather corset, and strapped to the bed panting for me. Now, get up those stairs, will you?'

She stood there, her hands clenched in painful tightness at her sides, hating him. 'No,' she said. 'No, you won't speak to me like that. Someone like you. You can't speak to me like that.'

'OK,' he said. 'I won't say another word. But if you don't get up those stairs, now, I'll lift you up and carry you.'

She followed him then, up the stairs, shaking with anger and helplessness.

The first two floors seemed unoccupied; the stairs were bare wood, the doors blank. But as they reached the second floor, he opened an unlocked door into a wide carpeted lobby, and the glare of lights met her eyes. In one of the rooms that led off the lobby, she glimpsed a girl with cropped dark hair and silver earrings sitting over a word processor. A slim, brown-skinned man with a glossy black ponytail sat on the desk, reading something to her as she typed. There were stacks of papers lying around on the floor, and maps pinned to the wall. They both saw Liam at the same time, and Rebecca saw how their faces registered surprise, and pleasure. The man came hurrying towards them and said, 'You've got them, Liam? You've got the papers?'

'I've got them,' Liam said softly, lifting the slim document case into prominence.

The other man's face lit up. 'We've nailed him, then. We've done it.'

For the first time since it had all started, Rebecca, standing alone and unnoticed in the shadows, saw the man called Liam smile.

Then she saw that the dark-haired girl had got up from the word processor and was coming slowly towards them. Her eyes seemed wide and haunted. 'You're late, Liam. We were getting worried.'

'Things went a little wrong. It took me longer than I thought. And then he sent some of his security stooges after me.'

'Oh, Liam –'

'But it's OK. I got away. As you see.'

Rebecca tried to run then. She was edging back towards the staircase all the time; and just as Liam spoke, she turned swiftly, intending to race down the stairs towards the door. But he was on her in seconds, as if he'd anticipated her every move. Rebecca could have wept with the futility of it, as his strong hand fastened round her wrist and he hauled her close to the unsettling warmth of his body.

'Let me go. Let me go, damn you –' She was almost crying with weariness and tension.

'I've told you.' He swung her forcefully round towards him, and his blue eyes burned into her. 'I can't let you go. You're only making things worse for yourself.'

The man with the ponytail was watching them with an anxious frown. 'Is she all right, Liam?' he said, in his soft, slightly foreign voice. 'She doesn't look like one of us.'

'She isn't. She's my reluctant driver. She's cold, and she's tired. Unfortunately, she'll have to stay with us, just for a while, even though it may hurt her aristocratic sensibilities. I need to talk to her. See that we're not disturbed, Petro, will you?'

'Sure, Liam.' Petro's expression was worried as he took one last look at Rebecca, still trapped in Liam's lethal grip. But Rebecca saw that the girl with cropped dark hair, who wore a tiny white lace top and tight jeans, was staring at her coldly, just as Janey had done.

Liam led her up one more flight of stairs. He let go of her wrist, apparently quite confident that she would know better now than to try and run. He walked to the end of a long uncarpeted landing and then he stopped at the foot of a spiral staircase.

He waited for her with one hand on the railing, and his blue eyes were dark, unfathomable. 'You're all right?'

His casual enquiry enraged her. 'Oh, yes. Of course. What do you think? How do you think I feel about being here, with you? You're a thief, aren't you? You stole something from that house this evening. Either that, or you messed someone up on some sort of deal, and that's why those people were after you. You're nothing but a criminal.'

'You've got it wrong,' he said.

'Then tell me. Tell me what's going on, will you?'

'I've told you,' he said, 'that the less you know, the better. Are you going to stand there all night? I need you up these stairs.'

The metal steps were hard and cold on her stockinged feet. As she climbed the last of them, gripping the handrail tightly, she saw that the spiral staircase opened into a huge stunning room. Lime-waxed floorboards stretched for forty, fifty feet, the whole length of the building; and four full-length windows looked out on to the dark gleaming magic of the river Thames. Rebecca caught her breath at the view; she'd been right about the river, though much good would her guess do her.

There was furniture here in plenty, though it seemed lost in the vastness of the room. There were richly coloured ethnic rugs, squashy cream sofas, chunky black rattan tables covered with papers and magazines, and a patchwork-draped bed in one corner. A guitar rested against the wall by the fireplace. There were no electric lights, but Rebecca saw that several big wrought-iron candlesticks took their place along the walls. Only some of them were lit, probably because the room glowed softly already with the reflection of the city's lights from the river's black-mirrored surface down below.

35

She'd once been to a party at the Docklands *pied-à-terre* of a rich designer friend of Annie's. This apartment dwarfed it. Some place he had here, in spite of his rough image. Whatever his activities were, they were profitable.

He'd moved towards the candlelight, and was opening up the briefcase he still held, leafing through the papers inside it. She stayed very still, but her eyes flashed round the room for another door, another exit.

There wasn't one. There was only one way out, back down those stairs, and she knew she would never make it.

Suddenly, she heard the sound of a powerful car, approaching fast through the silence of the night. Liam dropped the briefcase and made quickly for the window, his powerful body rigid with tension. Rebecca felt her own pulse pounding thickly with fear, felt her breath catch in her throat. 'I thought you said they weren't following you any more.'

He said tersely, 'Half of London might be after me by now. Stay here. I'm just going down to check that all the lights are turned off.'

As if there was anywhere she could go, Rebecca thought feverishly, her hand to her throat. By the time she heard his footsteps hurrying down the steps into the distance, her breathing was becoming short and laboured. A sudden, more familiar fear started to trickle like icy water down her spine. Oh, God, no. Don't let it happen here. Please.

As her lungs started to tighten, she plunged instinctively towards the windows, to see if she could open them, to get some air. She saw the arrowing beams of a car's headlights slashing through the darkness of the street below, heard the menacing purr of its motor cut abruptly short as the vehicle pulled up. Car doors slammed; then she heard several pairs of footsteps running up and down the street, rattling on doors, trying locked garages. The figures were ill-defined, shadowy, and far, far below her. She tried desperately to work at the window catch; but suddenly she heard Liam coming up behind her, and he was pulling her roughly away from the window, his strong hand clamped purposefully across her mouth.

'Don't even think about it,' he said, and she gasped for breath as his big palm closed her airways. 'You were going to call out to them, weren't you? Don't you realise you're in as much danger from them as the rest of us?'

'I wasn't,' she choked out as he pressed her relentlessly against his warm hard body. 'You don't understand. I wasn't going to call . . .'

By the time the car had roared away down the street, and he'd relaxed his grip on her, her breath was wheezing in her throat. He cupped her face with his hand, lifting it up to him. 'Dear Christ,' he said. 'Asthma?'

'Yes.' She nodded, her hand to her throat, as the whistling started in her blocked bronchial passages. 'Yes, damn you . . .'

'You've got an inhaler?'

'In – in my bag. Back of car . . .'

He was down the stairs, and back again in what seemed like less than a minute, diving through her tiny cluttered bag and holding the small plastic case of her inhaler out to her in silence. She grabbed it and clutched it to her mouth, closing her eyes as the blessed relief came slowly, oh so slowly, to her restricted airways.

He was watching her, his blue eyes dark, waiting till he could see the tension leaving her body. The shadows cast up from the gleaming expanse of river below the windows flickered across the room, across his face.

'You're all right, Rebecca?' he said.

'Yes. No thanks to you.' Her voice was still tight and aching.

He shook his head. 'I told you. I had no choice.'

'No,' she responded bitterly. 'I suppose all criminals

say that, don't they?' She had lifted her head now, and was running her hands through her hair, her eyes half-closed as she let her lungs fill with searing air. Then her eyes snapped wide open. 'How did you know my name?'

'It was on your inhaler.' He was moving closer to her again. 'Sit down, Rebecca. You're shivering with cold and shock.' He was pushing her almost gently towards one of the settees. She sat down right on the edge. He shrugged his leather jacket off and wrapped it quickly round her shoulders; as he did so, his fingers brushed the bare flesh of her arm, and she leapt as if he'd burnt her.

He assumed she was afraid of him. She was, of course; but there was also some emotion much darker, much more frightening than that.

He said, 'Believe me, if I could explain, I would.'

'But you can't, can you? You're a thief. You were in that house, taking something that didn't belong to you. I don't want to know any more. Just let me go, for God's sake.'

'I can't do that, either. Not till the morning. You've got to stay here, with me.'

She hunched herself in his jacket, in despair, and twined her red-painted fingernails together. 'So what are we going to do all night? Count bloody sheep?'

The minute the words were out of her mouth, she regretted them. He was looking at her silently, his blue eyes very dark, and her pulse leapt and raced at that look. It burnt her, because it was full of silent, rigidly controlled male desire.

Oh, God, she thought, in utter anguish, make him stop doing this to me. I hate him, and yet just looking at him makes me think of long, slow, achingly mean sex. That face, that cruel, beautiful mouth. And his body – lean, power-packed, made for unspeakable pleasures.

'You shouldn't swear, Rebecca,' he said softly at last.

'It really doesn't suit you. Anyway, what do you normally do all night?'

Even his hard south London voice ravished her, making all her pleasure points pound. 'I sleep, of course,' she snapped back.

He grinned, relaxing at last, and started walking slowly towards her. She was mesmerised by the glimpse of work-hardened muscle sliding and tensing beneath his thin shirt as he moved. He stopped. For a moment, she thought he was going to kiss her. She imagined the feel of his hard warm lips on her mouth, on her breasts, and other places that made her almost shake with impossible desire.

Christ, she was mad to react like this. He was hateful, hateful. She longed for him to show some male weakness, to make some crude, arrogant advance on her, so she could tell him exactly where he belonged, with his rough, cheap clothes and his uneducated voice and his scruffy long hair. In the gutter.

He raised his hand, and she felt herself tremble in anticipation. The smile was still on his lips as he used that same hand to point casually at the bed in the corner. And he knocked all possible insults from her mind as he said, 'Sleep, then.'

The silence that followed was broken by footsteps on the staircase leading up to the room. A voice – Petro's voice – called out, 'Liam. The phone for you. I think it's important.'

The man Liam nodded, and turned quickly towards the steps. Rebecca, her throat dry, called out quickly, 'Where are you going?'

He turned. 'I have things to do. People to speak to. But I'll be back. And the door downstairs will be locked all night.'

With that, he left her. She heard his footsteps echoing more and more faintly as he made his way downstairs to answer the phone. Rebecca sat there alone, hunched up in the darkness in his leather jacket, her mind and body turbulent. She gazed out through the huge windows at the glimmering pewter surface of the river far below. 'Don't you realise you're in as much danger from them as the rest of us?' he'd warned, almost shaking her.

From them? From who? From someone at the party? From the men who'd followed them?

Suddenly she remembered that the slim document case he'd clutched so tightly to his chest during their nightmare race through London was still lying on a small table near the fireplace. He'd thrust it down when he'd heard the car racing along the street outside. Surely the answer to at least some of her questions would be in there. Quickly, because she knew that he might come back up the stairs at any moment, she crossed the room to the table and opened it.

And she realised that whatever else she had expected – photos, drugs, money even – it wasn't this.

The document case contained some kind of company accounts: neat, boring, and official. She frowned, running her eyes down the dates and figures. There didn't seem to be much scope for criminal activity here. Perhaps Max, with his sharp financial brain, would be able to decipher it all; she certainly couldn't.

Remembering Max made her feel lonely and frightened. Thinking she heard the sound of someone moving about downstairs, she pulled out one of the sheets on impulse and folded it hurriedly into her little bag. Then she curled up on the settee by the window again, her mind spinning with confusion, a confusion compounded by weariness. What was going on? What was so important about these papers? She thought rather wildly of blackmail, of protection rackets, of some sort of company theft; but somehow Liam didn't fit the picture.

Why not?

Because you fancy him, Rebecca, a tiny voice whispered inside her head, and she shivered again. No. She couldn't fancy him. That was crazy. He was rough, mean and dangerous. She despised the sort of person he was, and she hated him for what he'd done to her. But what really frightened her most was the possibility that she already knew too much for him to let her go.

The moon was rising coldly over the tall silhouetted buildings on the other side of the river. She watched it, her mind aching with torment, her eyelids heavy with weariness.

Her despairing battle against sleep was the last thing she remembered.

She dreamed of Liam. Her dreams were heated, shameful, unspeakably erotic. In her dreams, he stripped her bare of all her clothes, and ran his strong work-hardened hands all over her body, assessing her in silence. Then he deliberately began to squeeze the soft buds of her nipples until they peaked and stiffened; as she cried out and shuddered with fierce arousal, he pulled her legs apart, and began to drive his tongue deeply, rudely into her yearning sex, filling her, ravishing her with hot moistness until she began to shake with impending release, and moaned his name aloud.

She woke abruptly. She was aware of a sudden stabbing sense of loss that he wasn't there, and she despised herself for it, because girls like her didn't go to bed with men like him, ever. And then, she realised two things: firstly, that she was in the bed in the corner of the big room, covered by a crisp sheet of thick white cotton; and secondly, there were two other people up here, a man and a girl, sitting in the far corner by a window. There was music; the man was idly strumming a guitar.

Someone had lit all the candles now. They glimmered softly against the bare plaster walls of the immense room. There was a faint exotic scent in the air: patchouli,

41

or some kind of incense, perhaps; and there was a low fire burning in the big open grate at the other end of the room. Rebecca's blood raced hotly as she stirred beneath the smooth clean sheet and realised that Liam must have carried her over here while she slept and covered her up. At least she was still dressed.

The music stopped. The man who wasn't Liam said, 'Hush. I think she's waking.'

Rebecca froze, closing her eyes. Another voice, female and scornful, said, 'No. Oh, no. Women like her aren't used to stirring before noon, are they? They get up just in time for lunch and the next shopping expedition.'

Rebecca was instantly aware of danger in that voice. She knew it must be the girl with dark close-cropped hair she'd seen earlier, working at the computer. Keeping her eyes tightly shut, she tried to relax and let her breathing seem natural, though her heart was hammering.

The voice of the man who'd been playing the guitar was kinder, and slightly foreign; she realised he was the man called Petro. He said, 'Liam said she was OK. He said, if she woke, we were to look after her.'

The girl said, shortly, 'I'm getting rather tired of Liam's taste for stupid little rich girls. I think she should be taught a lesson.'

There was a moment's silence. Then the man said, 'This one's different, Cass. Liam said she helped him out, drove him here when he was getting away from the men who were chasing him. The girl's had an asthma attack or something. That's why she's still here.'

'She's had an attack of wanting to slip her hot hands inside Liam's jeans, more like. He always seems to have that effect on girls like her.'

'You're jealous, Cass,' said the man quietly. 'Stop letting the bitterness show through. You're jealous. It spoils you.'

The girl gave a sad little laugh. Rebecca heard her

42

say, at last, 'Sorry, Petro. It's just that – well, I care about Liam.'

'We all do. Don't we?'

'And I don't want him getting into trouble –'

'He's always in trouble. But he'll be all right. He knows what he's doing.'

'He certainly does. He's got the papers,' said Cass in quiet jubilation. 'In spite of those bastards who tried to stop him, he's got them.'

Rebecca lay on the big bed in the far corner of the room, scarcely moving, scarcely breathing. Those papers again. Whatever they were, they must be desperately important.

Suddenly she realised that utter silence had fallen. She wondered, for one moment, if the people had gone. She opened her eyes again, very carefully, and saw that they hadn't.

Cass and the man Petro were in each other's arms, on the woven rug before the fire, kissing. Cass's close-cropped hair gleamed sleekly in the flames. Sitting cross-legged facing the man, she brushed his cheek lightly with her lips, then leant forward to release his penis from his jeans. It sprang up from the zippered opening, its shaft dark and throbbing against the smooth white T-shirt he wore. Gently, lovingly, Cass caressed it, then bent to take it in her mouth.

Rebecca felt a stab of liquid longing piercing her loins. The girl kissed the man's cock tenderly. The man, sitting with his strong legs enclosing Cass's slender frame, gasped with pleasure and leant forward to slide Cass's stretchy lace top from her shoulders, cupping her small breasts with his hands. Then he pulled off his T-shirt; the girl, leaving his penis for a moment, rubbed her long nipples excitedly against his bare flesh.

He was muscular and sleek; his skin was the colour of rich, pale coffee, and his glossy black hair was tied back tightly from his face to reveal the prominent beauty of his cheekbones. The woman kissed him on the mouth, then returned her attention to his jutting penis; it was strong, and slightly curved, and was shiny with her saliva. Avidly, she wrapped her lips round the swollen glans, then slid her tongue firmly up and down the lengthy shaft, taking as much as she could of its length into her mouth, pulling the opening of his jeans back yet further to caress the heavy sac of his balls.

Rebecca lay curled on the bed, very still, her body thrumming with sexual tension. Her breasts ached painfully, and her tight black dress was chafing at her nipples until they were as hard as pebbles. Her vagina pulsed and clenched, meltingly liquid.

Oh, God. Now the girl Cass had pulled away from Petro, Rebecca could see her breasts, with their erect teats that were startlingly long and dark. Petro's eyes were on them too; he was licking his lips slowly. Cass was pulling off her jeans. She wasn't wearing anything else, wasn't wearing knickers. Still watching Petro's face, she began to rub with slow lascivious delight at her quim right in front of the man's hot eyes; he moaned again, and his huge straining penis jerked in frustration. Then the girl was lifting herself with glee to squat astride him, rocking herself gently to and fro to ease the stout length of his cock between her sex-folds, catching her soft lower lip between her teeth and dreamily closing her eyes as his glorious thickness impaled her.

Petro was muttering softly to himself now, clasping her tight little buttocks tenderly in his big hands, lifting her up and down on his penis, his eyes fastened on her thrusting nipples. Rebecca, moistening her own lust-dried throat, could see the base of his sturdy cock gleaming darkly each time Cass raised her clenching loins. She wished it was her, wished she could feel that lovely strong shaft driving up into her. In despair, she reached quietly for her own aching breasts, carefully unfastening the top few buttons, rubbing at the tautly erect nipples, squeezing and pulling at the stiff little nubs of flesh. But the sweet pleasure of her own silent caresses only made the insistent ache between her thighs all the more tormenting.

Cass was coming now. She threw her head back and uttered sharp little animal cries, lifting herself feverishly then grinding down again on to the man's sturdy root. Her small breasts bounced pertly with every movement, and her earrings jingled faintly. Her hand slipped to the abundant bush of dark hair at her groin, and she started to rub frantically at her clitoris. Rebecca could hear the slipperiness of her juices as her fingers worked greedily up and down.

The man bowed his head to lick at her long, stiff teats. 'There, there, my Cass,' he muttered as he steadied her with his strong hands. 'Feel me, feel my hard cock driving up inside you. Dance on me, my sweet one. Devour me.'

For a moment, Cass went very still. Then she began to cry out, her face flushed with excitement, her eyes wild as her orgasm consumed her. She rode frantically on Petro's stiffened cock, and her cries pierced the candlelit air.

She was subsiding at last, still whimpering. Petro, with stupendous self-control, continued to drive himself gently in and out, caressing her clenching vagina and prolonging her orgasm until Cass seemed almost senseless with pleasure. She sank her cropped head against his chest, her hands still clutching his wide shoulders.

'Oh, Petro,' she muttered. 'That was fantastic. Just fantastic.' She nuzzled his smooth cheek with her mouth. 'What can I do for you, to repay you?'

There was a moment's silence, as a log crackled and spat in the fireplace. Then, with an icy shock that froze her heated body rigid, Rebecca realised that Petro was looking over the top of Cass's head, straight at the bed in the far corner, straight at her.

'You could help me to get a taste of *that*,' he breathed softly.

Cass twisted her head sharply towards the bed. 'She's awake?'

'Oh, yes.'

'She's been bloody watching us?'

'She certainly has.'

No good pretending now. Rebecca dragged herself slowly up from the pillows, holding the sheet against her breasts, because there wasn't time to button up her dress. Her gaze was defiant, but inside she felt weak at the way they were both watching her. The man was amused and aroused; the girl was angry. She'd eased herself away from Petro's lap, and his penis, still engorged, swayed threateningly. He rubbed it idly, maintaining his huge erection, as he silently watched Cass pull on her jeans and stalk over to the bed where Rebecca was.

'You cow,' she said. 'You dirty little cow. You've been watching us, haven't you? Have you been playing with yourself as well? Wishing you had Petro's big cock up your tight, upper-class little arse?'

Rebecca was pale, but her voice was composed. 'You woke me up,' she said coldly. 'What the hell was I supposed to do? Say, "Please stop shagging and making such a noise?"'

Cass slapped her cheek. It wasn't the pain but the humiliation that cut Rebecca to the quick. Petro meanwhile was walking towards them, the lower half of his sleek body clad in jeans; but from the unbuttoned fly, his heavy erection jutted menacingly. Rebecca's heart thumped.

'Hey, Cass,' he said in his musical voice. 'Leave her. She's Liam's, remember?'

'So she thinks,' said Cass bitterly. 'She's yet to learn that Liam just uses little rich girls like her for fun, then throws them away. Especially the ones who are sluts, like this one. Look at her, Petro. Just look how her eyes are fastened on your cock, how her face is all bright with longing, wanting you to fuck her!'

She pulled angrily at the sheet. Rebecca clutched at it, but she was too late. Cass tugged it back triumphantly and tossed it aside. Rebecca's crumpled dress was unbuttoned to the waist; her breasts peeped out, soft and warm and rosy-tipped. Her hem was rucked high, revealing slim golden thighs above the lace tops of her torn black stockings. She felt exposed, degraded, and horrifyingly aroused.

'See those breasts, Petro,' Cass was saying triumphantly. 'Just see those tight little nipples. She'd have anybody right this minute, anybody!'

It was true. Rebecca knew her body betrayed her. She was exquisitely aroused. The beautiful brown-skinned man was gazing at her hungrily; Cass was stroking his stupendous erection, which jutted, heavy and smooth and ripe, towards Rebecca's trembling body. The plummy head of his penis was rigid and glistening; a tiny tear of moisture oozed from its pulsing eye. Rebecca tugged the sheet back tensely over her naked breasts, but she knew her glowing eyes, her desire-swollen mouth, must still give her away.

She said coldly, 'I could hardly help observing your activities, could I? I rather assumed I was meant to watch.' She turned over languidly. 'If you must know, I found it all rather tedious –'

Cass ripped the sheet from her shoulders. 'Slut. Little rich stuck-up slut. And Liam thinks you're special. Uncover your breasts for us again, slut.'

Rebecca's hands gripped the edge of the sheet. 'No.'

'Uncover them, or I will. Hold her, Petro.'

Petro reached out to hold Rebecca's wrists. She struggled uselessly against him; his big hands were strong and warm, making her skin tingle. Beneath his touch, her gold bangle chafed at her soft flesh like a manacle. Cass ripped away the sheet to reveal Rebecca's breasts once more. Petro groaned aloud, his black eyes burning on them, and Rebecca shuddered anew at her naked exposure, her helplessness. She felt Petro lifting her hands gently but remorselessly above her head and pressing them back against the wall. Her breasts were stretched high and taut, and she realised with despair that her crests were starting to stiffen hungrily. The man's long throbbing cock was dangerously close to them as he leant across her; its swollen heat seemed to burn her exposed flesh. She squeezed her eyes shut. Oh, God; her loins were melting again, and the silvery moisture was seeping dangerously from the silken flesh folds at the joining of her thighs. Her tiny black panties were already wet; they chafed almost unbearably against the sweet throbbing of her engorged clitoris.

The silence and the darkness overwhelmed her. She opened her eyes again to see that Cass's hand was on Petro's massive penis. Slowly, her eyes never leaving Rebecca's anguished face, Cass began to masturbate him. As the velvety foreskin slid to and fro, his cock swelled and grew afresh, the eye at its glossy tip pulsing with desire. Cass chuckled with satisfaction.

'You like this, rich girl? You'd like to feel this man's penis filling you, fucking you? Of course you would. Petro's beautiful, isn't he? Let me give you a taste of his sweet, hard flesh . . .'

Carefully, Cass continued to rub at the hard penis, and Rebecca struggled anew against the man's relent-lessly firm grip on her wrists. Then she froze, quite breathless, as Cass started to guide his stupendous shaft against her breasts, circling the sticky glans slowly around her hardened nipples, each in turn. She cried out as his penis gently caressed each stiffened nub, pushing the little stems of flesh deliberately to and fro, causing a sweet, almost painful delight to shoot through all her nerve endings. She strained her arms against

Petro's grasp, his willing prisoner, and arched her body against him, silently begging for more. She rubbed her thighs together convulsively, feeling her tight panties caressing her vulva like a warm hand. She longed for penetration.

And all the time Petro watched her with burning eyes as Cass, grinning, made his dusky cock caress Rebecca's yearning nipples as tormentingly as if they were her clitoris. Slowly but strongly, Cass glided her fingers up and down the man's long shaft, always pressing the swollen glans to Rebecca's breasts. The man braced himself and began to shudder. He threw his head back, his eyes glazed in ecstasy. His sleek hips jerked, once, twice, and his semen began to shoot out in hot liquid bursts.

With a calculating smile, Cass circled the man's spurting penis in the silky pools of liquid that gathered on Rebecca's breasts. Rebecca squeezed her eyes shut, knowing they must see all of the incredible, shameful pleasure she was experiencing as his glossy phallus slid about on her sensitive flesh, pushing her hardened teats from side to side. She suddenly thought of Liam's aggressively masculine body. She imagined him standing there at the foot of the bed, drawing her stockinged legs around his waist. She pictured him sliding his own silky-strong erection deep into her hot stickiness, ravishing her with slow and deliberate strokes, his callused fingers teasing the throbbing bud of her clitoris with remorseless skill.

She couldn't help herself. As Petro continued to spend his seed rapturously over her tight nipples, she clenched her thighs together fiercely and started to feel the sweet pleasure of her own climax flooding her tense body. She imagined herself squeezing her inner muscles round the steely thickness of Liam's plunging cock, as Cass continued to rub her breasts with Petro's jerking penis. She heard Petro gasping for breath as the last of his semen spurted; then she felt his magnificent erection subsiding reluctantly as her own dark ecstasy died slowly away. He released her hands at last.

Horrified by what she'd allowed to happen, she opened her eyes to see that Cass was staring at her flushed sticky body with a mixture of contempt and triumph. Rebecca clasped her hands across her naked breasts, hot with shame.

'As I said,' Cass declared. 'Just the same as all the rest, in spite of her money and her posh voice. A dirty little slut...' As she spoke, her hand was exploring Rebecca's thigh, rubbing up against her panties. Rebecca flinched and gave a little cry as Cass cupped the soaking fabric and probed the sticky puffiness of her labia. The woman's fingers pulled, explored, hooked the gusset aside, remorselessly tracing a delicate and almost agonising path between Rebecca's slick flesh-folds. One finger drove into her vagina, thrusting mockingly.

'She's ready for more, Petro,' Cass announced gloatingly. 'See how moist, how open she is down here. Use your tongue on her, Petro. Lick her juices. You like doing that, don't you?'

Rebecca dived to escape, twisting her hips free of Cass's mocking exploration, rolling over to fling herself from the bed.

And then she realised, at precisely the same moment that the others did, that they were no longer alone. Liam was standing at the far end of the room, at the top of the staircase. His hand was gripping the iron rail; his face was hard and expressionless in the candlelit shadows.

Rebecca froze. Cass and Petro too had gone very still, very quiet.

Liam was the first to speak. He said, in a voice that was soft and dangerous, 'I told you to watch the girl, Cass. I told you to let her sleep; but not to speak to her, not to touch her.'

Cass's green eyes filled with scorn. 'Sorry, Liam. But you didn't warn us what she's like, did you? She couldn't get enough of Petro's cock, just now. Do you really want all the details?'

Rebecca started to get up from the edge of the bed, her arms clasped across her naked breasts. 'It's not true,' she whispered. 'It's not true.'

'Oh, God,' drawled Cass, 'she begged him for it, Liam. Begged him to drive his cock right up between her wide-open legs, while I played with her breasts. She said it was the best screw she'd ever had. Quite honestly, it seemed the only way to keep her quiet.'

Petro was silent at her side.

Liam's eyes were like slate as he gazed at them all. 'I think,' he said at last to Cass, 'that you and Petro had better go back downstairs. Petro, bring us some coffee, will you? I'll speak to you both later.'

Cass said quickly, 'She'll lie to you, Liam. But it's true, what happened. She was begging for it –'

Liam repeated, 'Downstairs.'

Cass shrugged maliciously. 'OK. But I warn you. The sooner you're rid of the bitch, the better.'

She sauntered across the big room, her tight little bottom clenching provocatively beneath her jeans, and made her way down the stairs. Petro followed her, still silent, not meeting Liam's eyes. Rebecca didn't look up either, from where she was sitting on the edge of the bed; but she could hear Liam's slow, deliberate footsteps coming across the room towards her.

'Well?' he said.

She realised that she was shivering violently now, even though the room was warm. Slowly she lifted her face to meet his gaze. 'Let me go,' she said. 'I've done nothing. I know nothing about you, or your hateful friends, or your business with those stolen papers, or why those people were after you. Let me go.'

He said, in that drawling voice that stripped her quite

bare, 'You want to go? You surprise me. According to Cass, you were having the time of your life. It certainly looked like it when I came in.'

'The time of my life?' she flashed back. 'Shall I tell you what happened, Liam? What really happened? When I woke up, Cass and Petro were in the room, over by the fire. They thought I was asleep, and they started to have sex. They taunted me – Cass taunted me – when they found out I was awake.'

'So you joined in with them. Did you enjoy it as much as Cass said you did?'

She caught her breath. He must have seen her mind-wrenching orgasm. How could she deny it? 'It was pretty much as I'd expected,' she retorted coldly. 'What interesting low-class company you keep here. According to Cass, you fuck her pretty regularly as well. Why are you holding me a prisoner? Why can't I go? What else am I to be subjected to? If you must know, I joined in with the sordid little games they suggested because I thought that it might give me a chance to escape from here. Can you blame me?'

He said harshly, 'Did they force you? Are you trying to tell me that they forced you? If so, I'll deal with them, believe me.'

She sagged back against the bed and in a low voice she said, 'No.'

Instead of replying, he walked slowly towards the fireplace, to pinch out a candle that was dripping wax on the floor. Rebecca suddenly saw that dawn was starting to spread silvery-grey fingers across the London horizon, outlining the ghostly profile of the half-finished buildings on the far side of the river. Somewhere a ship's hooter sounded: lonely, haunting in the silence.

He turned back to her and the chilly light caught his face, accentuating his hard, high cheekbones and cruelly sensual mouth. Her pulse started to leap and pound again. Oh, God, why did he affect her like this when she despised him so much? It was him she'd imagined driving his lovely strong penis into her as Petro spurted his seed over her aching breasts; him she'd wanted in her arms. Oh, please, she prayed. Don't let him guess it.

Petro came up then, with two mugs of coffee. He handed them silently to Liam, without looking at Rebecca, then turned and left again. Liam brought one of the mugs over to her.

She almost pushed it away. 'I don't want it.' Her voice shook. 'I don't want anything from you, or your hateful friends. I despise all of you.'

'Suit yourself,' he said. 'But if you've any sense at all, which I'm beginning to doubt, you'll drink it. You're shivering with cold.'

He put the coffee down on the bedside table. It smelt fragrant, tempting. She took it in silent, bitter rage and drank some. Then she put it down again. 'You promised me earlier I could leave,' she said. 'When can I leave this hateful place?'

He'd moved away from her to prop himself against the broad ledge beneath the window, clasping his own coffee loosely between his hands. In the early morning light that poured through the glass, his well-washed jeans seemed to cling to his narrow hips and heavily muscled legs like a second skin; Rebecca tore her eyes from them with an effort.

He said, 'I told you. You can't go yet. Those people who are after me aren't the police. They're more dangerous than that.'

'But why are they after you?'

'They want me to stop talking about something I've found out. In other words, they want my silence.'

His words struck her as improbable, pompous almost. She said scornfully, 'You seem to have an inflated idea of your own importance. Unless you're a criminal, which you keep telling me you're not, how can someone like you have come across something that's so terribly important?'

He watched her for a while with his calm blue gaze, seeming oblivious to her scorn. 'Perhaps it's my job,' he said.

Rebecca gazed at him incredulously, her arms still folded tightly across her breasts as if in defence. 'Your job!' she exclaimed. 'But you're a thief. You stole those papers in that briefcase over there, from someone at the party. You're a thief.'

'How do you define theft, Rebecca?' he said softly. 'I would guess that the financial activities of most of your high-class friends wouldn't bear much investigation, would they? Whether you're talking about tax evasion, clever accountants, or the exploitation of workers, it's all crime; but the difference is that your kind get away with it.'

She leant forward, her anger driving away any remnant of caution. 'So you and your friends are honest? How can you dare to try and tell me that, after what you've put me through tonight?'

His eyes narrowed slightly, but he replied, calmly enough, 'I thought you were enjoying yourself earlier.'

'No!' She'd sprung to her feet now, her face warm with humiliation because she knew he was thinking of Cass and Petro. 'No. I told you, it was hateful –'

'Spare me the denials,' he said. 'That's the best sex you've had in years, I should think. I've bedded enough of your kind to know. It seems to me that women like you have a secret fantasy about having good rough sex with a man so far below you that he's got to crawl on his hands and knees to get anywhere near you: a man you wouldn't even look at in normal circumstances. Sort of novelty value, I suppose –'

'Stop it,' she breathed, her hands clenched tightly into fists. 'Stop it, will you? I'm not interested in your low-life bedroom antics –'

54

'Aren't you?' he said.

Her heart thumped as his blue eyes mocked her. Somewhere deep in her groin, a pure, erotic pulse of desire was throbbing. 'Look,' she said, 'look, if you prefer to have sex with women who have money instead of brains in order to feed your inadequate ego, then that's your problem. I'm not impressed. I'm not interested, either, in the tacky business that's been going on tonight, those papers you stole. Believe me, there's no way I'd choose to repeat any of what's gone on tonight to anyone. I just want to forget it as soon as possible. So can I go now?'

'No,' he said.

Her heart started to pound again slowly, thickly. She was frightened of him. She was frightened of what he did to her, of what he might do to her. Her limbs felt heavy, heavy as lead; her mouth was dry. She said at last, 'You can't keep me here for ever, you know. People will come looking for me. Soon they'll report me as missing. I'll be more trouble than I'm worth.'

He said, 'I don't want to keep you here for any longer than I have to, believe me. You can go in a few hours, as soon as I've made some phone calls. Providing, that is, that you give me back something that belongs to me.'

'You're joking. How could I have anything of yours?'

Instead of replying he started to walk slowly towards her with a casual male grace that mesmerised her. In the grey shadows of dawn, his hard-boned face was predatory, like a jungle cat's. He said, 'You seem to have forgotten something, don't you, Rebecca? I believe it's hidden in that expensive little bag of yours.'

Oh, no. She froze in horror. The sheet of paper from the briefcase. He knew. She'd forgotten all about it – she'd picked it up in a moment of madness – but he knew. How? He must have gone through her things when she was asleep. He was hateful, hateful. Clutching her bag, she leapt towards the stairs, but he was there well before her, his wide-shouldered frame completely blocking her escape. She pushed at him frantically but he caught at her wrists, holding her with effortless, frightening strength. Her bag fell to the floor, spilling open, and still she continued to struggle desperately.

'The front door's locked,' he told her. 'It's no use trying to escape.'

'Let me go. Let me go –'

'Calm down. You'll make yourself ill again.'

Suddenly, the sound of a distant police siren ripped through the grey early morning mist outside the window. It tore at her already frayed nerves, making her cry out in fear. He caught her in his arms, holding her close, saying urgently, 'It's not for us, this time. It's not for us.'

She leant into him, shuddering, and his body was warm and strong against hers. 'Oh, God,' she whispered. 'Oh, God, Liam.'

'Hush,' he said, one hand supporting her narrow waist, the other stroking her sleek copper hair back from her face. 'It's all right, Rebecca.' He tensed suddenly. 'Do you need your inhaler?'

'No . . .'

'I swear it will be all right.' His voice was urgent. 'You're quite safe now, I promise.'

But she wasn't safe. Not from the sudden rip-roaring spasm of desire that gripped her whole body; not safe from the terrible weakness in her limbs that melted and flowed like honey as he held her close; not safe from the nearness of his cruel yet sensual mouth, as he fiercely touched her forehead with his lips and sent burning shivers shuddering through her.

Then they were kissing. No, not kissing, but devouring each other, tongues stabbing and twining in erotic demand. His big hands were running swiftly, possessively up and down her back, rustling against the raw black silk of her dress. She stood on tiptoe, arching herself against him, twining her fingers round his neck, moaning hungrily as his mouth ravaged hers, his strong tongue darting and probing between her willingly parted lips in insistent, unmistakable male demand.

He smelt clean, of supple leather and sun-kissed skin, edged with the faint tang of lemony soap. She was shaking with desire when he finally withdrew. 'Please,' she muttered. 'Please don't leave me.'

He held her a little away from him, his blue eyes dark and burning above his hard-edged cheekbones. 'Rebecca. If I stay, you know what will happen?'

'Yes,' she whispered, 'yes.'

'You're sure? Quite sure?'

She nodded, biting at her swollen lip. 'Yes. Oh, God, yes. And Liam, I didn't let Petro fuck me. They played with me; it was a sort of game, and it's true, I can't deny, that I enjoyed it. But I didn't let him fuck me.'

Suddenly he picked her up, and carried her over to the shadowy bed in the corner. All the way, he covered her face with kisses that inflamed her. With strong, sure hands, he unbuttoned her dress and peeled the crumpled silk away from her body, kissing and licking at her fiercely jutting nipples that thrust so hungrily towards him, drawing them into his mouth and abrading them with his teeth until dark spasms of pleasure tore through her, while his stubbled jaw rasped at her aching breasts. She cried aloud in longing, rubbing her legs against his strong thighs, feeling the coarse denim of his jeans stroking her soft skin as the folds of her labia parted and swelled.

He held her in his arms, restrained her. 'Gently,' he said, in his quiet, husky voice. 'We've got time, Rebecca. We've got time.'

She was trembling with need as he lifted himself carefully away from her and moved down her body. His tongue trailed deliciously down her stomach, pausing to caress the button of her navel with deliberate kisses.

'You are beautiful,' he said. 'You have a beautiful body.'

'No,' she whispered, half-laughing, half-crying with the surging waves of desire that were making a mockery of her self-control. 'No. I'm not thin enough. I need to lose some weight . . .'

'Beautiful,' he repeated, correcting her; and then he was easing down her tiny silken panties, feeling her swollen flesh with his fingers, slowly, as if it delighted him. A delicious languor spread through her body as his tongue pressed between her thighs and eased its way into her warm sex, running slowly up and down her aching furrow until Rebecca arched herself against his face and opened herself to him.

'I'm coming,' she muttered tensely. 'Oh, I'm coming.'

He lifted his head, his sensual mouth gleaming with her juices, his navy blue eyes hooded with pure male desire. 'No, you're not,' he said. 'Not for a long time yet.'

She was embarrassed. 'I'm too eager,' she whispered. 'I know I am.'

'No, you're not,' he said quietly. 'You're luscious and lovely, Rebecca, and I want this to last for ever.' He started to peel off his own clothes: his soft white shirt, his patched jeans, his navy boxer shorts. His body was beautiful: sleekly muscled, golden-skinned, narrow-hipped. As he eased his shorts down over his powerful thighs, Rebecca felt a fresh surge of sheer desire as she saw his magnificent penis springing up against his taut stomach.

He was beautiful. Long, thick and strong – Annie's favourite mantra about the guy of her dreams. The words floated through her lust-hazed mind. His strong face, with its exquisitely carved, faintly stubbled jawline and jutting cheekbones, looked almost tender as he drew her into his arms again and kissed her with lips that tasted shockingly of her heated sex. His tousled blond hair fell forward from his face, brushing her cheeks tantalisingly. She moaned in his arms, and rubbed her aching breasts against his chest, revelling in the feel of his hard body against her nipples.

Already, his hair-roughened leg was nudging its way meaningfully between her thighs. She rubbed against him luxuriantly, feeling the velvety bulk of his balls, the hot strength of his taut shaft. Slowly he inserted the glossy head of his cock between her sex-lips, pushing and probing in her slippery juices, stretching her, parting her. She gasped with bliss as at last he slid into her, filling her yearning passage with hard male strength.

He held her very still with his hands, pinning her loins beneath him, so she was impaled on his rigid penis. He gazed down into her breathless face with sleepy eyes; but she knew that he was wide, wide awake. 'Is that good, Rebecca?'

'Oh, yes. So good.' Max, and the other lovers she'd had, only asked her that when they wanted compliments. Yet, incredibly, she felt that Liam was asking her because he cared.

He smiled at her, saying, 'I'm glad.'

'Liam. Oh, Liam.' She was gasping with delight as his steel-hard cock throbbed within her. 'I thought you said you could never fancy me. I thought you hated me.'

His eyes burned her. 'Shall I tell you, Rebecca, when I first wanted you?' He was starting to move his penis in and out of her, letting it work its own dark magic against her silken inner membranes, driving her into a slow exquisite frenzy as he spoke. 'I wanted you the moment I saw you climb out of that car. As you swung your legs to the ground, I saw the line of your lovely golden thighs above your lacy stocking tops, saw the tiny black silk triangle of your panties, scarcely covering your sex. I wanted you then. I wanted to push you back into that car of yours, and spread your gorgeous long legs wide apart against the leather seats, and fuck you slowly, deeply, until you called out for me, and came for me, in front of all those watching people. Then I wanted to turn you over, and ravish your lovely high-class little arse . . .'

Rebecca was horrified and thrilled as his voice rasped huskily in her ear. His hands were on her rounded buttocks now, kneading them, pulling them tenderly apart; she could feel her stretched anus rippling with shameful heat as she imagined the dark pleasure of his huge cock invading her there, imagined him penetrating the tight little ringed orifice with his stiffened flesh. Her vagina clenched hungrily around him and her juices flowed freely as her clitoris throbbed with pleasure. He smiled mysteriously and suddenly pulled himself out, his velvety glans just caressing her slippery vulva.

She wanted to weep for emptiness. Her mouth was swollen and bruised from his kisses and her amber eyes were huge with arousal as she whispered, 'Is that why, Liam? Is that why you followed me to my car?'

'No,' he breathed, caressing her cheek with one lazy finger, his eyes on the thick gold bangle that circled her wrist. 'Ah, no. I thought you would still be at the party with some rich lover. I had to get away quickly, you see, because I'd got what I wanted, but someone had spotted me; so I was on the run, as simple as that. Any car would have done.'

'Any?' Her face, absurdly, fell.

'I didn't have time to make a choice, Rebecca. But your car was special. And so are you.'

He started to pinch one of her taut raspberry nipples sharply between his strong finger and thumb. It was as if he was playing with her clitoris, so direct and painfully exquisite was the sensation.

'Oh, Liam. For God's sake, take me again, will you?' She was half-laughing, half-crying with pleasure. He pulled her with gentle strength to the edge of the bed and spread her thighs apart, taking his time to gaze at the intimate folds of flesh beneath her carefully trimmed little triangle of coppery pubic hair. Rebecca could feel his eyes devouring the glistening pearl of her exposed clitoris and she stirred with agonising need. She could see his cock, hard and straining, throbbing against his taut belly.

'This is it, then, sweetheart,' he murmured, his voice rough with desire. He lowered himself a little, positioning himself with care. Then, as Rebecca writhed on the bed, he eased himself into her, and started to drive his thick shaft into her, again and again, teasing her, delighting her with its potent strength. She clutched him to her, and cried out wildly as his thumb reached into her moist sex to press against her clitoris, sending white-hot needles of pleasure through her.

'Lift your legs,' he said. 'Wrap them round my body. Let me fuck you properly, Rebecca. Let yourself go.'

She hesitated, smelling the scent of her own juices as he lifted his hand to brush his thumb against her lips. 'You make me feel dirty,' she whispered. 'Good, but dirty.'

He gave a hooded smile. 'Sex should be dirty. Has nobody told you that? Relax. Forget your inhibitions. And yes – that's it –'

Almost shyly, she lifted her legs, and he hooked them quickly over his powerful shoulders. Then he crouched over her, driving his long penis in so hard, so deep, that the hairy root of his shaft ground relentlessly against her exquisitely swollen clitoris, sending a wave of ecstasy like molten fire flooding through her veins. At the same time, his hands were caressing her uplifted buttocks, stroking up and down the crease that separated them. Before she realised what he was doing, his strong forefinger had found her bottom-hole and was driving in sweetly, deeply, in time to the pounding of

61

his cock. Rebecca writhed on the double impalement, felt the impossible sensations of heavy pleasure rippling through her captive body; then she began to tremble and utter little incoherent cries of bliss. He watched her with burning eyes as her climax overcame her.

All the while, as she shuddered and spasmed beneath him, he continued to slide his penis deep within her, and his finger pressed even more urgently into the tight rosebud of her anus, until she felt she was drowning in a warm sea of delight. She lay back in his arms at last, limp and sated with pleasure. His whole purpose, it seemed to her, was to rouse her, to watch her and tend her through her searing ecstasy, while his own body stayed hard, deliberate, utterly controlled. Not like Max, coming after the first few thrusts. Not like anyone she'd ever known.

He kissed her, his lips hard and warm, and she felt the driving pulse of his own urgency at last, heard his heavy, almost ragged breathing as his penis tensed and swelled deep within her. She moulded herself gladly to his strong body, letting him take her with almost savage strength as he lost control at last and thrust powerfully to his own release. She loved the feel of his manhood jerking and spasming at her very heart.

He drew her gently up on to the bed and held her tightly in his arms after that, stroking her face. She felt sleep starting to claim her as she lay there, languorously pressed against the heat of her body, and at first she tried to fight it. But he kissed her, saying, 'It's all right. Sleep if you want to. We've got hours yet.'

'You've got some phone calls to make, you said.' Her eyes were wide open now, alert with fears that had only temporarily been submerged. 'What are those papers you've got, Liam? I looked at them. I took one because I wanted so badly to try to make sense of all this, but it made no sense at all to me. Are you going to blackmail someone?'

'No,' he said. 'I'm simply going to tell the truth. And people don't always like the truth. I swear to you, I'm planning nothing worse than that. Trust me.'

He kissed her with tenderness; Rebecca, reassured, lay back in his strong arms, her body warm and deliciously fulfilled. He gazed down at her in silence. After a while he touched her arm, close to the bracelet that encircled her wrist.

'My turn for questions now. Who gave you this, Rebecca?'

She felt herself colouring slightly. 'Someone I know. His name's Max Forrester.'

'The banker?'

She tensed, pulled herself upright. 'You know him?'

'Relax. I know him by name, and I've seen him around. He often goes to Les Sauvages in Soho, doesn't he? It's one of my favourites, too.'

The look on her face must have betrayed her disbelief, because he laughed and said, 'You look horrified. Isn't someone like me allowed to enjoy good food? It's not a prerogative of the upper classes, you know.'

She blushed. 'I'm sorry. I'm stupid. It's just that I wouldn't have thought it was your kind of scene.'

'Perhaps it isn't. But I like to widen my horizons now and then, for the purposes of my job.'

'Your job?'

'I'm a journalist.'

'A journalist?' She was aware that she was stupidly echoing him. He laughed at her open amazement.

'Yes, a journalist. I told you earlier it was my job to find things out, things that people would rather were kept secret.'

'You mean gossip? Scandal-mongering? Paparazzi-type stuff?'

'No. Oh, no.'

She frowned, not understanding, not sure that she really wanted to understand. She ran her palm down the line of his lean lightly stubbled jaw. 'You're being mysterious, Liam. Will you explain it all to me some day?'

'I think you might understand it all quite soon,' he said. 'Do you belong to Max Forrester, Rebecca?'

His finger was gently circling the pulse points on her wrist, just below the bracelet. She gazed back at him.

'No,' she said. 'I don't belong to anybody.'

He smiled. 'Glad to hear it.'

He laid her back down against the pillows, and held her in his arms until sleep claimed her at last. Then he gently kissed her forehead and covered her with the sheet before quietly dressing himself.

Daylight was creeping in like a ghost through the tall windows, and the fire had died down to ashes by the time he finally left the silent room.

Chapter Three

*R*ebecca was woken by the rhythmic blaring of a car horn down in the street below. Only taxi drivers blasted their horns like that, she reflected with growing irritation as the sound gradually penetrated her luscious dreams. She surfaced slowly, stretching her arms, thinking, for just a moment, that she was back in her own bedroom. Then she saw the vast vaulted ceiling over her head; she felt the bright morning sun pouring in through the windows that overlooked the Thames, and she remembered everything.

Liam. Where was he? She leapt to her feet, acutely aware of her nakedness, reaching already for her clothes.

Someone was knocking now at the front door, down at street level. Whoever it was sounded impatient. Putting her dress on, and buttoning it frantically, she ran to look out of the window, and saw both the idling taxi and its driver, pacing impatiently to and fro. Then someone opened the front door; Rebecca couldn't see who it was. Was it Liam talking to the driver? It must be. Soon, he would come up to be with her again. Her body throbbed with the memory of his warmth.

She decided to go down and meet him, to let him know she was awake. She looked down at her skimpy little black dress and her spike-heeled sandals, and a slow smile spread across her face. Not really the kind of thing to go down to breakfast in at – she glanced at her watch – oh, God, nine in the morning. She must still look as if she were dripping with sex. Suddenly she caught sight of Liam's shabby leather jacket, lying on the back of the chair. She pulled it on. It smelt warmly, deliciously of her lover. She closed her eyes, and felt his strong wicked hands on all her secret places again. Perhaps she'd forget breakfast, and suggest bed again. But who was the taxi for?

She didn't have to wait long to find out. As she hurried down past the empty floors towards the front door, she saw not Liam, but Stevie, the gentle-looking guy with long brown hair who'd taken her car away last night.

He watched her coming down the stairs with anxious eyes; then he said, 'I'm sorry. I should have come up for you earlier, only I didn't like to wake you. There's a taxi waiting outside for you.'

For her? She didn't understand. 'Where's Liam?' she said abruptly.

Stevie looked embarrassed, and that was when she started to guess. 'He's gone. He had to leave, really early.'

Of course. Hadn't he told her he had things to do, calls to make? But Stevie must have seen the sense of loss in her eyes, because he went on quickly, 'The taxi's for you. Liam told me to order it.'

So that she could join him, wherever he was? Her heart leapt again. 'Where am I to go?'

He looked puzzled, his brown eyes like a faithful spaniel's. 'Why, to your home, of course.'

'Of course.'

'Trust me', Liam had said. She felt suddenly flat with

disappointment. 'I suppose the fact that you've got my own car garaged close by is quite irrelevant to all this?'

'Liam had to take your car.' At least he had the grace to sound ashamed. 'He said he needed it urgently. But you will get it back.'

Oh, what a fool she was. So Liam had left without her, in her own car, and didn't intend her to follow. Feeling sick at the unfolding betrayal and at her own stupidity, she said, 'I suppose you do realise that I could go straight to the police and get you all charged with abduction and car theft?'

'Yes,' said Stevie with patient gentleness. 'But Liam didn't think you would.'

No. No, of course he knew she wouldn't. The police would laugh in her face once they realised she'd allowed, no, begged the man who kidnapped her to screw her senseless. A journalist? No way. That was probably just his way of putting a romantic gloss over his dubious activities as some kind of shady dealer, a conman, perhaps even a common thief. No wonder he made enough to live in a place like this and dine regularly at Les Sauvages.

Just then, the taxi driver marched in through the half-open door. 'Look,' he said. 'Am I getting this fare or not?' Then he caught sight of Rebecca; his eyes widened appreciatively.

'Well,' he said. 'Let's be going, shall we, darling?'

Rebecca hesitated. She was damned if she was going to give in to them all, and let them get away with it. She turned back to Stevie and said in a low voice, so the taxi-driver couldn't hear, 'I want my car. I swear I'll go to the police and tell them about everything if I don't get my car back.'

'Liam will get it back to you,' Stevie said quickly. 'Really, he will, and very soon. He's not a car thief, believe me.'

And then another door opened into the hallway and

Cass came out. She looked bright, almost triumphant as she gazed at Rebecca. 'So you're leaving us. A word of advice,' she said. 'Don't bother getting in touch with Liam again, will you? He won't appreciate it.'

At least that gave Rebecca the impetus she needed. 'Get in touch?' she breathed incredulouly. 'You're joking, of course.' Turning her back abruptly on Stevie and Cass, she walked out into the street to where the taxi was waiting.

The driver was already opening the back door. 'Where to, darling?'

'Take me to Kensington Church Street, will you?' She climbed in and closed the door firmly, hoping to curtail any further conversation; but he was talking again as he got into the driver's seat.

'A bit of shopping? Now, that's nice.'

'No. Home.'

'Ah.' He grinned salaciously as he sat behind the wheel. 'Got a bit of sleep to catch up on, have we?'

Rebecca pointedly didn't reply. Instead she opened her bag, searching for her comb and her bronze lipstick. Angrily she pulled her comb through her hair. Damn Liam, damn him. She'd fallen for it all: the harsh captor bit, the sudden kindness, the almost violent, lust-kindling urgency of his seduction technique. She leant back and closed her eyes.

The taxi driver, horn blaring, was forcing his way relentlessly through the rush-hour traffic of the City. The sight of the ever-ticking meter caught her eye, and a fresh anxiety assailed her. She looked quickly into her purse – almost empty, as she knew it was, except for a used tube ticket and a till receipt. She leant forward apprehensively and tapped on the glass.

'The man who phoned you, for the taxi. He didn't pay you in advance, did he? With his credit card, or something?'

The taxi driver was busy cutting up a smart and

expensive grey saloon. The saloon driver blasted his horn angrily, and the taxi driver gestured at him through the open window. 'Pay? No, he didn't pay,' he told Rebecca suspiciously. 'Got a problem with that, darling?'

'No, no,' said Rebecca quickly. 'I just wondered, that's all. Some people do, you see. Pay in advance, I mean.'

The taxi driver turned round to leer. 'I bet they do,' he said.

Rebecca turned quickly to look out of the window, ignoring him. A forlorn hope, if ever there was one, to imagine that Liam might have told Stevie to pay for the taxi. She remembered the way Liam had looked at Max's thick gold bracelet last night. No doubt he assumed she was rich enough to pay for a whole fleet of cars.

She suddenly realised that the hateful driver was still leering at her in his rear view mirror. She became acutely conscious of her smudged mascara, her still-swollen mouth, and the highly visible upper curves of her breasts, pushed upwards by the restriction of the tight little dress. Flushing with annoyance, Rebecca quickly drew Liam's leather jacket across her chest. The woollen lining scratched delicately at her skin, like his lovely, knowing fingers. God. She moved her thighs restlessly on the scuffed seat, aware of the silken moisture that lingered in her secret places, still haunted by the memory of pleasure so acute that it had scorched itself forever on her senses. Sex with Liam had been superb. She'd never felt so vital, so alive, so gloriously dirty. Yet he'd got his friends to kick her out of his place with an unpaid-for taxi, as if she were some cheap tart he'd brought in for the night.

The anger and humiliation seared her anew. But then, reluctantly, she began to smile. OK, so he'd seen her as a challenge – posh, superior, out of his league. Well, hadn't she seen him as a bit of rough? Hadn't she been

deeply excited by the novelty of being bedded by a
south London wide boy who called himself a journalist
but was really on the run from the law?

Good for Liam. He'd got what he wanted, and so had
she. It wasn't as if he'd forced her. She coloured a little,
remembering how she'd clutched at his lovely tight
buttocks to force his cock harder inside herself. And
he'd enjoyed it just as much as she had, she was sure.
She remembered the spasming of his thick lusty penis
and smiled slowly. We're still even, Liam, she whispered to herself. Oh, yes.

Knightsbridge was as crowded as ever with shoppers
and tourists. Her driver crawled impatiently alongside
the sightseeing buses and dark-windowed limousines,
reaching Kensington Church Street at last and turning
off with a squeal of protesting brakes into the quiet little
road where she lived. She gathered herself to get out,
still thinking, rather dreamily, of Liam, but she came
back to earth with a bump when the driver told her the
fare.

'Hang on a moment, will you?' she muttered, and
began to hunt for her front door key.

'Oh, I will, darling,' he assured her flatly. 'I'm not
going anywhere until I've been paid, believe me.'

She found her key at last and pounded up to the first
floor of the Victorian mews cottage she shared with
Annie, praying that her flatmate would be in, and
solvent. If not, it would have to be the fantasy pot. No
one had won it for at least two weeks, so it would be
brimming.

Annie was in bed. Solvent she might be, but she was
also fast asleep, so it was the pot. She rushed to the
kitchen to ransack the little blue china bowl, and hurtled
downstairs again.

By the time Rebecca had paid him, shut the door on
his final leer, and dragged herself wearily up all those
stairs again, Annie was awake. She'd pulled on a green

silk kimono-style dressing gown, and was gathering her long blonde hair back from her face, yawning with sleepy delicacy as she waited for the kettle to boil.

She turned huge reproachful blue eyes on Rebecca, then looked meaningfully at the empty china bowl. 'Becs, darling,' she said in her husky upper-class drawl. 'You've pinched our pot. We always said, never. Not even for the sweetest taxi driver ever.'

'I've not pinched it,' said Rebecca, flopping thankfully on to the nearest kitchen stool. 'I've won it, Annie. Oh, I've won it. The fantasy of the year. The decade . . .'

Annie's eyes grew even wider. 'Not Max. Surely not Max?'

'No!' Rebecca gestured impatiently. 'I don't even want to think about Max. No, somebody quite different, Annie. Someone I don't even know. You see, last night I was kidnapped.'

'Kidnapped. You're serious, aren't you, darling?'

'Yes. Absolutely serious.'

'Weren't you completely terrified?'

'Yes. At first I was terrified out of my mind. But then this man, the man who jumped into my car and made me drive him across London, he turned out to be OK. More than OK. In fact, he was utterly, utterly gorgeous.'

'Oh!' Annie looked enraptured. 'Thick, strong, and long?'

'Oh, yes. Oh, most definitely yes to all three,' breathed Rebecca.

Half an hour and three coffees later, they were still both sprawled comfortably on Annie's crumpled bed, the only surface in the entire house on which there seemed to be sitting space, while Annie extracted, with huge delight, every last shred of detail from her friend.

'So these people – the well-endowed guy, Petro, and the girl, Cass – they held you down on the bed, while the man rubbed his dick against your breasts?' Annie was radiant with lust.

Rebecca grinned. 'They knew I was enjoying it,' she explained. 'In a way, I challenged them to do it. I'd already watched them, you see, having sex together. And I told myself I might be able to escape if I distracted them.'

'Cunning. But really, you just fancied this Petro like mad?'

'I suppose I did, yes. Wouldn't you have done?'

'Oh, God, yes. Petro sounds divine . . .' Annie wriggled deliciously on the rumpled bed. 'And then Liam – this gorgeous, blond rough-diamond type in leather and jeans, who's up to some shady business and who kidnapped you – he carried you back to the bed after you'd tried to escape, and made love to you?'

'Yes.' Rebecca's voice was softer now. 'He was glorious, Annie. Sort of earthy and – wicked. Up to no good, I'm afraid. He tried to spin me some yarn about being a journalist, of the fashionable scruffy kind who's out to expose the evils of modern-day capitalism or something, which couldn't possibly be true. But who cares about the lies, when he was such a glorious lay?' She picked idly at the counterpane and sipped some more coffee. 'Apparently he's got this thing about rich upper-class girls like me. I'm just another one to add to his list, unfortunately. But he was worth it.'

'Better than Max?'

'Christ, yes.' Rebecca sighed wistfully. 'And that reminds me, Annie. Max won't help us out. I asked him last night.'

'Oh.' Annie's shoulders slumped. 'Back to reality with a bump, then. By the way, Max must have rung you earlier this morning – there's a message on the answerphone. I only got in at nine.'

'You only got in at nine?' teased Rebecca. 'Who were you with all night? Rich, gorgeous, eligible?'

'Rich, gorgeous, and a shit. The usual.' Annie looked suddenly sad. 'He's on television, and he spends more time admiring himself in the mirror than he does looking at me. The kind I usually fall for. Unfortunately.'

Rebecca said quickly, 'He didn't hurt you?'

'Only my pride, I suppose.' She laughed wistfully. 'We'd had a wonderful meal at that new place in Covent Garden, you know? Then he took me back to his flat, which was divinely expensive, all oriental carpets and mirrors and fabulous antiques. Anyway, he brought out the champagne, ready chilled, of course, and got me to strip for him. Apparently he has this thing about fair-haired, ex-convent school types like me. He was lounging back on one of his big leather settees, not undressed, but most definitely unzipped – I could see him rubbing his huge dick slowly up and down while I was doing my usual wanton seductress bit. And then, just when I was really turned on, waiting for him to call me over and pull me on top of him, he called out to someone, and a gorgeous Filipino girl with slanting black eyes came sidling sleepily out of one of the bedrooms, looking quite adorable in a flimsy silk nightshirt.' She sighed ruefully.

'Well, this man – I call him Lucifer to myself, Becs, because that's who he reminds me of, a sort of mad, bad fallen angel – he told me that he wanted to see us both together. With, you know, whips and things. He got out more champagne, with his cock still waving around, all ready for us, and told us to get on with it.'

'So, what happened?' Rebecca knew, very well, that she would hear everything. She settled back with her coffee and tried not to keep thinking longingly of Liam as the lust curled at her entrails.

Annie grinned. 'I'm sure you can guess – you've been with guys like him, haven't you? He had us spanking each other, basically, with some leather paddle things he keeps locked in one of those antique cabinets dotted around the place. Then, when I was really wild with excitement, and my bottom was all tingling and red, he turned the Filipino girl on all fours, on that priceless antique carpet, and took her himself. I had to watch. Imagine, Becs. There I was, wildly turned on, and I had to sit back and watch as he slid his long cock in and out of her little arse.'

Annie sipped at her coffee, and tried to smile. 'It was great fun, of course. He's desperately attractive, really demonic – like Lucifer, as I said. Dark, wild-eyed, well-hung. And the girl was certainly athletic too. She's obviously used to his ways. You can imagine, though, how I felt, being left on the sidelines.'

Rebecca could imagine, only too well. It would have been like her watching Petro and Cass together, watching Petro's long penis sliding in and out of Cass's eager sex while she longed for him herself. She said, softly, 'I can't imagine you were left on the sidelines for long, Annie.'

'Christ, no,' Annie drawled in her deliciously plummy accent. She stretched herself on the bed, grinning lasciviously. 'You know what I'm like, don't you? I made my feelings fairly plain, and Lucifer offered me a vibrator, told the girl to go and get it from her room. He stood there fondling his huge erection, damn him, waiting for her to come back, and there I was, naked and practically panting for him. Really wet, you know? Anyway, she came back with this huge rubber dildo, and then he sprang on the girl again, humping away at her, while I watched rather jealously and used this great purring phallus on myself. Pathetic, isn't it? I could see him turning his head to look slyly at me, watching me as I shuddered around the thing. Anyway, after Lucifer had finished driving his silky great dick between her buttocks like some demented demon, he grinned at me and told me I might be lucky next time. Then, would you believe, he pointed out to me that his private video

74

camera had been going all the time. He certainly got his money's worth out of me last night.'

'The sod,' exclaimed Rebecca, shifting herself a little because she was feeling warmly aroused herself at Annie's tale. 'Oh, Annie. You can find someone better than that, surely? There won't be a next time with this guy, will there?'

Annie looked uncomfortable, but her wide innocent eyes gleamed with lust as she said, 'He's picking me up tonight. He's promised it will be just the two of us.'

Rebecca sighed. Annie was as drawn to men like that as a butterfly to nectared flowers. But who was she to preach, when she'd enjoyed delicious sex only the previous night with two gorgeous men she'd never met before, who were more than likely criminals?

'Enjoy yourself, then,' she said. 'And invite me round when you've got him tamed, will you? He sounds rather appetising.' She sipped at her coffee, discovered it was cold, and pulled a face. 'Anyway, to get back to mundane reality, what sort of message did Max leave for me, can you remember?'

Annie rearranged herself on the bed. 'Oh, he asked you to ring him. Muttered something about the party last night not being much of a success, and would you fancy a meal with him tonight, or words to that effect. That's why I was so surprised when you said you'd split with him.'

Rebecca was surprised too. 'Are you sure you heard him properly? We split, all right. As I told you, I made the mistake of asking him if he'd buy the lease off our grasping landlord. He said no.'

'Well, perhaps that's why he wants to take you out for a meal,' said Annie hopefully. 'Perhaps he's changed his mind.'

'Pigs might fly. More likely he's remembered some money I owe him. Anyway, I'm not going to ring him back till much, much later. Let him stew. Right now,

I'm going to shower, and get myself together. I'm too exhausted to even think of Max.'

'You can watch last night's all-action video, if you like. Lucifer gave me a copy.' Annie smiled enchantingly. 'Tell me what you think of my performance, Becs, seeing as it's the only acting assignment I've had in the last six months.'

'What, and drive myself crazy with unsatisfied lust? No thanks, Annie. Some other time, perhaps?'

She went to shower and wash her hair, then dressed herself in a plain beige suit, the kind her mother would like. The rest of the day stretched ahead, without sex, without shopping or friends: in fact, without any kind of pleasure quotient, as she set her mind to getting a job.

Annie, who'd trained at drama school, had already left the flat to go to her job as a waitress in a fashionable Knightsbridge brasserie 'while I'm between TV assignments' as she told everyone airily. Ever the optimist, Annie had been born with a silver spoon in her mouth, being the daughter of a beautiful and well-known socialite who was related to some of the best families in England.

But then divorce had struck, and Annie's father, a suave diplomat, had moved on. Annie's mother, while still very much the social butterfly – she wrote a diary column for a well-known gossip magazine – was totally impractical with the reduced allowance she was now living on, and Annie was unable to rely on her any further for financial help. Just like me, really, thought Rebecca sadly. Born into a seemingly gilded life, she was in fact left with very little with which to support herself. Max had suggested that she use her connections, but even they didn't seem to stretch very far. And her education at an exclusive girls' boarding school had been wildly expensive, but left her with little in the way of useful qualifications.

Because she had a smattering of secretarial skills, she decided to try the agencies, but they were unimpressed by her lack of certificates and experience, and the money they were offering wouldn't even pay the rent, let alone anything else. The woman who interviewed her at one particular agency couldn't even be bothered to get her name right.

'So, Rachel,' she said, lighting a fresh cigarette with rather agitated, red-taloned fingers, 'you have some keyboard skills, and experience of receptionist work, have you?'

'Not Rachel,' said Rebecca with cold patience, 'but Rebecca. I've told you that already.'

'Sorry, darling. Oh, hell,' she said, stubbing out her just-lit fag, 'could you come back again tomorrow? Only I'm in a bit of a shambles at the moment. Just got back from Mauritius yesterday, to find the bloody flat's been burgled. And the insurance company are playing up, because they say the place shouldn't have been left empty for two weeks, not in SW1.'

'I'm sorry,' said Rebecca, stiffly gathering up her bag and her woefully brief CV. 'I'll go.'

'Come back tomorrow, Rachel darling!' The woman was already punching out a number on her phone. 'Tell you what. If you really want to earn some money, set yourself up in some sort of house-sitting agency – all my friends are desperate for someone really reliable to look after their homes while they're away. Christ, at least we might be able to insure ourselves then – Hello? Hello, is that you, Isobel? Listen, darling, you'll never guess. I've been burgled again . . .'

She waved her free hand carelessly at Rebecca, who was already letting herself out.

Rebecca visited the rest of the agencies on her list with growing depression. As she made her way laboriously across London on the tourist-filled tube, struggling to find the right change for the ticket machines and constantly fending off the unwanted attentions of various unattached young men who seemed to latch on to her like sellotape to the wrong side of wrapping paper, she wondered bleakly if she'd ever see her car again. Most likely not. She would, at least, have the satisfaction of telling her bank manager that it had been stolen. But then she remembered that if she claimed it was stolen, she would have to report its loss to the police; along with, presumably, everything else that had happened last night. The obvious option, of course, was to retrace her steps to the Docklands apartment where she'd spent the night, and tackle Liam face to face. She remembered Stevie's earnest expression as he'd said, 'Liam's not a car thief. He's not.'

Oh, shit. How could she believe any of them? She did some shopping in Bond Street on her way home, defiantly stretching her credit card to its limit. Then, still feeling flat with depression, she got the tube to Kensington High Street and walked the rest of the way home.

And as she turned the corner into the little mews street where she lived, she stopped and blinked. Her car was there. It was parked close to her house, next to a meter. Some money had been put in, but it had run out, and a parking ticket fluttered aggressively beneath the wipers. Rebecca picked it up, feeling a little dazed. She unlocked her front door and found, lying on the door-mat, an unmarked envelope containing the keys, together with the usual pile of bills deposited by the postman.

So Liam had been here. She tingled at the thought. He knew where she lived. How? Her handbag, of course; her address was in her diary, and on her inhaler. He'd have made sure of all that last night. He didn't seem to miss a thing.

With an effort, she humped her carrier bags and all the bills inside, and dropped them on the kitchen table, feeling on edge, unsettled. He could at least have left a note. But why should he? He didn't want to see her again. That was quite plain.

Depression always made her starving hungry. She flicked on the TV in the sitting room, and, resolutely ignoring her decision to diet, went into the kitchen to make herself a huge, comforting bacon sandwich. The thought that Liam had been here continued to pull at the back of her mind, unsettling, arousing.

OK, she told herself angrily, as she sank into a squashy sofa with her sandwich and idly flicked over to the news. So he'd been gorgeous-looking, and an extraordinary lay. He had a lovely cock; he knew exactly how to use it; and he spoke to her like dirt. Novelty value, a bit of rough, that was all. Best to forget him, as soon as possible.

But she couldn't. Her mind kept wandering back to him like a child within reach of a tantalising pile of forbidden sweets. And it almost made it worse that she'd got her car back, because it told her so flatly that he didn't ever want to see her again.

As Rebecca demolished her sandwich, Annie rushed in to get ready for her date with Lucifer, because it was her night off from the restaurant. Her blue eyes glowed with anticipation.

'Be careful, Annie,' said Rebecca.

'Oh, I'm all right, darling. I don't think he's seriously weird, you know? Anyway, I might as well make the most of him, because he's going abroad soon, to film some glossy holiday feature in the Bahamas. He even asked me if I wanted to look after his flat while he's away.' She grinned. 'Probably so he can fantasise about me playing with myself on that huge leather sofa of his.'

Rebecca was suddenly alert with interest. 'Do you think he might pay you?' she said quickly. 'For looking after the flat, I mean?'

Annie smoothed down her long, floaty summer dress and said vaguely, 'Don't know. I'll ask him, shall I?

He's going away for a whole month. How about a hundred a week minimum for flat-sitting?'

Rebecca remembered the woman in the agency saying, 'All my friends are desperate for someone reliable to look after their homes while they're away. Christ, then at least they'd be able to insure themselves . . .'

'It sounds OK,' said Rebecca slowly. 'It sounds very much OK. Sound him out, will you? But wouldn't he want references or something, if he's leaving you in charge?'

'He knows Mummy. Everyone knows Mummy. She still writes that social column, you know, and he thinks she's fantastic.' Annie grinned. She swung her bag over her shoulder. 'I'd better be off, anyway. See you later.'

'See you later. Have a good time, now.'

The house seemed very empty when she'd gone. Rebecca finished off her bacon sandwich, mentally counted the calories, then thought inevitably of Liam. To distract herself, she wandered to the kitchen to scrounge again, wondering what else there was to eat. Picking up a yoghurt to check the sell-by date, she was only vaguely aware of the TV news filtering slowly through her food- and Liam-obsessed brain as the announcer droned his way smoothly through the financial headlines. 'And there's been a major setback in the City for businessman Hugh Raoni's newly floated Green Company . . .'

She dived back into the sitting room to stare at the screen, a spoonful of yoghurt halfway to her mouth.

'. . . It has been revealed, through anonymous sources said to have been initiated by an unnamed journalist, that the Green Company actually has shareholdings in several spheres, such as waste disposal and road building, that are quite at odds with its supposedly eco-friendly image. Company chairman Hugh Raoni has declared himself shocked by the revelations, and has denied all knowledge of his subsidiaries' involvement in these fields, saying he was badly misled by his fund managers. Nevertheless, shares in his prestigious Green Company have dropped badly today . . .'

Rebecca was suddenly leaning forward, yoghurt quite forgotten, gazing at the screen. There was an interview with Raoni, who mouthed platitudes. He looked just as she'd imagined him from Max's description: handsome, well-groomed and beautifully dressed. He oozed confidence just as his suit shouted money, and he brushed aside today's catastrophic collapse as a minor setback. She remembered how Max had enthused about the man. 'It's the future, Rebecca,' he'd told her confidently. 'Big money, like Raoni's, is all going on corporate environmental performance these days. Everyone's going ethical. It's the only way to be.'

Rebecca suddenly remembered Liam saying to her in his calm, clear voice, 'Those people who are after me aren't the police. Oh, no. They're far more dangerous than that.'

'Why are they after you?' she'd asked.

'They want to stop me talking about something I've found out. It's as simple as that.'

Rebecca sat back, her mind snapping sharply into focus. Yes, it was simple.

No wonder Liam had been on the run last night. He was a journalist after all, just as he'd told her; and those anonymous sources the newscaster had referred to were in the slim briefcase that he'd clutched to his chest all through their mad midnight drive through London. Thanks to Liam, Raoni had been stripped, temporarily anyway, of both his eco-credibility and a hell of a lot of money. Rebecca let her breath out slowly. Why hadn't she realised that it was Hugh Raoni himself that Liam had been after? Hugh Raoni, the smooth, smiling power-broker who had told Max that Rebecca wasn't good enough for him.

As the newscaster droned on, she realised that she

was clenching her fists so hard that her nails were digging into her palms.

'Oh, well done, Liam. Well done,' she breathed. She wished she'd believed him when he'd started to open up to her, and then he might have told her more. She wished she'd trusted him. She wished that she could see him again. She knew, too, that just seeing him wouldn't be enough.

She still had his jacket. She stroked it absently, like a child with a security blanket, her mind hazed with memories of the delicious pleasure its owner had brought her. It was still only seven o'clock, and the empty evening stretched interminably ahead. The phone rang, and she leapt towards it, hoping for a moment that it might be Liam. Leaving it on the answering machine, but ready to pounce, she heard Max's suave cultured tones, and was aware of a crushing sense of disappointment. He wanted her to ring him, as soon as possible, because he wanted to talk to her about the party. He sounded so smug, so damned complacent, that she longed to throw the phone out of the window. 'Stop using up the tape, you bastard,' she muttered under her breath, storming back into the kitchen to make a coffee before he'd even finished.

It was no good. She'd be fit for nothing until she'd tracked Liam down and spoken to him again. It could well be that he wouldn't be at all pleased to see her, because she already knew far too much about his key role in the Raoni affair; but she was prepared to risk that.

Anyway, she told herself, she needed to give him back his jacket.

Changing quickly into some pencil-slim cream jeans and a black T-shirt, she grabbed her keys and the jacket and hurried down the stairs to her car. She rolled back the roof to let in the evening sunshine, and felt her spirits lift as the engine purred sweetly into life.

The sun-warmed London streets were still thronged with cars and summer tourists weighted with cameras. She crawled through heavy traffic along Victoria Embankment, then headed east towards the Isle of Dogs, following the line of the river, passing the familiar outline of Tower Bridge silhouetted against the evening sunshine. As soon as she reached West Ferry Road and the residential developments that adjoined it, she began to slow down and look around more carefully.

She knew that the house had been close by the river, so if she combed the area methodically, she would find it, surely. If only she'd taken in more of her surroundings last night, or this morning, even, when the taxi carried her away; but she'd absorbed so little, because her mind had been preoccupied with other things. Liam, mostly. She pressed on, her eyes straining at street names and directions, starting to grow hot and tired and frustrated.

Then, just when she was about to give up hope, she found the road she was looking for. She recognised the tall façade of the newly-refurbished warehouse building; the big, gleaming windows that looked out over the river from beneath heavy concrete lintels. She recognised, too, the untidy clusters of cement mixers and other evidence of building work; in fact there was a group of yellow-helmeted workmen just tidying up, a little further down the road, who watched with interest as Rebecca's sleek open-topped car coasted slowly towards them.

This was the house, set in the middle of the terraced row. She recognised the unpainted door, the pile of empty milk bottles gathering dust. She parked and got out, carrying Liam's jacket over her arm like a talisman, and walked slowly towards it.

'No one there, love. It's empty.'

She jumped as she realised that the builders had drawn near, grinning at her. They weren't wearing shirts, and their work-hardened bodies were brown and sheened with sweat. Rebecca suddenly remembered Annie's fantasy, and pushed the thought away hurriedly.

'The apartment up there's not empty,' she said, pointing. 'I know there are some people living in this one.'

One of the builders moved forward. 'You're right,' he said, 'there is someone there usually. She lives here by herself. The rest of the apartments below her aren't finished yet. The lads and I have noticed her because she looks rather young to have a big place like this all to herself.'

By herself? Rebecca's mind was working desperately. Surely Cass didn't own this house? 'Do you know her name?' she asked sharply. 'Please. It's really important.'

'She's called Chloe,' said another man, stepping forward. He looked as if he might be their boss. 'Chloe Masters. She's a writer, or something. Nice lady: always friendly, always has a word for the lads. She's away on holiday at the moment; her place has been empty for a couple of weeks now.'

'No,' said Rebecca. 'That's not possible. I know there were some people here, last night.'

'Must have been ghosts, then, love. Or squatters. There's been trouble before with squatters along this street; it will be better when all the places are done up and occupied. There was no one when we got here this morning, that's for sure. No one was here yesterday when we knocked off either. We'd call the police if we saw anyone suspicious hanging around.'

'All right,' Rebecca said. 'Thank you.'

She turned back to her car, heavy with despondency. This had been the house, she was sure of it; but Liam and his friends had vanished without a trace. Could they be squatters, just using the house at night-time, when the builders had gone? They certainly hadn't seemed like the sort of people to live in a place like that.

But then, nothing had been as it seemed in the last twenty-four hours. It was as if the whole episode was a figment of her imagination, a fantasy indeed.

One thing was certain. There was no way at all she could get in touch with Liam again, to tell him that she understood now, and wished she had trusted him. And she knew, without being told, that there was not the remotest possibility of him getting in touch with her.

Perhaps it was just as well.

Twilight was muting the brashness of the London streets by the time Rebecca got back to her house. Still feeling unsettled, she put her car in the garage then went to open the front door with her key.

Then she stopped. There were lights on upstairs, and she could hear music playing.

She froze, her hand on the door. Annie was out. She herself had not left anything on, she was sure of it. Perhaps it was Annie, back early from Lucifer's den.

The door was certainly unlocked. She pushed it open warily and went up the stairs. Through the open door into the tiny kitchen, she could see that the kettle had recently boiled. Her own washing-up still sat in the sink, reproaching her.

Then she heard the sound of voices, coming from the TV in the sitting room. She looked through there and saw Max, lounging on their squashy white settee in his dark business suit, the remote control in his hand. She'd forgotten he had a key, it was so long since he'd used it. He looked round at her, and grinned. He clicked the off button, and she realised he'd been watching a video.

'Made yourself at home?' she said somewhat coldly, eyeing the bottle of white wine he'd helped himself to from the fridge, and the half-empty glass.

'Hi, Rebecca. I've been ringing all day, leaving messages. Where've you been? Busy shopping? Gossiping with your friends?'

She was stung by his casual complacent air of owner-ship, after the things he'd said to her last night. And his assumption of her lightweight activities goaded her into an outright and utterly spontaneous lie. 'Neither. I've been working, actually,' she said, dumping her bag on the coffee table and running her hand absently through her hair.

'Really? You've got yourself a little job, then?'

He said it with such amused indifference that she was bridled into complete rashness. 'Not exactly,' she said. 'Actually, Annie and I are setting up our own business. We're going to look after people's homes for them while they're away. I've got several clients lined up already.'

'I'm sure you have.' He grinned. 'Come here, Rebecca.' He'd reached to click on the video again, and he stretched one arm out to her possessively. His sleek regular features were set off dramatically by his expen-sive silk shirt and Savile Row suit, and Rebecca felt her pulse tingle warningly. Oh, God, she hated him after last night, after what he'd said, what he'd done. But he was still so attractive, damn him.

She sat reluctantly next to him, keeping her distance, trying to work out what he was after. Then she saw what was playing on the screen. It could only be Annie's video, the one she'd casually mentioned this morning. The picture was a little blurred, and the setting was dark; but it was still clear enough for her to see Annie, and the Filipino girl, and the man who must be Lucifer, all writhing purposefully on the thick cream carpet.

'Oh, God,' she said. 'It's Annie. It's hers. How dare you come in and put it on, Max?'

He laughed and pulled her closer. 'It was in the machine already. Relax. I just flipped on the video channel while I was waiting for you, and there it was. Large as life. Larger, perhaps.'

Rebecca watched, riveted, only vaguely aware that Max was pouring her a glass of wine, and refilling his own. She found herself gazing mesmerised at Lucifer; she couldn't see much of his face, but his cock was huge. Just as Annie had described, he had the slender young Filipino girl naked on all fours, so her long black hair curtained her face. Her body was a warm olive colour, and Lucifer was fondling her buttocks, caressing the crease between her thighs with the blunt head of his rampant penis. Max passed Rebecca her wine; she drank it numbly, then felt the chilled potent liquid fizzing through her veins.

'Fine company your friend Annie keeps,' said Max. Rebecca realised his voice was husky, as if he were already a little out of control. She glanced instinctively at his lap and saw a bulge pressing against his crotch, signalling his blatant arousal.

'How long have you been watching this, Max?' breathed Rebecca accusingly.

He grinned, and loosened his red silk tie. 'Long enough. It's your friend Annie next. Look.'

He was right. Annie moved centre-screen, her long fair hair hanging in a tumble of curls around her delicate face and naked shoulders. Her breasts were pert, pink-tipped, flushed with desire; she moved slowly closer to the camera, revealing more of her body, and Rebecca saw, with a jolt of shock, that her friend was gently rubbing a huge rubber dildo against the mound of her sex.

'Max,' she said urgently. 'Max, we shouldn't be watching this.'

'Why not? Relax, angel. She told you about it, didn't she? And she left it in the machine, for God's sake. She wants you to see her at her rampant best, wants you to join in next time, probably . . .' He broke off and leant forward. 'Christ, that's incredible. Just look at that.'

Someone, probably Lucifer, had swung the camera round from its swivel mounting so that it was focused on the Filipino girl, on all fours, looking up at the lens expectantly. Then Lucifer was behind her, his face tense, his hands grasping at her buttocks. His penis nudged between her thighs, grossly distended. As Rebecca and Max silently watched, he pulled her bottom cheeks apart and drove into her well-primed vagina. He thrust with vigour, his red shaft glistening with her juices as it drove in and out; Rebecca watched, aware that she was holding her breath.

Oh, God, she wanted some of that. She felt her own vagina tingle and swell, was aware of a strong, almost painful pulse throbbing there as she imagined that giant rod of stiffened male flesh pounding deeply within her. Max, beside her, had also gone quite tense; his arm had crept round her, drawing her close and, with his eyes still fastened on the screen, he was pulling Rebecca closer, sliding his hand under her clinging black T-shirt, pushing aside the cotton of her bra and feeling and stroking at her hard little nipples until she wanted to cry out at the delicious spasms of longing that were shooting through her.

Annie had moved into the picture now. With exquisite feline grace, and a look almost of innocence, she eased herself into position so that both Lucifer and the Filipino girl could watch her as they copulated. She was holding the rubber phallus with one hand, and stroking at her sex with the other, splaying the swollen pink lips beneath her little mat of downy blonde hair so that her arousal was blatantly apparent. Rebecca saw that Lucifer was still driving his enormous cock into the Filipino's rear; but his eyes were on Annie.

Slowly, with a mischievous grin, Annie leant back a little, her haunches settling on the soft carpet, her shoulders resting against a settee. Her legs were wide apart, her knees delicately raised. Then she licked the dildo, running her tongue round it lasciviously to moisten it; and she began, with a little sigh of longing, to drive its thick bulk deeply into her vagina.

Silently, Max took Rebecca's hand and put it on his groin. She could feel his penis, like an uncoiling serpent, hard and hot through the fabric of his clothing. Oh, God, she wanted him. At least, she wanted someone. She was wet and slippery between her thighs, and her breasts ached with the heavy tension of arousal. Her eyes were glued to the flickering screen. She saw that Lucifer was pumping frantically now, hugely aroused; his swollen balls were slapping against the Filipino girl's rump, and the girl beneath him was writhing, arching her head in ecstasy. Annie, darling Annie, was in a world of her own, happily driving the huge rubber phallus in and out of her vagina, while using her other hand to squeeze and pull at her stiffened nipples, her eyes closed with bliss.

Suddenly Lucifer pulled out of the Filipino girl. Rebecca was surprised, because she didn't think he'd climaxed yet. He hadn't. She gasped as she saw him rub his engorged cock frantically against the girl's taut silky buttocks. Then Rebecca saw him throw his head back in a silent cry, and his penis leapt and spasmed as his semen jetted forth over the girl's olive skin. Annie, too, was working frantically at herself with the dildo as she watched his cock in rapt fascination; Rebecca saw her rosebud mouth growing slack and her blue eyes becoming glazed with pleasure as she turned the purring motor on to fast, and pumped her hips against the hard rubber cock with frenzied glee.

The picture faded. Instantly Max was on her, his mouth hot against hers, his tongue plunging possessively between her lips, tasting faintly of minty toothpaste and expensive white wine. Rebecca stretched out swiftly beneath him on the settee, uttering soft little moans of delight as he pushed up her tight black T-shirt and tore aside her tiny bra and nipped at her hard raspberry nipples with his teeth.

'Oh, God, Max,' she muttered. 'I need you, now.'

Almost shaking with desire, she pulled her tight cream jeans down to her knees, feeling deliciously imprisoned by her restrictive clothing. She heard the rustle of the condom packet – he'd come prepared, then – and a moment later she felt the silky length of his stiffened penis throbbing against her belly, then sliding downwards to find the warm flesh-folds that were already wide open for him. He drove straight up into her and held himself there, filling her immediately with such delicious, toe-curling pleasure that she was almost delirious with joy.

'Please fuck me,' she muttered, her legs still trapped beneath his heavily muscular ones, so he had to take her at an oblique angle that made the shaft of his cock rub tantalisingly against her soaking clitoris. 'Fuck me hard, Max.'

He did. His penis was long and hard as iron as he thudded into her again and again. His fingers squeezed her nipples, driving her wild with a sweet pleasure that was deliciously mingled with a hint of pain. His mouth was hot and possessive over hers. She clenched herself tightly round him, feeling the hard friction of his cock; at the same time she lifted her hips, trembling in an agony of arousal, and felt herself begin to topple over the edge. An excruciating orgasm roared slowly through her body as his lengthy penis continued to drive darkly into her.

He came quickly after that, his breathing ragged, his cock spasming jerkily. Their bodies were sheened with sweat as they lay fused together.

Max kissed her, nuzzled her. She clung to him, warm and replete. Perhaps she'd misjudged him last night. Perhaps she'd not understood him properly. He was still a glorious lay, and he still, it seemed, wanted her very much.

She pulled herself up at last, and so did he. She nestled into his shoulder. 'That was delicious, Max,' she said. 'But we shouldn't have watched it at all. It's Annie's. It's private.'

'Relax, angel,' he drawled. 'I keep trying to tell you. She knew we were going to watch it.'

Rebecca went suddenly cold. She pulled away a little from Max and struggled to pull her clothes into some semblance of respectability. 'She knew? How?'

He refilled her glass of wine and handed it to her. 'She rang me earlier today, while you were out,' he said casually. 'Said she was worried about us, worried that you wouldn't ring me back, or something. She suggested I let myself in, open up some of the wine in the fridge, and have a look at the rather interesting video she'd left slotted in.'

'So – Annie planned all this?'

'She didn't want us to split, sweetheart. Neither do I.'

'That wasn't the impression you gave me last night, Max. What does Janey Franklin think of all this?'

He shifted, looked a little uncomfortable. 'It's nothing to do with her. I told you it was an open-ended thing with Janey.'

Rebecca wondered, somewhat sourly, if Max had got wind of the fact that Janey had been humping someone else rather frantically in the loo at the party last night. But she said nothing, just drank her wine.

After all, she had her own secrets to keep. She wondered if Max had any idea, any idea at all, that the unknown journalist who had sent Hugh Raoni's shares crashing into free fall had in fact stolen the incriminating documents from the house last night, from under Raoni's nose, while the party was in full swing. She wondered what he would say if he knew that Rebecca had spent the night with him.

She said carefully, 'Hugh Raoni doesn't think too much of your connection with me either, does he? Though, from what I've heard today, he's got rather a lot of other things on his mind.'

Max suddenly ran his hand through his sleek dark hair. 'Christ, yes. I'd almost forgotten – that video of Annie's drove it from my mind. I meant to tell you earlier, angel. There was some trouble at the party last night; Hugh Raoni was burgled. Some shitty little intruder got in during the party, stole some important stuff Raoni doesn't usually keep at home – papers, documents. Whoever it was had some nerve, and inside information, too, to know the stuff was there that night. The thief took exactly what he wanted from Raoni's study: some highly confidential reports submitted to Raoni by one of his top managers, who's boss of a waste disposal company that's going to be hauled before the courts for discharging toxic stuff into local rivers. Raoni was going to take the papers to his office this morning, and work with some accountants to disassociate the dodgy waste-disposal set-up from his Green Company, and obliterate any evidence that it was ever anything to do with him. But this sneak-thief made any cover-up quite impossible, and the mess has landed firmly on Raoni's own doorstep. Raoni's in quite a lot of trouble, as you might have heard on the news.'

'Yes,' said Rebecca. 'Yes, I have heard.'

'Caused a catastrophic fall in his company's shares. All done very deliberately; the timing couldn't have been worse.'

Rebecca said carefully, 'Didn't anyone see this man at the party? Didn't anyone check on him? Surely it was obvious that he was an intruder.'

Max shrugged. 'Nope, no one noticed a thing. He must have fitted in well. It was only when someone found Raoni's study door wide open, with papers scattered around, that one of the security guys Raoni had paid to mingle with the guests realised something was badly wrong. By the time he raised the alarm, the thief was tearing off down the road. Several of Raoni's men gave chase, but the guy got away, because there was a car waiting down the road for him. A fast one. Raoni's men got their own car and gave chase for a good distance, but then they lost him. Raoni was livid.'

Rebecca's heart was thumping slowly, almost painfully. 'I must have gone before all this happened. Did Raoni stop the party?'

'No. Only a few people like me knew about it. Most of his guests didn't even realise anything was wrong. Raoni was hoping, I think, to smooth things over, and get the stolen papers back before any damage could be done; he had a few leads to follow, a few addresses to check. But none of them worked; and, as you saw from the news, the damage was done all right.'

Rebecca hesitated. 'Do they have any idea who he was, this man, this intruder who stole the papers? They said on the news that he was a journalist.'

Max's aristocratic face twisted with scorn. 'He calls himself a journalist, but the radio news station that he first contacted with the story says that he's a member of one of those green activist groups – admittedly a little bit cleverer than most of the hairy weirdos of his kind, but still scum, living off taxpayers' money, hitting out at people like Raoni, who provides hundreds of jobs and services for people. And all because they're jealous of his wealth.' He laughed sneeringly. 'I can just see him. A hairy, dirty computer buff in an anorak – probably got some weird name, too, like Terrier, or Scout, something out of a comic strip . . .'

No, thought Rebecca wildly to herself, no, his name's Liam.

She sat back, pretending to sip at her white wine, but all the time she was experiencing a renewal of sheer exhilaration at what Liam had achieved. However Max and his friends might try to sneer at him, he was enterprising and courageous. That chase had been for real. What would Raoni's men have done to Liam, if they'd caught him? They wouldn't just have taken the papers back and wished him goodbye. Oh, no.

She said carefully, 'So they know this man's a journalist with an interest in environmental issues. But that hardly narrows the field, does it? Has Raoni any more clues as to who it was who stole those papers and gave them to the press?'

'No, but he's sworn to track him down if it's the last thing he does. These green warriors, or whatever they call themselves, are elusive little shits – they work under false names, false addresses.'

'Raoni's not putting the police on to this man, or his accomplice, the one who drove the car?' She felt rather dizzy at the revelation that they all thought she was Liam's accomplice.

Max laughed. 'The police? Christ, no. Raoni wants to sort this out in his own way. And anyway, he has got something on this guy to follow up – Raoni told me this afternoon, when I rang him from the bank about a loan he'd been wanting to fix up. Apparently, our eco-warrior friend broke his story to a radio news station at nine this morning, by phoning one of its reporters, then arranging to drop off the parcel of incriminating papers about the waste disposal company at a pre-arranged place. The reporter he spoke to is a quick thinker, a smart man who professes to be keen on environmental issues, but is a damn sight keener on ready cash. He saw that there could be money in all this, and arranged for our guy to ring him again in a couple of weeks or so, and fix another meeting – he promised him some airtime for prominent environmental issues, that sort of thing. Then the radio reporter, Pete Harmsworth, rang Raoni, and offered to sell him the meeting time and place, as soon as he knows it. For a good sum, of course. Raoni will have his henchmen waiting.' He smiled thoughtfully. 'I wouldn't give much for our eco-warrior's chances, once Raoni knows his identity.'

Rebecca forced herself to ask the question. 'Why? What would Raoni do?'

Max got up and knelt in front of the video player to rewind the film. 'What do you think, sweetheart? This devious little greenie has lost Raoni millions on the stock market, not to mention his eco-credibility. Raoni's powerful. I should think he'll have the guy thoroughly, and nastily, beaten up.'

'But – but that's criminal, Max!'

Max straightened up gracefully. 'So who's complaining? It would be made to look like an accident. A very spontaneous accident.'

In two weeks. Oh, God.

Max was reaching for his jacket, stretching his elegant limbs. 'I haven't eaten yet, and I don't suppose you have, have you? Come on. Get showered and changed and I'll take you out to a restaurant. There's a good new Japanese one down in Knightsbridge that everyone's raving about. Come to think of it, perhaps I'll join you in the shower, and we'll work up a really good appetite.'

'No. Thanks, Max, but I've already eaten,' she said, lying desperately.

'Well, we'll just go for a drink, then.'

She struggled silently for an excuse. She wanted to be alone, to absorb what she'd just learned about Raoni's plans for Liam, to think how to help him. Would he even want her to help him, she wondered, when he'd bundled her out of his life so quickly? But she couldn't just let him walk into the trap Raoni had devised. She couldn't.

She wished Max would just go. Perhaps she'd made a bad mistake, letting him think that they could just carry on as before. She said at last, 'I'm sorry, Max, but I've got a lot to do. I've really got to get on with some phone calls, and catch up with things.'

He drawled, 'What sort of things? I didn't realise you had such a packed agenda.'

She floundered, then remembered, clutching like a drowning non-swimmer at a piece of straw. 'Why, this flat-sitting business I told you about. There's some paperwork to sort out, that kind of thing.'

His handsome face looked sulky suddenly. Almost like a spoilt schoolboy, a very rich public schoolboy. Nobody ever said no to Max, especially not a female, and he obviously didn't like it.

'You don't think you're taking this thing a bit seriously, Rebecca? Sounds like a joke to me. Forgive me, but I can't quite see you and Annie running a fully-fledged business.'

'Can't you?' she stood there facing him with her hands clenched at her sides. 'Oh, can't you?'

'No, quite frankly. What are you going to call yourselves? You'll have to make sure people don't think you're setting up some seedier kind of service, you know – especially with Annie's penchant for the exotic.'

'You seem to enjoy her proclivities as much as anyone,' she said, looking at the video machine. 'And we're setting everything up professionally.'

'Oh, yes?' he jeered. 'And what are you calling yourselves?'

'In House,' she said rather wildly. 'While you're away, we'll make sure things stay.'

He laughed. 'Got any clients yet?'

'Er – several possible ones, some enquiries . . .'

His mouth curled in scorn. Just then, the phone rang. She picked it up distractedly. 'Hello?'

'Becs, darling, it's Annie. Listen, exciting news – Lucifer really does want us to look after his flat! One hundred pounds a week, like you said.'

Rebecca felt the smile widening her face. She reached for the pen and notepad that were miraculously close by for once, and said clearly, for Max's benefit, 'One hundred a week. It's not up to our usual rate; but I suppose, as he's a friend of yours, we can make an exception. What's the address, Annie?'

She repeated the exclusive Belgravia address with inner glee, watching Max's jaw drop as she did so. 'Fine,' she said. 'Tell him it's on then, Annie.'

'Rebecca, is Max still there? How did things go?'

'All right, Annie. Yes, I'll speak to you later. Bye. And – take care.'

She knew Annie would understand that she couldn't talk. She blessed her, for her opportune call. Her blood fizzed with unexpected excitement at the thought of her wildly improvised idea actually coming off. She put the phone down and said casually to Max, 'That was Annie, talking about one of our clients.'

'So I'd gathered.' He looked reluctantly impressed. 'Perhaps it's not too bad an idea after all, Rebecca. Certainly the two of you must have lots of connections between you. Got any cards? I could move a few for you, if you like.'

She shook her head, realising that she was getting rather good at this lying business. 'Actually, they're at the printers. They're due tomorrow. I'll let you have some, Max, of course. And now, as I said, I need to get on with some phone calls.'

He frowned, the sulky child again. 'OK. Guess I'll have to find someone else to take out to dinner.'

He would, too. Janey Franklin, quite possibly.

But somehow, Rebecca didn't mind quite as much as she should have done. She didn't have the time.

Because, as she showed Max to the door and absent-mindedly accepted his light but lingering kiss on her cheek, her mind was full of Liam. She had to warn him that the radio reporter he trusted was in fact about to betray him, was going to lead him straight to Raoni's henchmen. But where was he? Who was he? And how could she hope to find him, before Raoni did?

Chapter Four

Moonlight glinted on the broken surface of the lake as Petro swam sleekly through the dark water. Cass sat watching from some rocks at the water's edge, clasping her hands round her knees, breathing in the leafy scents of the velvety July night. The tall beech trees arched like a canopy behind her, their interlaced branches breaking up the brightness of the stars. It was as hot and sultry as midday, even though it was past ten.

Petro waded slowly towards her, the little wavelets rippling around his strong torso. Lake water streamed from his long black hair to his glossy brown shoulders. 'You should come on in,' he said. 'It's warm.'

He came a little closer, then stopped. The water came to his thighs. Cass could see the black pelt of hair at his groin where his long phallus nestled, sweetly vulnerable compared to the rest of his body. She shivered suddenly in her cropped shirt and jeans. 'The trees, Petro,' she said. 'I can't stop thinking about the trees. They won't really be allowed to destroy them, will they?'

'Not while we're here to stop it.' He looked pointedly towards the little camp in the clearing: the cluster of tiny tents, the battered motor homes, drawn together for solidarity. There would be more. This was only just the beginning. 'And Liam,' added Petro earnestly, 'will be here soon. Won't he?'

Cass laughed, a little bitterly. 'You say his name as if he's some sort of hero, some mythical fantasy figure – Liam saves the world . . .'

Petro shrugged. He started walking towards her again, running his hand through his sleek hair, sending more sparkling drops of water showering around his shoulders. 'He's doing pretty well so far, isn't he? He all but destroyed that bastard Raoni, with the information he got about the secret activities of his precious Green Company. Do you know how he found out that Raoni would have those documents at his home, on the night of that party, instead of in his office safe where they're usually kept? He chatted up one of Raoni's middle-aged secretaries, that's how. Screwed her senseless. A man of many resources, is our Liam.'

She said obstinately, 'He should be here now, with us, telling us what to do.'

'Cass, you know he's not like that. He has his own agenda. Leave him to it. He'll be here in his own good time, to tell us what to do next; and then he'll be gone again. He's a loner, a leader, and meanwhile we're to settle ourselves down here for as long as it takes. And it's not always too unpleasant, is it?'

He was sitting beside her now on one of the rocks, rubbing a big navy towel across his shoulders. He was staring absently at a moonlit cove a little further round the dark lake; Cass looked to see what had caught his attention.

She might have guessed.

Some girls had come from the camp, to play at the water's edge. They were a fair way away from Cass and Petro, but it was quite obvious that the girls were very much aware of them – of Petro, at any rate. Both of them had long blonde hair, which glittered in the moon-light like silver, and they wore cropped denim shorts, and sleeveless T-shirts. They were sisters, but they could have been twins. Just as Cass turned to look, they were kicking off their canvas espadrilles and tentatively wading into the shallows, laughing and splashing.

Cass watched Petro watching them. He'd turned his back to her while he pulled the towel across his shoulders, and she absorbed the lovely muscular strength of his tight buttocks, the rippling play of muscles in his back.

Cass felt the sexual hunger gnawing at her loins. She was still bitter about Liam, and the time just over two weeks ago that he'd spent with that rich bitch Rebecca, when she'd hoped he'd spend his last night in London with her. There'd been no need for it. He didn't have to fuck the girl – she'd have done anything he'd asked anyway. Most women did.

Two weeks, since she'd last seen him.

She found herself wondering, in her jealousy, if Liam had perhaps stayed behind in London in hopes of seeing the rich girl again. He should be here now, whatever Petro said about him having a different agenda. They'd planned it weeks ago, all of them, Cass and Petro and Stevie and the rest, to move from London to this latest demo site in Berkshire, where plans were going ahead to drive a ring road through beautiful woodland that was hundreds of years old. The protest was starting to draw attention from all over the country. The road was to be linked to a huge out-of-town shopping centre, full of concrete and cars and poisonous fumes. Cass hated cars. She'd hated, almost more than anything, seeing Liam in that rich girl's car, because he looked for a moment as though he belonged in it, in that world.

'It has to be like that, Cass,' Petro had told her urgently when she commented on it. 'He has to fit into their world, otherwise he finds out nothing, and we're working in the dark. Don't you see?'

'No,' she'd said stubbornly. 'I don't see.'

She'd heard them, that night in the Docklands apartment. She'd heard the hateful, rhythmic pounding of the bed as Liam shafted the rich cow while she moaned and writhed beneath him, obviously enjoying every inch of his long, lovely cock. Just as Cass used to. She'd get him back. She had to.

Petro was drying himself rather absent-mindedly now as he stood there beside her at the water's edge. Looking up at him, she saw that his penis was stirring with life against his thighs; Cass, turning, saw why.

The two girls who were splashing about a little further round the lake had taken their clothes off now. They were playing in the shallows, stooping to hurl water at each other, laughing and shrieking as they hopped about on the smooth water-washed pebbles. Their bodies were slim and brown, their pert breasts crowned with prominent dark nipples, and the moonlight hung in shivering droplets on their naked skin. They kept glancing, with teasing eyes, at Petro, who stood transfixed.

'Go on,' said Cass dryly. 'They've been watching you all day. Make them happy.' She was used to their type. Camp groupies, the others called them mockingly, because they treated the protest camps like some kind of holiday. They came only in the summer, and stayed only as long as the weather was hot and dry. They helped themselves to wine, shared spliffs, and got themselves screwed by the hunkiest of the regulars, of whom Petro was always a favourite. Liam was the prime target; but he, thank God, tended to scorn them, and even if he did take them to his bed, he didn't usually spend more than a day or two at a time at the camps. Poor old Stevie, who had stayed on with Liam in

London, always watched them rather wistfully. Unlike Petro, he was always too shy to make his mark.

'Go on, Petro. Join them,' she said again.

Petro needed no further telling. In fact, he was quite relieved to get away from Cass, because she was sometimes heavy company, especially when she was hung up about Liam. It was a mistake for anyone to get hung up about Liam.

Hesitating only briefly about whether to haul on his jeans or pull the towel round his waist – both a little tricky, because by now his erection was quite prominent – he decided on impulse to plunge back into the lake and approach them that way. As he swam towards the girls, his sleek brown body was like a seal's cutting through the dark water.

He saw that the girls were pretending not to see him, but he knew very well that they had. They were engaged now in a mock tussle, trying to tip one another into the water; they were laughing aloud as their lovely little breasts rubbed wetly against each other. Oh, you sweeties, thought Petro rapturously and, by the time he got to his feet to wade the rest of the way, his cock was throbbing wildly.

They were still pretending not to notice him as he emerged from the water; and that suited him, because he loved watching their play-fight. The girls had only arrived at the camp this morning with their new expensive rucksacks and designer jeans – 'Shallow little tarts,' the scruffier, older female veterans had pronounced scornfully. Petro had been too busy talking with some of the other protesters about the likely route of the road, and whether tunnels would be too dangerous this time, to talk to them. But he kept seeing their laughing blue eyes turned towards him, and he found out that their names were Marianne and Lucy – two sisters, both at university, both looking for some excitement for the holidays. Both real blondes, too; he could see the downy triangles of pale pubic hair at the apex of their luscious thighs.

Suddenly they turned to face him, arms entwined, still laughing. 'Hi,' breathed one of them softly, her eyes straying mischievously to Petro's stupendous erection. 'I'm Marianne. This is my sister, Lucy. You're Petro, aren't you? The musician Petro. We know about you. We've heard about Liam, too. Is he here?'

'No. I'm afraid not,' said Petro, trying hard not to be jealous, because Liam was always the one all the camp followers asked for. He had some kind of enigmatic eco-hero reputation; hardly any of them had met him, or even seen him, but his fame – or notoriety – had spread, especially among the female sex. 'He's not here yet, unfortunately.'

'Never mind.' The one called Lucy looked down slyly at his rampant cock. 'Do you think you can manage both of us, at once?' She ran her hand over her slick wet breasts, and Petro smiled widely.

Cass, who'd been watching, lit a cigarette and settled herself back in a mossy hollow so they couldn't see her. Their antics brought back memories of her first camp, four years ago. It had been a sizzling July, just like this one; the camp had been a hotbed of idealism and seething lust. 'It always gets like this in summer,' one of the older men, a forty-year-old bearded university lecturer, had told her as he shared his joint with her. 'A hint of rain, of cold, and the party's over – most of them melt away, come September. It's only the true protesters who slog it out in the mud, the cold, the dirt. Are you going to be a true protester, Cass?'

She had been sure of it then, just as she was sure the blonde pair, who'd got Petro on his knees now on a smooth turf-covered clearing just near the water's edge, weren't. She'd let the lecturer, whom she admired greatly because of his intelligence and his idealism, ease her out of her cumbersome eighteen-year-old virginity. She'd not had much idea, really, what it would be like, because she'd never thought much about sex; she'd been brought up to believe she was too thin and plain to be of interest to men. But he'd plied her with wine, and told her she was beautiful; she'd been shocked by the plethora of new sensations as he'd so carefully eased his stiffened penis between her thighs. He'd thrust gently for a while, filling her with a searing sensation of longing; then he'd become distraught, almost speechless, and he'd thrust and trembled his way to orgasm with swift intensity, leaving her guessing, hoping that there was more, much more.

She soon found out that there was. The lecturer went home then, to his family. Cass meanwhile threw herself into sex, and discovered she had a voracious appetite; she also discovered, to her surprise, that many men found her boyish looks and her small long-nippled breasts surprisingly attractive. But there was still something missing.

Then Liam arrived, and she knew what she had been waiting for.

She watched the girls with Petro. They would go back to university in a few weeks and boast to their friends about their commitment to the environmental cause; when really, all they were committed to at the moment was Petro's rather spectacular cock. Cass watched as Marianne bent over it, swirling its plummy head with her tongue, cupping his fat balls with her fingers and engulfing his throbbing shaft with her soft lips. She could hear the girls laughing, exclaiming over its size; Lucy was watching her sister avidly, playing with and squeezing her own nipples, saying, 'Save some for me. Save some for me, Marianne.'

Petro, stretched out on the turf, was groaning hoarsely as the girls licked and nipped him, playfully running their hands all over his brown sinewy body. Cass watched, feeling her own body quickening, feeling a little pulse of desire like an opening flower in her own secret parts. Petro was good, but not as good as Liam. Oh, no.

When Liam had arrived at the camp that summer four years ago, she'd known he was someone special. Not just because of his looks, which were spectacular even among that camp of young, exuberant students; but because everyone turned to him for guidance, for advice, even the older ones. The older women, veterans of Newbury and Greenham Common, mothered him to his face, and lusted wistfully after him from afar. The younger ones just lusted after him. He was elusive, secretive; he never spent more than a day or two at the camp, because he preferred to keep his base and his contacts in London. She heard he'd got a sparkling degree from the LSE, and could have had his pick of lucrative careers; but he laughed when she asked him about it, and said he was too young to sell himself to anybody.

Once he brought a girlfriend with him from London, where he did some writing on environmental issues. The girlfriend was a beautiful, sophisticated American called Ruth, who stayed close to Liam wherever he went around the camp, and made it quite plain that she was the one sharing his tent at night. Cass hated her. Ruth came from a rich New York background; she was only playing at all this, unlike Cass, who came from a poverty-stricken home on a Peckham council estate with an abandoned mother who'd struggled to bring up three kids alone. She'd hated Ruth, just as she hated Rebecca now. Why did Liam need them like that, when he made no effort to shake off his own working-class roots? Couldn't he see that to them he was just an accessory, a novelty?

One night, on learning from her friends that Ruth had

gone back to London for a few days to be with some relatives who were over visiting from the States, Cass made her way to Liam's little tent. She'd scrubbed herself in the nearby river, and shaved herself till her pale skin was like silk, and rubbed sweetly-scented baby oil into her body. Then she'd crept into his dark tent, and pulled off her jeans and T-shirt before Liam had even properly opened his eyes. Her body was skinny, she knew – too skinny for some men – but her nipples were long and dark, which usually excited them hugely, and her appetite for sex was rapacious.

Liam had stirred sleepily as she'd crept in. She'd watched him for a moment, luxuriating in his peacefulness, in her aloneness with him. In his sleep he'd pushed the blanket back from his body, so it lay in folds round his sleek hips. She'd adored the breadth of his shoulders, the nut-brown hardness of his nipples, the quilted muscles of his lean stomach. His face, in sleep, looked younger, and the hard perfection of its contours was softened by dreams. Gently the naked Cass had bent to peel the blanket further back from his body, and saw, with a shock of delight, that he already had an erection in his sleep. His penis had been heavy and dark against his belly, its silken tip reaching to his navel. With a little sigh she had bent down beside him and begun to press hungry kisses against his strong thighs, his stomach, his balls. She'd taken each of the velvety globes in her mouth, sucking and licking at the tender, hair-roughened skin. He'd woken, then. His sleepy blue eyes had widened in surprise; and then he'd smiled.

'Cass,' he'd said.

She'd taken his penis in her mouth, drawing it deep into the back of her throat, her insides trembling with a fresh surge of desire as she felt its thickness, its sheer male strength throbbing against her lips. She'd run her tongue round his cock-tip, and flickered over its tiny eye; she'd felt his body surge and ripple beneath her.

106

Oh, God, but he was beautiful. Her loins had spasmed urgently, melting with the sweet dark ache of desire; her little pleasure bud had throbbed angrily, and she'd longed to feel his stiffened rod of flesh deep within her.

He had still been smiling sleepily, running his hands through her close-cropped dark hair. Then his fingers had slid to her small boyish breasts and had begun to pull at the long brown teats until she was trembling with arousal. She'd needed him inside her, needed him to fuck her. She'd gasped and shivered, lifting her head from his straining cock, her mouth swollen with desire for him. The juices of her arousal ran sweetly between her thighs.

He'd said softly, 'I can't promise you anything, Cass.'

The glow of Cass's little torch, which she'd set on the ground beside her, played over the curving golden muscles of his smooth torso, over his mane of sleep-tousled hair. His eyes were lazy but warm, crinkled at the edges with smiling into the sun, their irises an incredible dark blue. His mouth was strong and passionate. The thought of it working on her breasts, on her sex, had made her almost convulse with need.

'When is she coming back? Ruth?' she'd said.

His face had become suddenly serious. 'I don't know. And I haven't promised her anything either, sweet little Cass. I travel alone. It's safer that way.'

Not tonight, you don't, she'd muttered to herself, and she'd wriggled sinuously up his body, legs straddling him so he could see the hungry pink folds of her splayed sex. She'd bent to kiss his mouth hard, twining her tongue with his, letting him taste his own cock. His answering kiss had been warm and strong and powerful, just as she had known his fucking would be. She'd felt his tongue plunge strongly up into her mouth, probing and thrusting in a delirious simulation of intercourse, and knew she had to have him, now.

His dusky penis had been nudging hungrily up

between her thighs. She'd sat astride him, feeling for its bulky thickness, guiding its saliva-moistened head against her sensitive vulva, shuddering with joy as it slipped against her prominent clitoris. Then she had lowered herself on to him, and begun to take his shaft into herself, while his hands played tenderly with her breasts.

Oh, God, he had been delicious. So thick, he'd speared her, stretched her to the very limit. So long and hard; she'd been able to move up and down on him as if he were an oiled wooden shaft, there solely for her pleasure. She'd ridden him faster, feeling the thickness of his cock chafing her pleasure-bud; then she'd slowed down, afraid he was going to come, as other men did, because of her frantic riding of him. He had been tense, but in control, watching her from under hooded eyes, a slight smile playing around his mouth.

He had squeezed harder at her nipples, watching her, waiting; she had gasped aloud and writhed her sinuous body above him as the delicious pleasure-pain of his stimulation washed through her. He had moved his penis again inside her, driving her towards the edge; she had clamped her yearning vagina round its silken stem and thrown herself wildly up and down its stiff length, impaling herself again and again, reaching down to find her own slippery cleft and rubbing swiftly against the side of her burning clitoris, feeling it like a hard, swollen little pebble of need.

Then she had cried out as the almost unbearable sensations took over her body, and she exploded into orgasm, riding him dementedly as the bliss of his penetration poured through her. She had tried to muffle her cries, fearful they would wake the camp; Liam had helped her by kissing her, drawing her down on to his hard chest so her breasts were caressed anew, prolonging the bountiful sweetness of her explosion. She had felt the sudden harsh pumping of his cock as he clamped her body over his; she felt him jerking inside her, again and again and then he had held her very close, running his hands through her cropped hair.

'No promises, Cass,' he'd said quietly at last.

'I don't want any,' she'd returned defiantly. But that was not true, then or now.

Idly, with flickering lust, she thrust aside the memories and continued to watch Petro and the two blonde girls at the water's edge. Petro was not Liam, but he was a good substitute. Marianne and Lucy had got him on his back now, pinning him down; he was laughing, protesting, but made no real effort to escape. His penis was glossy from Marianne's tongue; the two girls were crouched over him, breasts swaying, pert bottoms raised enticingly in the air. Cass wondered idly which of them would take him first. It looked as if Lucy would be the lucky one; she was preparing to sit astride him, her long blonde hair curtaining her face as she gazed down at his hungry erection. She was playing with herself, pulling her sex-lips apart in readiness for his shaft to plunge inside her.

But Marianne was obviously determined not to miss out. She, too, was positioning herself over Petro, straddling his face.

'Lick me, Petro,' she muttered. 'Use your big tongue to lick me out, while you fuck my sister. I won't take long – ah, yes . . .'

And then her voice had died away, because Petro, with his usual vigour, was lapping hungrily at her sex. Marianne writhed happily about on his face, rubbing her soaking cleft against his mouth, his nose, his jaw; as his tongue thrust up high into her pulsing vagina, the tremors of a forceful orgasm took her over. At the same time, Lucy lowered herself on to his cock, licking her lips as the big shaft drove remorselessly up inside her; she thrust herself up and down on him, moaning with delight, and all three of them came together in a deliciously sticky mingling of limbs and lips and tongues.

Petro, smiling hugely, rolled over on to his side, clutching both the girls to him. 'Christ,' he muttered happily. 'I'm not going to be fit for anything, with you two around.'

They caressed him gently, their eyes meeting conspiratorially. 'Oh, yes, you are,' they promised.

Cass pulled herself up, suddenly bored with watching them. Girls like Marianne and Lucy were useful, without a doubt. They brought good publicity, and they were photogenic; the press loved to interview people like them. She must make sure, though, that Petro primed them with some facts, as well as his lively cock, during their stay here. They'd probably just homed in on the camp in search of sex and adventure; most likely they didn't even know what they were protesting about.

It must be well past ten o'clock. Slowly she started to wander back through the trees towards the camp, where the flickering candles and lanterns of the protesters cast a soft glow over the assortment of tarpaulin tents. The faint murmur of companionable voices drifted towards her through the thicket of beech trees, silvered by the moonlight; the members of the little band were preparing to settle down for the night.

Cass wondered if they ought to be thinking of organising a rota of people to keep watch. Stevie had mentioned it to her rather anxiously when they first set up the camp; but Stevie was always anxious about something. Admittedly, he had a point. But as far as Cass knew, the business consortium behind the proposed development was still waiting for planning permission to be finalised. Only then could the developers bring the court action needed to declare them trespassers.

Then, they would have to be on their guard. Then, whoever it was who was planning the hateful road –

and the score of developments that would be sure to cluster along its ugly length – would be only too eager to arrange for the protesters to be beaten away from the site before they got a real chance to get dug in with their tree fortresses and concrete anchors and tunnels. They'd have to prepare themselves for the arrival of the private security guards: big, brutal-looking men, in heavy blue uniforms that made them sweat, who treated the protesters like scum and made their own mindless contribution towards the destruction of the environment.

She must speak to Petro in the morning about tightening up their defences. They could start by embedding the trees with bolts and wire, to smash up the chain saws. That had worked on other sites, but would it work here? She wished, again, that Liam was here: not only because she wanted him, but because she was worried about him. Now that Hugh Raoni was finished, she knew that the next task on Liam's list was to discover who was behind the big anonymous business consortium planning to destroy Hegley Wood. She knew that people of that sort, just like Raoni, would not take kindly to any sort of investigation.

'Don't worry about Liam,' Petro had reassured her earlier. 'He has his own agenda. Leave him to it.'

She had no choice. After all, Liam had made it quite plain that, whatever he was up to in London, he didn't want her help.

The girl was sitting by herself in the Soho wine bar, looking bored and miserable. As usual, her pretty friend was already being chatted up, and she was left by herself. This was all the more noticeable because the wine bar was crowded, as it always was on a Friday night. The men hunted in packs, downing their chilled beers and openly eyeing up the females on offer. The girls were dressed in scanty little numbers showing lots of tanned thigh. Their faces were heavily painted, their mouths drawn in typical sullen pouts as they feigned indifference to the predatory males surrounding them; but really they were on edge, strung out for the slightest hint of an advance.

When the girl, whose name was Charlotte, saw the man approaching, she looked round to see who he was aiming for. She knew it couldn't be her, because he was utterly gorgeous. Tall and blond, with a body to die for, and deep blue eyes set in a suntanned face that seemed all hard-edged cheekbone and lean strong jaw. He walked with a kind of athletic lope that just naturally oozed sex at every step. His clothing was almost scruffy: faded jeans and trainers, and a clinging white T-shirt. But he had all the women – and a few gay men – slavering over him as if he were dressed in the ultimate designer chic.

He smiled at Charlotte, showing even white teeth, and she looked over her shoulder again nervously. He couldn't be smiling at her. She was horribly conscious of the rolls of puppy fat beneath her straining blouse, and of her slightly plump thighs that were unfortunately spread wider by the padded stool she was perched on. She wished she could go to the loo, to powder her nose and put on some more mascara.

Then he said, in a drawling south London accent, 'Hi. Can I buy you a drink?'

Her voice came out almost as a squeak. 'OK. Vodka and cranberry, please.'

He bought her a large one, and a small beer for himself. He chatted to her about the wine bar, asked her where else she socialised, where she lived, as though he were really interested. He bought her another drink, and another, until Charlotte was quite dazed. At one point, Charlotte's pretty friend headed back in her direction, and her jaw dropped with envy as she glimpsed the man. Charlotte, with very rapid, very expressive eye movements, made it quite plain to her friend Sophie

112

that she was on no account to come any nearer. In fact, Sophie could at that moment go and jump in the bottom of the Thames, as far as Charlotte was concerned.

He told her his name was Liam. He was a journalist, he told her; he did occasional factual pieces for magazines and newspapers, and had been involved with some TV research. At first Charlotte could hardly say a word back, because she was so overcome by the fact that he'd singled her out. She could barely even lift her eyes to his beautifully masculine face without feeling butterflies of lust at her stomach. Instead, her gaze kept flickering over his body, and that was every bit as dangerous. His soft cotton T-shirt seemed to just skim over the hard muscles of his chest and shoulders. His jeans clung tightly to his long powerful legs; there were some frayed holes around the knees, where she could glimpse dizzying patches of warm, suntanned male skin. His thigh seemed to keep just touching hers as he lounged gracefully on the stool next to her, sending electric shocks through her and rendering her quite speechless.

But gradually, as the vodkas took effect, she grew more relaxed and met his eyes with increasing confidence. OK, so she was slightly plump, but what was wrong with that? The bar was packed with stick-thin women, but this guy hadn't lifted his eyes from her face, except to order more drinks. He must like her short skirt and her tightly buttoned blouse, even though Sophie had told her earlier, rather cruelly, that she could see her bra showing through it, because of the way the buttons strained over her big bust. Under his blue gaze, Charlotte glowed and blossomed.

'I bet you've got an interesting job,' he said.

'Oh, no. I'm only a secretary.'

'Only? Too many people use that word.'

'Well –' and she felt her plump cheeks growing pink again '– it's quite an important job, really. I work for a big engineering firm – roads and things, new motorways

113

– and I handle lots of confidential information, you know?'

'Then I won't ask you any more,' he said gravely. He looked at his watch. 'It's getting rather late, isn't it? This place will be closing soon. I suppose we'd better be moving on.'

We? Charlotte felt herself shake with excitement. The thought of having sex with a man like this was the stuff of her dreams. Something to remember for ever. She wanted to pinch herself. 'You could always,' she said with a slight squeak in her voice, 'come back to my place.'

They travelled together on the tube to Camden, where her flat was. The carriage was crowded, so they had to stand, and she stayed very close to him, conscious of other women looking at his lean body and tousled blond hair with a kind of jealous hunger, then at her with disbelief.

She didn't care. She had a beatific, vodka- and lust-induced smile all the way home; and when she finally unlocked the door to her little flat, two floors up in an old Victorian mansion off Camden High Street, she could hardly even remember the way to the kitchen.

'Forget coffee,' he said, coming up behind her and slipping his hands round her waist, then running his palms up to slide over her tight blouse and across the ripe swell of her breasts.

Charlotte felt the sexual tension fizzing through her rapidly hardening nipples. 'Oh, Liam,' she cried out, turning to face him. 'Kiss me, please.'

He kissed her, in a tender but purposeful sort of way that made her go quite weak. He tasted lovely: of sun and cold beer and sex. She kissed him furiously back, driving her tongue against his, wrapping her fingers round his strong neck, and standing on tiptoe to try to match his muscular height. His hands were round her waist, pulling her hard against him, so she could feel

114

the glorious male hardness at his loins; she whimpered and pressed herself harder against him, feeling the soft little folds of flesh between her thighs tingling and swelling. The vodka swirled headily through her veins, along with the sheer exhilaration of lust. She reached for his lovely tight buttocks and pulled him closer, shutting her eyes dreamily.

He held her away from him and smiled gently down at her. 'I bet you're popular at work,' he said.

She tried to wriggle close to his hard warmth again, nuzzling her cheek against his chest, breathing in his clean male smell. 'Yes, I am. Stewart Bridges, he's our senior partner, says he can trust me with anything ... Oh, Jesus, Liam. Can we go into the bedroom?' She was reaching to pull his T-shirt up, almost ripping it in her frenzy, running her palms with breathless delight up and down the quilted muscles of his stomach.

He chuckled low in his throat and caught her hands. 'I suppose you just work on London projects? With building and design, I mean?'

'Oh, no,' she said, gazing up at him dreamily. 'We've got something big on in the country – Hegley Wood, it's called; Berkshire, I think it is. You might have read about it, you being a journalist and everything, because some people don't like it. They're going to chop down some trees, you see, to build a road and a shopping centre. As if a few stupid old trees mattered.'

'As if,' he agreed, his blue eyes almost sleepy. 'Which company is behind this Hegley Wood project, sweet Charlotte?'

'Oh, I don't know.' She was suddenly, drunkenly impatient. 'Several, I think. But we're not supposed to talk about it. And I don't want to talk about it, not now. Shall I tell you what I want, Liam?'

He was still holding her hands, still smiling. 'What?'

'This,' she muttered hotly. Pulling away, she sank to her plump knees in front of him. With a determined speed that amazed Liam, she tackled the buttons of his faded Levis and crooned with joy as she saw the bulge that was barely contained by his white cotton boxers. 'Oh,' she gasped, 'your lovely cock. Lovely, lovely cock . . .'

Her feverish fingers swiftly drew out his stiffening length, playing with him, cradling him joyfully. Liam braced himself calmly against her ministrations. Then she pulled away suddenly and tugged at her blouse and skirt, throwing them impatiently to the corner of the room. That was better. She was wearing a new bra, an underwired affair in white satin and lace, with smooth satin knickers and matching suspenders holding up her sheer white stockings. Her plump flesh billowed out from the confines of the lace; the swell of her generous breasts was sweetly enhanced. She knew she looked much, much better like this.

'Good,' murmured Liam, running his hands over her smooth white shoulders, reaching to tug gently at her dark nipples so that they peeped over the edge of her low-cut bra. 'Very good.'

'Glad you think so,' chuckled Charlotte, gazing at his rapidly swelling cock in wonder. Jesus, it was splendid. It was jutting towards her now in all its glory; darkly rigid, its underside swollen with veins. She felt her juices running hungrily and bent quickly to take him in her mouth, sucking, drawing on him until she felt him tremble. God, he was good in her mouth; thick, strong, male. She loved sex, and enjoyed it frequently – the wine bar was a good pick-up place – but a man like this hadn't come her way before, and she was going to make the most of him.

Backing away from him just a little, salivating at the glorious sight of his cock, Charlotte quickly pulled off her satin panties and almost leapt on to the sofa. There she lay facing him, pulling at her crimson teats so they protruded hungrily from the white lace of her bra. Then she lifted her stockinged legs high and wide, and fingered the silky folds of her sex, showing him how her exposed pink flesh was wet and ready for him.

'Fuck me, Liam,' she muttered, her eyes glittering. 'Oh, for God's sake, fuck me.'

He pulled off his T-shirt, so she could drink in the masculine beauty of his powerful torso. Then he advanced on her, rigid penis swaying, and knelt between her legs. He gazed at her breasts first, drawing the hard nipples into his mouth, swirling and sucking till she cried out with joy. Her splayed legs clamped round his hips, pulling him towards her; her empty vagina yearned for his solid male flesh, and he knew it. Gazing down intently at her flushed, excited face, he eased his long penis, inch by inch, deep into her honeyed sex.

She bucked and jerked against him, gasping with delight, scratching her fingers roughly down his back as she squeezed herself round him. The whimpers rose in her throat as he drew himself out, then drove his cock steadily and surely back in until she felt she could take no more of its exquisite length. She played with her own nipples frantically, rolling and squeezing them, her plump face rapt, her stockinged toes curling with joy; he pulled slowly out again, and she gazed in delight at the incredible length of his shaft. 'Oh, Liam. Let me have all of it. All of your huge cock inside me. Please . . .'

He drove into her hard, then, again and again. His finger slipped down to her splayed sex to stroke at her clitoris. She grasped her own breasts again, and jerked her hips frantically in time to his strokes, rising at last to frenetic orgasm as his lengthy shaft pumped in and out of her juicy passage. She arched her body and gave a long, whimpering cry as her climax overtook her; he held her close to him, still ravishing her with long, steady strokes, prolonging her ecstasy for ever, it seemed, until at last he buried his head against her billowing breasts and drove himself to his own convulsive release. She loved the feel of his powerful cock spasming inside her. She wanted it all to go on and on. She wanted to keep him here all night, but she knew she couldn't.

Even so, she hoped he would stay for a little while; coffee, perhaps, and then sex again, in half an hour or so. She pulled him close, nestling her breasts against the warm hardness of his chest. 'That was great, Liam,' she murmured happily.

He kissed her cheek. 'You were wonderful,' he said. 'You must have a lot of admirers.'

'Oh, a few.' She grinned. 'A lot of the older men at the office like to eye up my tits.'

'I bet they do.' He smiled back, stroking her breasts with obvious pleasure. 'Have you ever come across a man at your place called Raoni, Hugh Raoni? From what I've heard of him, he'd just adore someone with a figure like yours.'

'Raoni? Why, yes, I saw him, just the once. I was late in the office, catching up on some filing. Mr Bridges didn't know I was still there.' She yawned sleepily and curled up against Liam's shoulder. 'I heard Mr Bridges talking to this man Raoni about the Hegley Wood thing, the road and the shopping centre. Mr. Bridges looked cross at first, when he realised I was still around, but then he laughed, and told Mr Raoni I didn't know anything anyway, so how could I tell anyone; which is true, isn't it?'

Liam smiled. 'Of course it's true. Mr Bridges is very lucky, having someone as sensible as you to work for him.' He was putting her gently from him and standing up now. 'Look, Charlotte. I have to go now, I'm afraid.'

She'd known this would come sooner or later, but she was disappointed it was so soon.

'Tonight has been wonderful,' he went on. 'I really hope I'll see you again some time, but I have to travel a lot, you know?'

Oh, yes. She knew. She watched a little sadly as he drew on his clothes, and salivated again over the way his lovely tight buttocks moved beneath his jeans as he walked with that easy, narrow-hipped stride of his towards the door.

She sighed as she heard his footsteps going down the stairs. Why on earth had he picked on her? It was just so totally unreal. No one would ever, ever believe her. Food for her fantasies for months and months.

Two nights later Cass, bored and restless with the inactivity at the camp, and worried because there was no news of Liam, was sitting around a low-burning fire with the other women, drinking a little wine, and talking. A lot of them had been at Fairmile till the end, when the great oak was felled. Cass looked around, registering each tree as it spread its branches towards the moonlit sky. The same wouldn't happen here. It couldn't.

The wine and the talk hadn't suppressed her longing for Liam, but had stirred it painfully. Where was he? He should be here by now. She needed him. They needed him. She wandered a little way from the others into the darkness beyond the clearing, listening to the sounds of the night, the almost imperceptible rustle of the tiny forest creatures that lived in the undergrowth, the distant haunting call of an owl. She was wearing a cotton jersey and combat trousers; her skin felt warm and sweat-sheened in the sultry July night.

Suddenly she heard a vehicle revving noisily in the distance along the rutted track that led into the forest. Its headlights crested the brow of the hill, lighting up the night. Cass hurried towards it, her heart thumping. Everyone else was on the alert too; the camp was alive with figures, tight-faced in the darkness.

The vehicle, an ancient Land Rover, jolted along the track through the trees and stopped at the clearing. She saw who was driving it, and her heart filled with gladness. It was Stevie, with Liam at his side.

She hurried towards him, pushing her way through the others. 'Liam,' she breathed. 'You've made it at last.'

But he hardly seemed to register she was there, and his familiar face was bleak with anger as he swung himself down from the Land Rover and scanned the camp. Stevie hovered behind him, looking anxious.

'Were you all asleep?' Liam said at last, 'every single fucking one of you? We could have been anyone, Stevie and I, driving in on you: the police, security, paid wreckers like they had at Newbury . . .' He gestured to the dying fire, the empty wine bottles lying around it, and there was no trace of his usual sexy sleepiness. His eyes were icy cold above his hard cheekbones, and his hair looked almost unkempt, as if he hadn't slept. His shirt and jeans were dusty from the rough road. 'What do you think this is,' he went on, 'some midsummer's eve party, for Christ's sake? Unguarded fire, rubbish lying around, cheap wine – how many of you are drunk, or high? Haven't you even thought about setting up a watch? Don't you remember how at Fairmile the bailiffs came out of nowhere when most of the protesters were down at the pub, and hauled all the rest of them away before razing the camp to the ground?'

Cass stepped forward, her head held high, though inside she was feeling sick and cold. 'There's no one around yet, Liam,' she said defiantly. 'They haven't even got planning permission. We're on public land, so we're OK till the warrant goes through the county court and the sheriff's men move in. Aren't we?'

Liam said bitingly, 'This is public land, but the farm-land around us isn't, and the developers know it. They're moving in, Cass. They're setting up just down the road; we passed them on our way here. Portakabins, mobile phones, alarm systems, the lot. Compared to their set-up, this is a disorganised rabble. I thought you at least, Cass, would have known better. And where's Petro?'

Petro, Cass guessed, was probably in bed with the delectable sisters.

Liam's eyes burned into her. 'All right. I can guess.'

Just at that moment Petro appeared, dressed but looking sheepish. Liam strode over to speak to him, completely ignoring Cass. Cass walked over to the edge of the clearing and stood there, staring up at the sky through the interlaced branches. She didn't know how long she was there. It could have been ten minutes, or an hour. Then she heard footsteps, coming up behind her, and she knew instantly who it was.

'Get lost, Stevie,' she bit out. She felt sick with misery. 'I want to be on my own.'

He said hesitantly, 'Cass. I only want to help. Liam didn't mean to upset you.'

'He doesn't care what he does to me. He doesn't even want to fuck me any more.'

Stevie gazed at her, his brown eyes filled with compassion. 'He still cares about you,' he said. 'I know he does. It's just that he's so busy with everything.'

'He's too busy for me,' she spat out, almost shaking with hurt and disappointment.

'I'm not,' said Stevie quietly.

She laughed scornfully. 'Would you like to fuck me then, Stevie? Do you think I'm attractive?'

'Yes,' he said. 'But not when you talk like that.'

Cass felt quite frenzied, quite out of her mind, with the wine, and her longing for Liam, and Liam's blunt coldness to her. 'I won't talk, then,' she said in a hard little voice that was raw with her bitterness. 'I just want you to take me, Stevie, from behind. That's what Liam used to do, when we were together.' She crouched swiftly on the ground in front of him, wriggling out of her trousers, throwing him a look that was filled with challenge and contempt as the cool night air brushed

121

her bottom cheeks. 'He used to tease me,' she went on, 'said I had a bottom like a boy's. Do you like my arse, Stevie? Is your cock throbbing at the sight of it? Do you want me, Stevie? If not then, for God's sake, just go.'

There was silence for a moment. Then she heard him kneeling behind her. His hands, surprising her with their warmth and strength, were stroking her buttocks gently, nudging between her thighs at her silken sex. She shivered with sudden, acute longing.

'I want you,' he said. 'I've always wanted you.'

She felt a spasm course through her as his penis nudged its way into her silky wetness and slowly, strongly drove into her vagina from behind. Was this really Stevie, gentle pacifist Stevie with his devoted spaniel eyes, whom she'd always rather despised? She caught her lip between her teeth and shuddered.

'I'm not hurting you?' he said quickly.

'Christ, no. Get on with it, will you?' she muttered crossly; but already the melting warmth was starting to build up in her loins as she felt his cock pushing strongly in. He was tender, too, moving gently to and fro, filling her until she thought she could stand no more; then slowly easing out, till she wanted to scream with the empty ache of frustration.

She lifted her buttocks higher, begging wordlessly for deeper penetration, and she got it. At the same time, his strong hands moved underneath her shoulders to tug at her jutting nipples, just as she adored. Her vaginal muscles clamped luxuriously round his steadily pounding cock, and she began to climax, the voracious pleasure tearing through her as Stevie continued to drive his thick shaft deep into her very heart.

Christ, he was good. A really solid prick, and staying power too. He hadn't even hinted at coming yet; she wondered dreamily, as her own orgasm sweetly subsided, just how long he could last. Some day, she might test him further. But she wouldn't let him know that yet.

He was bucking away behind her now, his balls slapping at her rump, his shaft pumping furiously until, at last, with a little cry, he clutched her to him and shuddered to his own release. She could feel his lovely cock twitching hungrily away inside her.

She gave him just enough time to finish, then pulled abruptly away and started to tug on her clothes.

'Don't get ideas, will you, Stevie?' she said.

He was getting slowly to his feet. His gentle expression irritated her. Same old Stevie. Still, at least he had something going for him.

He said, 'Don't let Liam hurt you, Cass, will you? He's a single-minded guy. People don't count much with him. Only if they get in his way. Or if they've got something he wants.'

The pity in his voice, and in his eyes, made her angry. 'Look. Only one thing matters to me about Liam, and that's the fact that he's a fantastic fuck. OK?'

His brown eyes became shuttered, but she'd seen the hurt there. 'No doubt,' he said. 'But only one thing matters to Liam, and it's not sex. All he cares about at the moment is finding out who's behind this road. And he's just been telling us back there that he thinks he's on his way to finding out.'

'And?' Cass's heart was beating fast, because she cared too.

'The guy who's the big mover behind this road project could well be Hugh Raoni.'

She sat down then on a moss-covered log. 'No, Stevie. No. Liam finished him; Liam all but destroyed his Green Company.'

'For a while, yes. But Raoni's a rich, wily bastard with friends in high places. You know how Liam got those papers showing it was one of the Green Company's offshoots that was responsible for spilling toxic chemicals

123

into local rivers then trying to cover everything up? Well, Raoni's adopted a crawling tactic; he says he knew nothing about it, was deceived by his managers. So he's landed a paltry fine, and a slapped wrist, and a 'don't do it again' lecture.'

'But surely his company lost all its credibility?'

'So? He set up a new one, under a different name. We're talking big money here, Cass.'

Cass said slowly, 'So we're up against Raoni again.'

'Liam's no real proof yet that it is Raoni, remember? We've got to keep our heads down until he's absolutely sure, or Raoni'll destroy us.'

And Liam too, thought Cass with a little shiver. She pulled herself up. 'Is Liam planning to stay long at the camp, do you know?'

'Only a day or two. Then he's heading back to London. He's got a meeting with that radio friend of his who's sympathetic to our campaign here.'

Cass nodded. A day or two. That was all. She said, with an effort, 'You'd better go now. There'll be a sleeping bag in one of the tents for you. You must be tired. Go on – I'll be OK.'

'Sure?'

She smiled. 'Yes, sure. Thanks, Stevie. For talking to me and everything.'

She watched him walking back to the centre of the camp where people were still gathered, still talking in serious voices. Cass could see Liam standing in their midst. She clasped her arms across her chest, aware that she still ached with wanting him.

At last, she went back to her own little tent, to lie wide awake into the night.

The news that it could well be Hugh Raoni who was behind the planned destruction of this beautiful woodland made her feel sick, because it looked as if Liam was up against his old enemy again.

124

Chapter Five

'You're sure, absolutely sure, you don't know any journalist of that description?' Rebecca was curled on the settee in the sitting room, the cordless phone clenched between her cheek and shoulder as she drew yet another pencilled negative line through one of the few remaining numbers on her list. 'Yes – like I said, twenty-four or five, longish fair hair, called Liam. He has a south London accent – Yes, I know there are a hell of a lot of freelance journalists in London . . . OK, OK. Sorry to have troubled you. Thanks for your time.'

'All ten seconds of it,' muttered Rebecca tiredly to herself as she tossed the phone back to the far end of the settee. Yet another bored-sounding newspaper office. How many more were there? She must have tried at least twenty numbers, from the big dailies to the smallest local advertising sheets. And she'd made no progress whatsoever.

She leant back against the plump cushions and closed her eyes. Why had she even expected to? She guessed that Liam was only found if he wanted to be found. He probably used different names. He certainly seemed to have vanished without trace. His well-worn leather jacket, hanging forlornly at the back of her wardrobe, was her only reminder of him.

She knew no more than she'd already learnt from Max: that Liam had arranged a meeting in the very near future with a reporter from a local radio station, the same reporter he'd broken the story to about the total sham of Hugh Raoni's Green Company. Rebecca had tried to ring the station, but as soon as she mentioned the Green Company story, they clammed up on her, all but cutting her off.

According to Max, Liam was going to be walking straight into a trap, and she had no way, no way at all of warning him.

'It will just be made to look like an accident. A rather nasty accident,' Max had said. Oh, God.

It was early evening. Pigeons cooed sleepily outside, and the still-hot summer sun slanted obliquely through the windows. Rebecca had just showered and was wearing nothing but a tiny underwired lace bra and matching slip in deep rose. She ran her hands slowly through her newly-washed mane of coppery hair and thought longingly about sex. Correction; she was thinking about sex with Liam.

Liam obsessed her. It was two weeks since she'd been dragged so violently, so briefly into his world; and ever since then, all through the long hot days and short nights of the sultry London summer, he was there at the back of her mind, a constantly unsettling, acutely sexual presence. It's because you were in his power, she told herself. It's because you were thrown into a situation outside your experience, with people outside your experience. You were held a prisoner, you were forced to do those things.

Except nobody had forced her into anything, and she knew it.

Each night she fantasised about him coming to her in her bedroom, fantasised about having slow, earthy sex with him. She imagined him imprisoning her, stripping her naked, tying her up; making her kneel, with her arms tied behind her back so that her pouting breasts were thrust upwards; forcing her thighs apart, so that he could see her swollen sex dripping with fragrant love juices, while he slowly, silently drew out his rigid cock and offered it to her mouth, her aroused nipples, and finally her gaping vagina, pausing just a moment before driving his massive rod of flesh deeply in and out until she was crying, pleading for release.

She'd never felt like this before. She'd never before wanted to offer herself, to abase herself before a man who had become a figure of fantasy in the darkest recesses of her mind.

Was it because Liam was so different to the sort of men she was used to? Her upbringing had been privileged, wealthy; her friends had come from the same background. Max was just the latest in a long line of rich, socially acceptable admirers with cut-glass public school accents that were as sharp as their bank balances; working-class men were a race apart, to be giggled about, or to play a part in some rude fantasy of Annie's. 'Bet he's got a huge dick,' Annie would laugh to Rebecca if they noticed some burly bouncer or rough-voiced barman eyeing them up longingly at a club. 'I could keep someone like that as a kind of private stud, telling him to keep his mouth shut, and to give me a good fuck whenever I felt really desperate. No need to bother about converastion or meaningful relationships; just good dirty sex. What do you think?'

Rebecca had laughed. 'Keep it as a fantasy,' she advised. 'I think the reality could be somewhat disappointing.'

But Liam hadn't been disappointing. She couldn't get him out of her mind: the way he'd touched her, the way he'd spoken to her in his earthy, sensual voice; the way his glorious body, with his thick, strong cock as the final instrument of pleasure, had driven her almost out of her mind with lust. She caressed herself night after night with her fingers, vividly remembering the feel of his iron-hard shaft as he'd ravished her. Her silken vulva was hot and slippery to her touch, and achingly empty as she moaned between her cool white sheets and called out his name in the throes of her climax.

She was obsessed, too, with the thought of Raoni's henchmen moving in on Liam. She had nightmares about it, remembering Max's drawling, dismissive laugh: 'Oh, people like Raoni have their methods. It will all just be made to look like a very unpleasant accident . . .'

She had no more numbers to ring now, no more leads. She might even have considered asking Max for help; but Max had flown to Geneva for his bank, a couple of days after they'd watched Annie's raunchy video. He'd phoned just before he left for Heathrow, again offering some sort of reconciliation, but she wasn't sure she wanted one.

At least Max's jibes about the tentative house-sitting agency had stirred her into action. She and Annie had distributed a few classy and expensive business cards to friends and other contacts, and the bookings and the money were actually starting to come in, easing the hassle of the red reminder bills that kept thudding through the letterbox downstairs. Annie was staying overnight at the absent Lucifer's flat in Belgravia – 'easier,' she said airily – and Rebecca had a small but lucrative rota of Kensington and Knightsbridge friends who wanted plants watering or mail collecting while they were away on holiday. The healthy fees she charged were enough to pay off a few instalments on her car, and to ward off the landlord – a truly welcome respite.

She was getting up slowly from the settee, running her hands over the silk of her slip where it clung to her bare thighs and trying to stop thinking of Liam, when the door to the house suddenly crashed open and Annie came charging upstairs.

'This is truly a brilliant way to earn some cash, Becs darling,' Annie called out. This was one of her regular flying visits to home base, in between shifts at the restaurant where she still worked, and her night-time stay at Lucifer's flat. She looked radiant. 'It's money for nothing – Lucifer's flat is divinely comfortable. Last night, in that big bed in the master suite, we had such fun –'

'I thought,' said Rebecca, 'that you were staying there on your own.'

Annie blushed, then laughed. 'Much safer with company, darling. You know?'

'Lucifer's probably videoing you.'

'Well, he'll be getting value for money, then.' Annie was charging round the house, grabbing clothes and CDs and a bottle of white wine from the fridge while biting into an apple at the same time. 'Can't stop, must dash. You look lovely, darling. What you need is a man. See you.'

She flew out, slamming the door behind her. Yes, thought Rebecca sadly, she's right. I really need a man. But only one will do.

Two days later, Max Forrester, his business trip to Geneva at an end, flew into Heathrow at four and got a taxi straight to Janey Franklin's flat in Chelsea. As the cab ploughed through the heavy west London traffic, he found himself thinking rather guiltily about Rebecca. The trouble was, as Hugh Raoni had pointed out, that she really wasn't much use to him now that her family's wealth had all but disappeared. Whereas Janey had a lot of contacts, a lot of gossip, and was also very, very naughty in bed.

Which was straight where she took him.

'Successful trip?' Janey asked softly as she closed the door and drew the semi-sheer voile curtains across the bedroom windows. Her flat was close to the King's Road; he found it noisy and claustrophobic, but Janey loved the buzz of being in the middle of things. Without waiting for his answer, she started to peel off the pale apricot silk pants suit she wore. Underneath it, her voluptuous breasts were barely contained by an expensive lace-trimmed white bra that was cut low to allow her provocative dark brown nipples to peep enticingly over the top; her suspenders and sheer stockings emphasised her plump creamy thighs.

Max gazed at her, dry-throated. He said at last, 'You knew I was coming.'

'Oh, yes.' She smiled. 'Several times, I hope. You want to be punished, Max? You've misbehaved?'

His fingers were shaking slightly as he started to undo his tie. 'Yes,' he breathed. 'Oh, yes.'

The bed dominated the room. It was half-curtained with damask drapes in a rich shade of burgundy. Its frame was of ornately twisted black iron, and the bed sheets were of cream satin. Mirrors were set in the walls and ceiling.

'You know what to do,' she said. Her voice was rougher now. 'Undress.'

Max did so, and a slight sheen of perspiration glossed his elegant body, because he knew what was about to happen. Silently he lay face down on the bed, and heard the drawer slide open. It was always the same; the delicious frisson of apprehension, of fear, even.

She tied his wrists to the bedposts. Once, a few weeks ago, she'd tried to blindfold him, but he hadn't enjoyed that, because he liked to see her ripe body in the mirror; he liked to see her scarlet mouth, her proudly thrust-nipples, the swollen mound of her sex pushing against her tight panties. When she'd secured him, she moved back to crouch between his thighs. She gazed thoughtfully at the hair-whorled crease between his buttocks and the softly vulnerable pouch of his balls; then she began to beat him rhythmically with a flat leather paddle that was already lying beside the bed. He raised his head in shock as the first searing blow burnt through his buttocks; he saw her lush body in the mirror, bending over him with determination, almost like a fantasy-figure in her salacious underwear; except that the exquisite pleasure-pain she dealt was real. His muscles tensed like whipcords. Against the slippery satin sheet, his genitalia throbbed.

He knew what would happen next, and it did. She oiled his tight bottom cheeks with some perfumed liquid of her own, and pulled them apart. Then she used the thick leather handle of the stout paddle to enlarge his little puckered orifice, and drove it deeply into the tight tunnel of his anus. He lifted his hips and groaned aloud. His penis throbbed hotly against his belly, sliding on the satin sheet.

'If people knew about you, Max,' she said, in a voice that both soothed and scolded, 'what would they say? Oh, what would they say?'

He watched her trembling breasts. She was as excited as he was, he would swear; her big, taut nipples thrust strongly out over the rim of her bra, and her satin panties rubbed and slipped into her swollen crotch. She was leaning over him now, smelling of perfume and female musk; as she drove the thick leather shaft faster and deeper, the shameful heat of penetration began to possess him. Then she reached with an oil-moistened hand to turn him over on to his side. Swiftly she caressed his fat balls, rubbed at his straining cock; then she increased the pressure, her fingers slipping tightly over the ridge of his swollen glans, and he spurted in anguished bliss, again and again, his anus spasming darkly around the hard fat rod she still twisted inside him.

She untied him, tossed him a towel and stood back, her eyes gleaming. 'You're a bad case, Max. What would people say, if they knew that the rich banker Max Forrester likes to be beaten and fucked? You'll have to teach Rebecca some little tricks like that, won't you?' Then she sauntered over to a chair in the corner of the room, and sat back in it with her legs blatantly apart, already untying the laces at the sides of her panties. 'Lick me now, Max. Do it well,' she said.

Still naked, still trembling with the fruition of passion, he knelt between her plump stockinged thighs and used his tongue to pleasure her. He was hard and vigorous, because he knew that was what she liked. He lapped at her like a thirsty dog at water, tasting her juices, driving the tip of his tongue high up inside her vagina, until her face became flushed and her legs clamped round his shoulders. She jerked hard against his bony face, using his tongue as if it were a penis, gasping as she came.

She lay back afterwards, watching lazily while Max showered in the cubicle just off the bedroom, where she could see his streamlined body caressed by the jets of water through the lightly frosted glass. He came out at last, his dark hair slicked back to the nape of his neck and a thick white towel round his lean hips.

'How was Geneva?' she asked softly as he started to rub himself dry.

'Oh, the usual. Shares, investments, EMU talk – you know?'

'I know all that. I want the gossip, Max. Remember that party at Raoni's? What's the news on him, nowadays? How are the mighty fallen.'

'How, indeed.' Max had found another towel to rub at his hair. 'But people like Hugh Raoni don't give up easily. He's quietly planning his revenge, they say.'

'And another mega development scheme somewhere, no doubt?'

'He's keeping quiet and being very, very careful this time. But no doubt he is.'

Janey, suddenly restless, got up. Her big nipples were soft now, sinking back into the fullness of her breasts. 'OK, Max,' she pronounced. 'I'm going to have a bath – I'm off to a party tonight. You'd better be on your way.'

He was jealous. His cock stirred lasciviously between his thighs again as she turned her back on him and he saw her luscious buttocks. 'You're going with someone else?'

She turned to face him. 'Yes. What's wrong with that? I thought we'd agreed. We could see whoever we wanted, as well as each other. I don't like to be cramped, Max.'

'Of course,' he said stiffly. 'I'd better move, too. I've got a date as well.'

'Who are you seeing tonight?'

'Rebecca,' he said on sudden impulse, knowing it would make Janey more jealous than anything. 'I promised to take her out for a meal. Can I ring her from here, to check she's still expecting me?'

Janey shrugged, keeping her cool, though he could see by the gleam in her eyes that she was annoyed. 'Of course you can,' she said. 'Use the phone by the bed.'

Max tried Rebecca's number. 'Engaged,' he said. 'I'll get a taxi home and ring her on my mobile on the way.'

'OK. Wine and dine her well, won't you, Max?'

'I will,' he said, resenting the hint of amusement in her voice. 'She's still pretty keen on me, Janey. She was devastated when I talked about us finishing, so I thought, I'll keep her in tow, just for a while, you know? To lessen the blow.'

'Then try teaching her a few tricks, why don't you?' Janey grinned. 'The poor girl will never, ever know what you like unless you tell her.' She started to gather up her bathrobe, then cast him a mischievous glance over her shoulder. 'That is, if you *really* want her to know what you like . . .'

Rebecca had just got in when the phone started ringing. She'd been to visit four properties on her list that afternoon; her bag was carefully packed with keys and lists of detailed instructions, but she flung the lot heedlessly on the sofa and dived to snatch up the phone. 'Hello?'

It was Max. She'd hoped, as she always hoped, that it was Liam.

'Hi,' said Max. 'Sweetheart, I've been trying to ring you for ages. I've just landed at Heathrow; I'm in a taxi, on my way back to my place. Can I see you tonight? How about a meal?'

Rebecca hesitated. 'I'm not sure, Max. It's a bit of a rush; I've just got in from work. Where were you thinking of?'

'You decide. I'll take you anywhere.'

Still she hesitated. Then suddenly, out of the blue, she remembered Liam saying, 'I've seen Max at Les Sauvages. It's one of my favourites, too . . .'

She drew a deep breath. It was too much to hope, of course, that Liam would be there tonight. But what other hope had she? She said lightly, 'OK, Max, if you're paying. We'll go to Les Sauvages.'

He chuckled. 'I might have guessed you'd go for an expensive one. OK. I'll ring and see if they've got a table. Put something nice on. And we can discuss things over a good meal. I've been thinking about you, a lot.'

Rebecca was rather agonisedly aware that the only person she'd been thinking about was Liam. Putting the phone down, she wandered slowly to her bedroom, and began to undress for a shower.

It sounded as if Max was hot for her again, as if Janey

Franklin was well and truly out of his life now. That was some triumph, at least.

The Soho restaurant was suitably crowded, with just enough of a buzz of waiters hurrying, and the *maître d'* scolding, and glimpses of a thronged kitchen through the latticed swing doors, to make all the clientèle feel that they had, in fact, chosen the best possible place in London to dine that night.

Max was as attentive as Rebecca had ever known him; as if he were anxious to prove something to her, or to himself. They'd had a drink in the crowded basement bar below the restaurant; then they'd moved up here, and he'd instantly commandeered the best table in the room, along with the most experienced waiters. He'd even summoned the chef himself to explain the mango salsa that was served with the pan-fried blue fin tuna; then he'd plied Rebecca with chilled Chablis and made sure that the waiters hovered ready to refill their glasses.

She sat in her chair, nibbling at the grilled goat's cheese starter then picking half-heartedly at the blue fin tuna with its sesame seed crust and accompaniment of crispy noodles. She was realising rather distractedly that she didn't really fancy Max any more.

At one time, she'd have been squirming in her seat with excitement at having him so close, so attentive. It wasn't as if anything had changed about him; he was as plausible as ever, still glossed with a patina of glamour from his Geneva trip, from brushing with people with the kind of power only money could bring. She knew he'd expect her to come back with him afterwards to his Pimlico apartment, to have sex with him. His long lean thigh pressed suggestively against hers, and his dark eyes burned on her lips, her throat, her breasts. She was wearing a new dress, a body-skimming sleeveless sheath in silky black crêpe; simple in style but divinely cut so that it clung to her high bosom and narrow waist like a second skin. It made her feel sexy, alluring, an utter temptress. But she didn't want to tempt Max.

This is stupid, she told herself fiercely, stabbing with her fork at the mango salsa in its piquant dressing of fresh lime juice. You've got one of the most attractive, most eligible men in London gazing at you with come-to-bed eyes, and all you can think of is someone else, some low-life journalist you'll never see again, someone from a world so different it might as well be another planet. Put a little effort into it, Rebecca. You need Max, in all sorts of ways. Use him, just as he's used you.

His hand was lingering now on her thigh beneath the heavy damask table cloth, slowly easing up the silky material of her dress. He was running his fingers lightly up and down her bare knee, just as he used to love her to run hers up and down his cock. He must be pretty desperate, she thought rather acidly, because he even asked her attentively about the flat-sitting agency. When she told him casually that they were thinking of setting up a small office, with a part-time secretary to handle the phone calls and paperwork, he appeared impressed, but in a condescending sort of way that irritated her. Even the way he summoned the waiter irritated her.

At one time, she'd have given anything to get this sort of attention from Max. Now, all she wanted was to see Liam again. She toyed hesitantly with her crème brûlée.

'I don't suppose,' she said, trying to keep her voice light, 'that you've heard anything yet about whether they've caught up with that intruder who stole the papers from Raoni's house?'

'On the night of the party, you mean?' He dabbed his lips carefully with his napkin; another habit of his that got on her nerves. 'No. You keep asking me about him. Why are you so interested?'

Careful, Rebecca. 'It's fairly natural to be interested, I would have thought, when it all happened so close to us – when we were actually in Raoni's house at the time of the theft. And you told me that the man responsible was meeting up again soon with the radio journalist who broke the story, and that Raoni was going to set his heavies on him. Has that happened yet?'

Max drank more wine. He looked impatient. 'Not as far as I know. But I only work for one of the many banks that Raoni has dealings with. I'm not a private detective. Let's go soon, shall we? We can have coffee back at my place, Rebecca. God, I've missed you. Have you missed me?' He leant closer, pressing his lips lightly against her cheek, and Rebecca was suddenly aware of a strange, heavy, almost sweet smell that clung faintly to his skin – like a woman's perfume. 'Do you know what I want to do?' he went on. 'I want to take your clothes off, slowly, and spread your legs wide apart while I play with your pussy. I want you to take my cock in your mouth while I drive you wild with my fingers, stroking your pussy and your breasts. Then I want to fuck you hard, so hard you'll cry out again and again . . .'

As he whispered, he was gripping her hand and moving it up his taut thigh to press it against his groin. His voice was hidden by the noisy hum of the busy restaurant, his actions concealed by the long damask tablecloth.

But Rebecca was no longer listening to him. She was hardly even aware he was talking to her, because she'd just seen someone, just caught sight of a face across the crowded room that made her almost forget to breathe. A man was seated over at the far side of the restaurant with a beautiful girl at his side. The girl was studying the menu, and the man was looking at it with her, pointing things out knowledgeably. He was dressed in a clean but crumpled white shirt and cream-coloured jeans; his tie, which was knotted loosely around his unbuttoned collar, was the only concession to the rigid

137

dress code of Les Sauvages. He had sun-bleached fair hair that was almost fashionably unkempt, and his dark blue eyes were turned intently on the girl at his side.

Liam. Rebecca drew a deep, unsteady breath. Her heart, which appeared for a moment to have stopped beating, began to thump hard against her chest with force that almost hurt her. Liam turned, then, and saw her gazing at him. His face registered nothing except a slight narrowing of the eyes. He looked at Max, then slowly turned his attention back to the menu. What had she expected? That he'd jump up and run across the room to greet her? Most likely he hardly even recognised her.

Nevertheless she was trembling visibly with shock. Max, his eyes hot with lust, his fingers still pressing Rebecca's fingers against his penis, was saying huskily, 'I'll tell the waiter to bring the bill and get us a taxi. Then we can head back to my place as quickly as possible –'

'No,' she broke in rather desperately. She didn't know what to do. She just knew she couldn't go without speaking to Liam. 'No, I don't actually want to go yet, Max. I'd love to have a coffee here first, and a liqueur – please. I like it here so much, I just want to stay here a little longer . . .'

He looked disappointed, and puzzled. But then she increased the pressure on his groin, and whispered, 'We've got all night.' So he quickly summoned the waiter and ordered coffee and Cointreau for both of them.

And all the time, Rebecca was gazing across the room at Liam, thinking, I must speak to him. I must warn him, about the danger he's in.

He didn't even look in her direction again. He was turning all his attention on the woman he was with, and Rebecca couldn't blame him. She was beautiful, with classy features and silky shoulder-length dark hair, and a slender figure that was enhanced by a long-sleeved mini-dress in toffee-brown cashmere. She never seemed to take her eyes from Liam's face, even when she was eating.

Rebecca could only watch, stunned by the jealousy and desire that swept over her. Her body was flickering slowly into arousal, like a fire curling with the first delicate little tendrils of flame; her breasts felt warm and heavy beneath her thin dress. And it wasn't Max who was making her feel that way.

Max had finished his coffee and his liqueur, and was looking at his watch impatiently. She asked him swiftly for some more wine and some petit fours.

'You never have them,' he said. 'And don't forget the calories, Rebecca.'

'Spoil me, Max,' she said lightheartedly, but inside she was feeling sick, sick with apprehension.

Max ordered, then caught her looking across the crowded restaurant at Liam. He looked too, and his face tightened. 'I'm not surprised you're staring at him,' he said. 'He would look more at home on a building site or a student demonstration than in an exclusive restaurant like this. Look at his hair – it hasn't been cut for weeks. And I thought jackets and ties were compulsory. I'll just speak to the *maître d'* about it.'

Rebecca wanted to die. If Max started to make a fuss, she would never, ever get to speak to Liam. She sprang wildly to her feet, making her refilled coffee cup spill over into its saucer. 'I must go to the loo,' she said. 'I won't be long.'

She remembered that there were some toilets downstairs in the crowded cellar bar. She had to cross the restaurant to get to the stairs; she tried to catch Liam's eye, but he had turned to listen attentively to something his companion was saying, and all she could see was the back of his head, and the way his sinewed thigh in cream-coloured denim was touching the girl's leg. She could see other women nearby gazing surreptitiously at him, with the same hopeless longing as herself. Had he even noticed her? He must have done; but he gave no indication that he had. Close to despair, she hurried downstairs to the crush of the basement bar and waited in the forlorn hope that Liam might join her there.

He didn't, of course. Why should he? The seconds ticked into long, long minutes; people down here were watching her strangely, because she was without a man and without a drink. The beat of the background music thundered and throbbed in her ears; unlike the demure restaurant upstairs, this was a vibrant pick-up place, open to non-diners and to all tastes.

Rebecca went quickly to the bar and ordered herself a large vodka. She'd already drunk far too much, but what the hell. In near-despair she threw it back, feeling the ice-cold liquid burning down her throat. She clutched her glass for company. Oh, Liam, please, she prayed silently. Whatever you think of me, come down here, just for a few minutes, so I can speak to you.

A hand suddenly cupped her bottom, and an oily masculine voice whispered in her ear, 'All on your own, darling?'

Rebecca whirled round. The action made her feel dizzy after all the alcohol she'd consumed. A fat little man in a shiny suit stood there; his hand continued to stroke her bottom.

'You look lonely,' he continued. 'Looking for a good fuck and a bit of fun for the rest of the night, are you?' His finger rammed up the cleft in her buttocks. 'You could do a lot worse than me, I assure you. Satisfaction guaranteed . . .'

He licked his full lips, and Rebecca, with an exclamation of revulsion, threw the rest of her drink in his face; but it splashed back against her, and her expensive black dress was soaked with cold, pure vodka. Cursing, she wrenched away from his hot grasp and made a dive towards the ladies' room. There was no one else in there. She leant back against the wall, shaking with despair.

Then the door opened, and Liam came in.

She spun round, trembling with astonishment. 'What the hell are you doing in here?'

'Looking for you,' he said. 'From the way you kept gazing across at me so desperately, I assumed you wanted to speak to me. Or something. I see you're with Max Forrester; better not let him guess you're down here with me.' His eyes raked her. 'What on earth's happened to you? Why is your dress so wet?'

She was suddenly, agonisedly aware that the soaking fabric was clinging to her loins, her waist, her breasts; and under his hard blue gaze her nipples were starting, with cruel inevitability, to harden. She folded her arms defensively over her breasts, hating him for seeing her vulnerability, and for assuming that Max owned her.

'My dress is wet because some stupid fat oaf in the bar was trying to grope me,' she snapped. 'I pushed him away, and got most of my drink over me.'

His gaze flickered down to her high-heeled shoes. 'I told you. You shouldn't wear shoes like that. You look as if you're waiting for a fuck. You'll attract the wrong kind of people.'

'I certainly am tonight,' she acknowledged bitterly. 'One after the other. Look, Liam. I did want to speak to you, as it happens, though God knows why I'm bothering. I just wondered if you knew that Raoni was after you.'

That got his attention. But instead of answering her immediately, he went over towards the heavy chrome chair that sat in the corner of the room, and dragged it across the door, blocking it. Then he came back and faced her.

'I know Raoni's after me,' he said quietly. 'But he's not going to find me. Have you really got something to tell me? Or is there something else going on here? Some power-play with friend Max, for instance?'

She caught her breath. 'Max Forrester has got nothing, absolutely nothing to do with this. But I have got something to tell you, Liam, if you can be bothered to listen. Hugh Raoni knows that you're planning another meeting with that reporter from the radio, the one you told about the Green Company business. Raoni's going to follow you to that meeting, and set his thugs on you. I thought you might be interested, might want to get your own defences in order. That's the only reason I wanted to see you. That's it. I'm going now.'

But he gripped her shoulders as she started towards the door, his fingers biting into her bare skin. 'Raoni won't even know where we're meeting, or when. It's not been arranged yet.'

She pulled herself away as if his touch contaminated her. 'Well, now. You're not as bright as you think you are, are you? The reporter will tell him, of course. He's in league with Raoni. Raoni's paying him to inform him of the details. Got it?'

'How do you know all this?'

'Max mentioned it,' she said flatly. 'Max works for an investment bank Raoni uses. He hears things.'

Liam was silent for a moment, absorbing it. She found herself stupidly staring at the warm golden skin at the base of his throat, where his crumpled shirt was open and his tie hung loose. Suddenly she longed to kiss him there, to unfasten more of the tiny buttons of his shirt and press her lips against the firm beautiful curves of his chest. Oh, God. She was mad to think like this, she knew, because she despised him, just as he despised her; but she couldn't help it, because he reeked of sex. Even his harsh south London vowels ravished her senses every time he spoke. She remembered – had she ever really forgotten? – how sweetly he'd made love to her, sliding his lovely long cock into her sex again and

142

again; and she felt her nipples harden anew beneath her damp dress. Her tight little panties rubbed at her soaking cleft, betraying her arousal; he must see it too, he must. What a stupid, utter fool he must think her.

He said slowly, 'I would have been careful about the meeting, of course. But thank you for telling me. I'm not quite sure why you felt you needed to. I wouldn't have thought you owed me anything.'

'You've certainly made it plain all along that you neither expected nor wanted to see me again,' said Rebecca in a low voice. 'But – and it might surprise you to hear this – I don't like Hugh Raoni either. I heard, of course, that his company was in trouble because of some leaked documents, and I realised straight away that it was you who'd taken them that night at the party. I wish you'd told me more about it at the time. You could have trusted me.'

His blue eyes suddenly burned beneath his hooded lids. He said, 'I'm sorry. But trust is difficult when you're carrying information like that around with you.'

'I trusted you,' she said. 'Mistakenly, I think; you just use sex as a commodity, don't you, Liam? As a means of buying something, even if it's only silence. Who's the girl upstairs?'

'Her name's Chloe. She's just a friend.'

Chloe. Somewhere in Rebecca's Liam-hazed brain, a warning bell rang, but she couldn't place the name, and didn't particularly want to. She shrugged. 'So you'll be screwing her later, will you? What for, Liam? Some sort of information, I suppose. Or did you want her to drive you somewhere in her car? Well, I hope she thinks you're worth it. You clearly think so much of yourself that I'm surprised you don't charge for your services.'

She thought she saw a glint of amusement in his hard blue eyes. 'As a working-class stud?' he said. 'No, I don't charge. Just tell me something, though, before you go back to Max Forrester. Is he a good fuck? I thought you told me once that you didn't belong to him; but, judging by the way he was groping you back there in the restaurant, he clearly thinks you do. If we're talking of paying for sex, is he really worth signing your life away for, Rebecca?'

'Yes,' she breathed, 'yes, he is worth it, and I'm not staying here a moment longer to listen to your insults.' She turned wildly towards the door, and only then did she realise that, in barring the door shut against intruders, he'd effectively locked her in. With him. He was already advancing on her with glinting eyes, and her heart started thumping.

'Shall I tell you something about Max Forrester?' he drawled lazily. 'I bet he's got a real thing about black stockings and corporal punishment. I bet he comes too quickly as well. Am I right, Rebecca?' Even as he spoke, his hands reached out to her wet dress, twisting and pinching her thrusting nipples through it. She almost fell back against the wall.

'What makes you think you're so good?' she cried out. His body was pinning her back now, his heavily muscled thigh insinuating itself between her legs, rubbing sweetly against the swollen mound of her sex through the thin fabric of her dress, setting her fragrant juices of arousal running wildly. His hips were nudging hers; she could feel the hard rod of his cock pressing against his tight jeans.

'I don't make value judgements,' he said softly. He'd bent his head, so that his sensual mouth was very close to hers; his blue eyes were hooded, amused, glinting with sex. 'All I remember is a beautiful girl, with amber eyes like a cat's, shivering with arousal in my arms, crying out again and again for me to fuck her. I remember her because I think she was the most exquisite thing I've ever seen. I've not been able to stop thinking about her since.'

She stared up at him in disbelief. She was trembling

with the effort of not falling into his arms. 'Really?' she scoffed. 'Come on, now, Liam. I thought you despised me. Those things Cass said . . .'

'What things?'

'Cass was there when the taxi came for me. She told me not to bother trying to get in touch with you. She told me not to make a nuisance of myself, because you didn't want to see me again.'

His eyes were suddenly hard. 'Cass,' he said at last, 'took a dislike to you. I didn't. The only message I left was for Stevie, instructing him to get you home safely. Cass can be cruel. I'm sorry.'

Rebecca stared up at him, her heart thumping. Someone tried the door, but it was jammed by the heavy chair. 'Out of order,' called Liam. 'Try the other one.'

'We must go,' Rebecca said rather breathlessly. 'Max – your friend – they'll wonder where we are –'

'I'm going nowhere,' said Liam softly. 'And neither are you. I think we have unfinished business.'

He pulled her to him almost roughly, except that his touch didn't hurt her at all, and he kissed her hard. His tongue ravished the inner softness of her mouth; she moaned at the back of her throat and instinctively twined her hands round his neck, feeling the springy thickness of his hair, the warmth of his skin. Nibbling at her cheek and throat with his mouth, sending shivers of longing through her, he pulled up her damp dress round her waist, almost ripping it with his strong hands; it was Rebecca herself who tugged down the tiny shoulder straps, so her wildly expensive garment was a crumpled twist of fabric around her waist. Liam's eyes became dark as midnight when he saw her naked pouting breasts; and when he bent his head to kiss them, to draw them into his mouth and abrade them with his tongue and teeth, she felt a pleasure that was almost as sharp as pain flooding through her body.

'Please,' she whispered as she leant back against the tiled wall, 'oh, please . . .'

She could already feel the hardness of his penis pressing against her flat belly through the fabric of his jeans. He was stroking his hand hungrily between her thighs, rubbing his fingers against the soaking flimsiness of her panties, driving his fingers through her crisply curling pubic hair and catching the side of her swollen wet clitoris with his thumb; she thrust herself again and again at his hand, on the brink. Swearing softly under his breath as he struggled with his own garments, he managed to unbutton his fly, and she felt his cock, hot and hard, throbbing against her bare skin; she moaned and reached down to touch it, wrapping her fingers round the thick shaft of flesh.

He pushed her panties roughly to one side, almost ripping them, so her swollen sex-lips protruded obscenely. Then he was lifting her, and she could hear the rasp of his harsh breathing; the next thing she knew, the rounded tip of his cock was thrusting eagerly at her, sliding up between the juicy folds of flesh that shielded her sex. She shuddered with delight as the thickness of his lengthy shaft slowly impaled her.

She threw back her head, crying out. He caught her cry with his kiss, at the same time lifting her, effortlessly supporting her against the wall, so she was able to twine her bare legs around his muscular hips. She gazed down raptly to where they joined, seeing the root of his massive cock driving slickly in and out of her engorged flesh. He withdrew almost completely, and she felt dazed with the pleasure of gazing at his long glistening shaft, that was paying such glorious homage to her.

'Oh, God,' she said weakly, 'this is just so rude. Someone's knocking at the door again, Liam. They'll break it down . . .'

'No, they won't. There's another loo at the far end of the bar. They'll go there. And this isn't rude, it's

146

beautiful. You're beautiful, Rebecca, every bit of you. I want to make you cry out. I want you to get such pleasure from my cock, you can barely stand it.'

Sobbing with excitement, Rebecca thrust her hips towards him again, begging for his iron-hard penis to penetrate her anew. He lowered his head again, to bite and lick at her breasts, while she grasped his strong shoulders. Still supporting her against the wall, he reached with one hand to rub at her hungry, sex-swollen clitoris, sliding its little hood back and forth with an almost agonising finesse; she began to shake uncontrollably, her feet drumming against his back, her fingers digging into the hard muscles of his shoulders. The almost unbearable pleasure built up and flooded through her whole body. Again and again the long shaft of his penis drove relentlessly up into her very core; she clutched at him and spasmed around him all through her long, blissful climax; and at last, just as she was subsiding, she felt him grip her buttocks hard as he jerked with delicious potency deep inside her.

They stayed like that for long moments, trembling with the force of their release, their slick flesh still joined at thigh and hip. Rebecca opened her eyes at last and smiled weakly at him. 'We must go. Max will be down here soon looking for me.'

His head jerked up at that, and his eyes were bleak. 'Max. Always Max,' he said. 'Did you think about him just now, when you came?'

'No,' she whispered. 'I thought about you. I can't stop thinking about you, Liam. I always wondered if I'd ever see you again. I went back to find that house, the house where you took me that night, because I'd still got your leather jacket; but you weren't there. I thought I was going mad, imagining it all . . .'

He kissed her forehead tenderly. 'I didn't mean to hurt you. Never that.'

'What were you doing at that house, Liam? The

builders said it was empty, that the owner was on holiday –'

'Hush,' he broke in quickly. 'Listen.'

Someone was hammering impatiently on the door again. 'Is there anyone in there?' a strident woman's voice called out. 'Open up if there is, or we'll get the manager.'

Swiftly but carefully, Liam eased Rebecca's limp body to a standing position, and as she leant rather weakly against the wall, he started to button up his jeans again. 'Time to move on,' he said. His voice was brusque, but his blue eyes were dancing with something very like amusement. And tenderness, Rebecca saw with a little jolt at her heart. 'Get into one of those cubicles,' he continued, 'and tidy yourself up.'

Pulling the fragile straps of her expensive dress quickly over her bare shoulders, letting its sleek length fall once more around her thighs, she nodded, and turned to do as he said. Then she stopped.

'Liam,' she said. 'I know I shouldn't ask you this. But that girl, the girl you're with, Chloe . . .'

'She's a writer, a journalist. Useful at times, but not tonight. She doesn't know it yet, but she's going home alone.'

She smiled up at him. 'So am I.'

He touched her lips with his forefinger. They were still bruised from his kisses. 'Some day I'll call for my jacket,' he said. Then the pounding at the door began again. Rebecca flew to bolt herself inside one of the tiny cubicles; and Liam swiftly dragged away the heavy chair that had been jamming the entrance. Two girls from the bar, scantily dressed, glittering with make-up and jewellery, almost fell through the door. They saw Liam, and froze at the sight of a man in female territory; then their eyes widened, and began to range over him with predatory interest.

'Repair man.' He grinned at them by way of explanation. 'Everything's in order now. Enjoy yourselves.'

By the time Rebecca got back upstairs to the restaurant, Liam was paying his bill, ready to go. The girl at his side was pulling on an expensive-looking jacket that matched her dress; she looked edgy, upset. Rebecca wondered if she'd had words with Liam because he'd been so long downstairs; if he'd really meant what he said, that he was going home alone. The stab of jealousy she felt as she saw the woman put her hand possessively on Liam's arm was so intense that she had to stop and pull herself together before heading over to Max. A writer. Chloe. She still felt it should mean something.

Well, it didn't look as if Max had missed her. He was talking to the *maître d'*, complaining in a loud voice that was meant to be heard.

'The standards you set for your clientèle can't be allowed to fall like this,' he was saying. 'If you have dress rules, you should stick to them.'

Liam, who was by now making his way towards the door with the girl at his side, turned round to look at him with cold narrowed eyes. Rebecca, feeling fingers of fear clutching at her throat, hurried across the room towards Max. 'Oh, for heaven's sake, Max, stop making such a stupid fuss,' she said in a low voice. 'Will you get my coat please? I'm sorry I was so long. I'm not actually feeling too good . . .'

But Max, stubborn with drink, continued his loud protest. 'There are people in here tonight,' he enunciated pointedly, 'who look as if they'd be more at home in the kind of cheap suburban hotel where travelling salesmen stay.'

He was looking straight at Liam. Liam turned to face him with the girl still on his arm, and said softly, 'Well. You should know.'

'What?' Max was bristling.

'I said, you should know. Salesmen's conference, that

kind of thing – that's what your suit reminds me of. Saved up for it for a long time, did you?'

Max lunged forward. 'Now, look here,' he snarled.

But Liam moved faster, and had caught him by the shoulders, and was pushing him back against the wall. He was the same height as Max, but much more powerful; and Max knew it. 'No, you look here,' Liam said. Everyone in the restaurant was staring spellbound; Rebecca felt ill. 'You're clearly drunk, so I won't press the matter. But you're right in saying this place should raise the standard of its clientèle. Starting with people like you.'

His eyes raked lazily over Max's helpless figure. Then he let him go. Putting his arm lightly round Chloe's shoulder, he guided her out through the door without a backward glance. Rebecca stood silent with misery as the waiters fussed, and the restaurant slowly returned to normal.

Max, looking rather white, blustered, 'He shouldn't be allowed to get away with this.'

'You were rude to him, Max,' said Rebecca tiredly. 'You insulted him.'

Max had started to sort out the bill. 'He should never have been allowed in this place. He was an insult to all of us, coming in dressed like that . . .'

As he pulled out his wallet to select a credit card, his mobile phone rang. He snatched it from his pocket and answered it tersely. 'Max Forrester.'

'Hello, Max,' a female voice purred. Rebecca, standing close, could hear every sultry word. 'Are you still at Les Sauvages? Got rid of that boring little Rebecca yet?'

'Janey,' said Max abruptly. 'Janey, listen –'

'I just wanted to tell you to come round again soon, darling. Any time you feel like doing something really, really dirty. Like the things we did this afternoon –'

Max snapped the phone off. He gazed at Rebecca

helplessly, for once lost for words. Rebecca, looking pale, was already collecting her jacket from the waiter, who held it out to her. As she slipped it on, she said, 'I'll see myself home, Max. They'll get me a taxi at the door. See you around.'

She went out quickly, just in case he should try to stop her. But that was a mistake too, because Liam was standing on the pavement outside the restaurant with the girl, and he was kissing her. In fact, from the way she'd twined herself around him, it looked as if he was virtually having sex on the street with his friend Chloe the writer.

That was when she remembered where she'd heard the name. Her mind flew back to the group of workmen gathered in the warm evening sunlight outside the Docklands apartment, when she'd driven back there in search of Liam. 'There is someone living there,' they'd informed her, 'but she's away on holiday. Her name's Chloe Masters – she's a writer. Must have been away for a couple of weeks or so now . . .'

Well, Chloe was most definitely back in town. Another of Liam's girlfriends, who'd more than likely given him the key to her place while she was away. No doubt she couldn't wait to get him back there tonight, either, judging by the way she was running her beautifully manicured hands across his wide shoulders, and fastening her mouth to his as if they were already in bed.

Yet another woman in thrall to Liam. Turning her back on them swiftly, in case they should see her, Rebecca changed her mind about waiting for a taxi and hurried off in the direction of the tube at Piccadilly Circus, feeling acutely and achingly depressed. What made everything worse was the way she'd thrown herself at Liam tonight, practically begging him for his body again. So he'd naturally taken what she had to offer – information and sex – and was duly grateful, but made it quite plain that that was it. He was offering nothing else, and that was the end of their arrangement. Time for him to go off home with the beautiful Chloe. Oh, he had been polite enough to deny it to Rebecca at the time, but that had always, quite clearly, been his intention. A working-class hero indeed; two women in one night.

Chapter Six

O ver the next few days, Rebecca was unable to get Liam out of her mind, even though she knew that she would probably never see him again. He'd told her he'd call, but he hadn't offered her any point of contact, any address or phone number. He still didn't trust her, and how could she expect him to? He must be more than aware that she could easily betray him to Max as the man who robbed Raoni's house and leaked vital information that cost the wealthy businessman millions. Whatever she might try to say to him to prove otherwise, she was on the other side. She'd been born on the other side as far as he was concerned.

She was afraid of being lonely those next few days, without Max, with Annie still based at Lucifer's and only her obsession with Liam to keep her company. It was perhaps as well that her days were becoming increasingly dominated by the house-sitting agency. She found it hard to think of as real work at first, because so many of the flats and houses she visited while their owners were away belonged to her friends, or to Annie's; but as the fees began to come in, and recommendations spread, and the paperwork bulged, it began to give her a certain kind of fulfilment she'd never found in working for other people.

Apart from Lucifer's flat, where Annie had stayed overnight, they'd decided to commit themselves to visiting only; usually in the morning and the evening, to see to basics like checking on mail and phonecalls. Annie advised Rebecca to charge extra for the client who asked her, very earnestly, to talk for at least ten minutes a day to her tropical fish, which she was convinced would pine without human company.

'Just do it,' Annie advised. 'But charge double for talking, Becs. After all, it's not included in our list of services, is it?'

Annie enjoyed herself hugely gaining entry, if only for a brief while, into other people's private domains. Lucifer returned from his filming assignation with a new girlfriend in tow, so Annie, who'd had her own kind of fun during his absence, philosophically took the fat cheque he gave her for tending his home and threw herself wholeheartedly into the expanding business. She cut down her restaurant work to a minimum, and Rebecca had to restrain her, during the busy August holiday period, from taking on too many clients.

'I just love it,' Annie enthused as she and Rebecca walked from the tube station one evening towards a small house in Notting Hill which belonged to a successful actor friend of hers. 'It's like being paid to have a secret window on other people's lives, isn't it?'

'Except they're not at home,' laughed Rebecca, pausing in front of the door of the house. 'Come on. Have you got the list and the key?' It was Annie's birthday, and they were planning on going on to a club later, so they didn't want to take longer than necessary. They had got into a routine of systematically compiling a checklist for each house in their care, containing vital information like the burglar alarm code, and a contact number for the owner, together with individual, often eccentric, requests. This place was fairly standard; their daily tasks were to sort the mail, water the pots in the sunny courtyard garden, check the answerphone, and forward genuine post to Annie's actor friend James, who was working on a TV series up in Scotland. Annie rang him most nights as well, to pass on messages from the answerphone; their conversations were lengthy and lively and very personal.

When she came off the phone, she was laughing and her eyes were aglow. 'James remembered it was my birthday,' she said. 'He really is a darling.'

Rebecca, who'd been watering the potted shrubs out in the sunny courtyard, nodded and refilled her jug. 'Just a good friend?'

'Just a good friend. He's gay, unfortunately for me, because he has the most gorgeous body. And he's generous as well; he's told us to help ourselves to a bottle or two of champagne from his fridge to celebrate my birthday. "Have a fantasy on me," he said.' Annie wandered happily through to the small chrome and white kitchen, found a bottle in the fridge, and began to unwrap the foil. 'That reminds me. We haven't played our fantasy game for ages.'

Oh, yes, we have, thought Rebecca rather wistfully, curling herself into a big armchair and taking the glass Annie offered her. At least, I have. How about sex with a rough blond hunk in the ladies' room of one of the smartest restaurants in London?

But she'd not told Annie, this time, and that in itself was a dangerous sign.

'Go on then, Annie,' she said, balancing her glass carefully as Annie filled it with the cold, foaming liquid. 'You, for starters. What's your latest?'

Annie draped herself carefully in the velvet settee by the window, where the golden evening sunshine poured in. She'd already drunk half her champagne, and her eyes sparkled as vivaciously as the wine. She laughed ruefully at Rebecca's question. 'You know me,' she said. 'Show me an out-and-out bastard and I'll go for him. I met a guy at a party the other night. He was rich, handsome, hint of Italian blood – reminded me of a mafia type, you know? I've been having fantasies about him ever since. The way he looked at me, Becs! As if he wanted to own me, to make me obey him, in everything!'

She poured herself more wine and leant forward a little, her cheeks warm. 'I imagined that I was his slave, and that I had to do everything, absolutely everything he told me – there, at the party, among his rich businessmen friends. I imagined that I had to undress, except for the little black G-string I was wearing; and I had to pose for all of them. Then he told me to go round and taste all their dicks. Of course, they all grew hugely aroused when they heard him tell me that; I had to unfasten each one's clothing, and savour each hard penis with my hands and mouth, while the rest of them gathered round to watch. And I knew that each one wanted, so badly, to fuck me . . .'

Rebecca shivered as the champagne started to course through her blood. Annie's tale was sending little lickings of desire through her. She imagined herself, almost naked, hot with sexual arousal, offering herself to a group of rapt, totally unknown men.

'Well-known nineties syndrome, Annie,' she said lightly. 'Independent, feisty woman, namely you, longs to be dominated, shamed even, as a release from the pressures of work and relationships.'

'But wouldn't *you* fancy it?' breathed Annie, her eyes shining. 'Go on, Rebecca, you'd love it! Imagine a crowd of power-suited men, all as gorgeous as Max –'

'Max isn't gorgeous. He's a two-faced toad.'

'Yes, all right, then,' said Annie quickly, who knew the story of Janey's phone call. 'You know what I mean. Anyway, they're all gathered round you, in this secluded, expensive house, with all these big dicks sticking out, and their tongues hanging out as well, because they want you so badly. They want to kiss you, to lick you, to run their greedy fingers over your breasts, to drive their massive penises up your tight arse – and you can go round, choosing the one you want, choosing what to do. It's power, in a way. Isn't it?'

Rebecca thought for a moment, feeling warm and a little breathless. She was wearing a black sleeveless top and tight indigo jeans that hugged her legs like a second skin. The smooth denim seemed suddenly like a man's hands, cupping her buttocks and chafing the warm mound of her sex. She felt her nipples tighten warningly; felt the trickle of her juices. She thought of Liam driving his lovely strong penis into her. She remembered him watching her face, waiting until she was ready to explode with mind-bursting lust.

'How would you choose?' she asked suddenly. 'If you had all those men around you, all those lovely bodies to choose from, how would you do it?'

Annie grinned. 'I'd go for size, of course,' she said, pouring herself more of the wine. 'I'd get them all to slowly rub their own dicks, you know? It would be gloriously rude, seeing all those men in suits, dressed perfectly for the office, except for the big meaty rods in their hands. I'd go round inspecting, tasting a little, running my tongue round the rim of their fat cocks, jiggling my breasts in front of their faces until they were panting with lust.'

'Don't forget their balls,' suggested Rebecca. 'You could look at them as well. Fondle them, feel how full they are.' She grinned. 'I should think by this stage, several of them will be ready to explode all over you.'

'If they do,' said Annie seriously, 'they're disqualified, of course. I shall go for a man with a big, thick-looking dick, lots of muscle, so I know he'll last. Then I'll let him rub it very lightly over my breasts, to make my nipples nice and stiff . . .'

Rebecca listened raptly. Her nipples were so hard already, she felt she would orgasm if someone just touched them. 'Then what?' she breathed. 'How would you take him?'

'I'd get down on the floor on all fours and lift my bottom to him. He could peel my panties aside and ram his dick up my wet juicy cleft. The others would be watching, slavering, pumping away at their own erect penises. I'd beckon one of them – the one who was next best – and I'd tell him to kneel in front of me while I took his angry penis in my mouth. Then I'd suck and suck, and the man behind me would ravish me like a great strong bull, pumping into me for all he was worth; and the men watching would rub their dicks frantically, their mouths hanging open, until they all exploded with lust, and their juices spat everywhere . . .' She sat back dreamily. 'Then I think I'd make them lick each other's cocks while I watched, purring away like a contented cat.'

'I bet you would,' smiled Rebecca, somewhat faintly. It was three weeks since she'd had sex with Liam. Three weeks, and her hunger for him was like a constant torment. 'So all this was started off by meeting this guy at a party? Did you tell him about your fantasy?'

'I sort of hinted.' Annie grinned. 'Just enough to get him interested, you know?'

'I should think he was. Interested, I mean.' She'd seen the effect Annie's stories had on men; they were usually knocked out by the combination of her angelic looks, her expensive Sloane accent and her wickedly dirty mind. 'Is he worth bothering with, though, Annie?'

'Mr Nice-Guy he isn't. But then, those sweet, genuine types don't turn me on. Unfortunately,' sighed Annie. 'What about your fantasies, Becs, darling? You seem a bit quiet – and you've been rather deprived of sex lately, haven't you, since Max's departure? Don't you miss him?'

'No,' said Rebecca. 'And yes, deprived is the word. If I told you that one night at a restaurant I grabbed hold of a man I hardly knew, and dragged him into the ladies' loo, and got him to barricade the door and fuck me up against the wall, would you believe me?'

Annie was watching her carefully. 'This is a fantasy, right?'

Rebecca tossed back the last of her wine and grinned. 'God, it's got to be. Nothing like that in real life, is there? Come on. I feel as horny as hell, but we've got to get moving. Shouldn't have had all that wine. Let's hope one of us can see straight enough to key in the code on the burglar alarm, otherwise we'll have the police around.'

'Police,' said Annie dreamily. 'Now, that reminds me of another fantasy . . .'

'Don't start! We've got a long night ahead of us – it's your birthday, remember? Some food might be a good idea, to soak up all that champagne.'

'We could go to Filipo's.' Filipo's was a pizzeria in Soho where a lot of their friends gathered. 'We could have one of his seafood specials, then find out who's going where, yes?'

Rebecca nodded. 'Must just pay a visit to the loo before we lock up. By the way, that Italian guy at the party, the one who set off your men-in-suits fantasy – are you seeing him again?'

Annie blushed. 'Perhaps. He's rather busy, but he said he would ring me. I think he knows Max vaguely. I was telling him I shared a house with you, and he said you and Max once came to a party at his house.'

Rebecca felt suddenly, horribly sober, and rather cold. 'His name?' she breathed.

'Hugh. Hugh Raoni,' said Annie cheerfully.

* * *

Some hours later, Rebecca sat tensely amongst a crowd of their friends as Annie flirted outrageously with every man she knew in the popular Covent Garden wine bar they'd headed to after Filipo's, and with some she didn't. Since Annie's news, it was as if her own appetite for partying had vanished as quickly as the champagne in her bloodstream.

Annie's mention of Raoni had frightened her. She hated Raoni anyway, because he'd told Max that she wasn't good enough for him. And she was worried, too, on Liam's behalf, because the fact that Annie had met Liam's enemy seemed to bring him much, much closer. OK, so she had been able to warn Liam away from that meeting with the journalist who'd been paid to betray his identity to Raoni; but that, she was sure, was only a tiny part of Raoni's campaign against the man who'd exposed his Green Company for what it was and cost him millions.

But why should you care, she rebuked herself silently, when Liam obviously doesn't care anything for you? Let him fight his own battles; he's obviously well used to looking after himself. And yet she couldn't stop thinking about him.

They'd called home before going to the wine bar, to get changed; Annie into a halter-neck body-clinging dress that made her look as if she'd been sewn into it, and Rebecca into a double-layer slip dress and high suede boots in matching black.

'Becs, you look gorgeous,' said Annie emphatically as they left the flat. 'Find someone really great tonight, will you? Get Max out of your system. Anyone would think you'd gone off real guys and just existed in that fantasy world of yours.'

Liam is my fantasy world, and he's not interested, thought Rebecca as she tried to throw herself into a party mood for Annie's sake. She found it harder and harder as a succession of eager men bored her to tears

160

with their efforts to impress her. At last, she fought her way across the crowded wine bar to Annie, who was clearly having a wonderful time.

'Annie,' she shouted, exaggerating her words to make them audible above the thud of the music, 'I think I'll go back home. I've got a headache – must be all that champagne earlier. You stay on – have a lovely time. Got your keys?'

Annie nodded happily towards the man she was flirting with. 'Yes, but I don't think I'll need them tonight. Sure you'll be all right?'

'Of course I'll be all right. Have a great birthday. I'll see to the house-sitting in the morning.'

Annie mouthed a grateful thanks, and Rebecca called a taxi back to Kensington. She felt tired and dispirited, and aching for sex.

At one time, she'd have stayed on with Annie, and had fun. The chances were she'd have found herself a man who took her fancy, and treated herself to a vigorous all-night session – no questions asked, no commitment, just the physical excitement and sheer indulgence of sex, with an amicable parting the next morning; perhaps to meet again, perhaps not.

The taxi was nearly at her street. She pulled herself quickly out of her reverie, aware that her breasts were aching now, and her mouth was sensitive, as if ready for some man's caress. Tough, Rebecca, she told herself sharply. Another night of celibacy beckoned. A hot bath, a good book and her fantasies were all that were on the menu tonight.

Sighing, she paid off the taxi driver and stood on the pavement in the warm night air, fumbling for her key as he pulled away down Kensington Church Street.

And then a man came out of the shadows where he'd been standing and said quietly, 'Hi.'

It was Liam.

Oh, God. It must be a fantasy, it had to be. She was

so startled, so astonished, that she dropped her keys. She bent to get them, clutching them to her almost defensively. He was watching her, a mixture of amusement and rueful apology on his face.

He said, 'Shall I go away, and come back again? Give you time to recover?' He was wearing a faded denim jacket, a soft white shirt and patched jeans. He looked as gorgeous, as delectable as ever. Her pulse, which had first started to race as dizzily as a wound-up metronome, settled down to a slow, meaningful thud.

'I know it's a corny thing to say,' she said rather breathlessly. 'But what the hell are you doing here?'

'I needed to see you. Can I come in?'

She shrugged, and managed, this time, to get the keys in the lock without dropping them. She led the way upstairs, flicked on the lights and registered, with a silent prayer of gratitude, that the house was, for once, tidy. She went to turn on the kettle. 'You're lucky I was back early,' she said coolly. 'I might have been hours yet. It's my friend's birthday.'

He propped his wide shoulders against the kitchen doorway and folded his arms as he watched her spoon the coffee rather clumsily into two mugs.

'I'd have waited,' he said. 'The only thing I was worried about was that you might have come home with Max.'

'I've not seen Max since that night at Les Sauvages,' she said curtly. 'Sugar?'

'I'm glad. Yes, please. I like your dress,' he replied, moving nearer.

She whirled round, the spoon in her hand. 'Look, Liam, what's all this about? What do you want?'

'I wanted to see you. I've been wanting to get in touch since that night at Les Sauvages, but I've been busy.'

The kettle behind her hissed away unnoticed. She stared up at him: a mistake, because she couldn't look at this man without thinking of sex, and she knew her body and her expression would betray her.

She turned quickly back to the coffee and said coldly, 'I've been busy, too. So you fancied a quick fuck again, did you? Sorry, Liam.'

His dark blue eyes danced, and she knew she'd blundered again. 'Well, yes, since you mention it,' he murmured. 'And not a quick fuck, but a slow one. Just as slow as you like . . .'

Little tongues of desire raked her warm skin. Her nipples puckered up with delight, as if they recognised his lovely, lazy London voice. A warning pulse of desire tugged at her loins, and Rebecca felt her legs trembling slightly as she poured the boiling water into the mugs. 'Really? And what's happened to your writer friend Chloe? Has she got bored with your self-proclaimed expertise?'

'No. She hasn't had the chance. I told you, I went home alone that night. I haven't seen her since.'

He was leaning against the doorway again, looking completely relaxed. She stirred some sugar angrily in his mug and shoved it towards him. 'I don't believe you.'

'Suit yourself. It's true.'

And then the phone rang.

She hesitated, afraid it might be Max; and then she remembered that neither she nor Annie had put the answering machine on. She flew into the little sitting room and grabbed the phone. 'Hello?'

The line was crackly, indistinct, but she realised very quickly that the caller was talking about one of the flats on their list. She stretched out to grab a pencil, and scribbled jerkily. 'Yes. Thank you for ringing. Yes, I'll be over straight away . . .'

Liam was watching her from the kitchen. His whole demeanour had changed; he was no longer lounging, but looking alert, concerned. 'Is something wrong?'

'Yes,' she said, already starting to rummage through the rows of hooks where she and Annie kept the keys to the flats and houses in their care. 'There's this flat Annie and I are supposed to be looking after; it belongs to a friend of Annie's who's on holiday. She's got lots of fish; she pays us to talk to them while she's away.' Liam's eyebrows lifted slightly; Rebecca hurried on, 'That was a neighbour, from the flat below, ringing to say that there's water trickling down through her ceiling. She's going demented, says the whole lot will cave in, or something. God, what am I going to do?' She ran her fingers distractedly through her hair. 'I'll have to phone an emergency plumber. It's eleven o'clock on a Saturday night – it'll cost a fortune . . .'

Liam said sharply, 'So you've got the key to this flat?'

'Yes – here.'

'Then let's get over there now. We'll at least be able to assess the damage, and we can turn the water off while we wait for a plumber. You can reassure the fish as well.'

She stared at him. 'Turn the water off?'

'Yes. At the mains.' He turned to her and grinned sleepily. 'Ever heard of a stopcock, Rebecca?'

Rebecca was reluctant to admit it, but in fact she had never been so glad of anyone's company as she was of Liam's that night. It seemed to her that he took care of everything, in a quietly competent way that made her feel more competent herself.

'We'd better take your car,' he'd said, making the first decision for her. 'We could wait a long time for a taxi.'

'I can't drive,' she said miserably. 'I've had too much wine.'

'I haven't. I'll drive your car, if you'll let me.'

She managed a wry little smile. 'You mean you're actually asking me, this time?'

He drove her quickly to the elegant row of converted

period flats in Chelsea where Annie's fish-loving friend lived. Rebecca got the keys out and hurried up the stairs, half-expecting to see torrents of water, Titanic-style, pouring down towards her; but there was nothing, only the agitated spinster who lived below, who was waiting for them in her doorway. She showed them the steady drip coming through the hairline crack in her ceiling, and eyed Liam with approval.

'You've found a plumber quickly,' she said.

Liam grinned; Rebecca said, 'Yes, he's a friend.'

They hurried upstairs, and Rebecca unlocked the door, turning on all the light switches so that the big opulently decorated flat was brightly illuminated. Liam went swiftly round each room. 'It's here,' he said. 'In the bathroom. There's a leak from the coupling at the back of the loo; the water's pouring out.'

Rebecca looked anxiously. The carpet was sodden. 'Oh, Christ. Is it just water?'

'Yes, don't worry. It comes down this pipe from the cold tank, to fill up the cistern. The leak probably started a couple of days ago, but you wouldn't have noticed, because so far the carpet's soaked most of it up.'

'What can we do?'

'It needs a new coupling. I'll try and get one in the morning. Find some towels, will you, to soak up the water? I'll find the stopcock, to turn everything off.'

She ran to the airing cupboard for towels, and blotted up as much water as she could, lifting the carpet to let the floorboards dry off. Then she hurried to find Liam, who was in the kitchen, on his back on the floor, struggling to turn off a tap under the sink. His patched jeans were covered with dust and a smear of oil ran across his once-clean shirt; his long legs were sprawled out crookedly as he wrestled with the stubborn metal. She tried very hard not to look at the all-too-masculine bulge at his groin. He pulled himself up at last and smiled at her.

'That's it,' he said. 'Water's off. Emergency over.'

'I really don't know how to thank you, Liam. If we hadn't got it fixed tonight, the damage would have been awful. Annie's friend would have been furious.'

He brushed some dust off his jeans. 'She should be grateful. If you hadn't been on call, the old lady downstairs would probably have panicked and landed her with an enormous bill for emergency plumbers. There are a lot of cowboys around.'

She felt strangely shy with him. 'How do you know? About plumbing, I mean?'

'I don't really know a lot. Just the bare essentials, but it comes in handy.'

The kitchen was small; he was standing close to her, so close she could almost feel the heat of his body. She reached up to touch a smear of dirt on his cheek, unable to stop herself. 'You've ruined your clothes,' she said quietly.

His eyes blazed at her touch. 'So have you,' he said, touching her bare shoulders with his hands as he gazed down at her sheer black slip dress, sodden from her efforts to dry out the bathroom. 'And you're soaked through.'

So I am, she thought rather desperately, instantly aware of the melting lubrication between her thighs. She was so aroused by his nearness, she almost forgot to breathe. His hands were softly kneading her shoulders, sending shivers of longing through her. She lifted her mouth to meet his, her hand creeping around the waist of his jeans, her fingers searching their way beneath his shirt to feel the warm smooth skin. He cupped her face with his hands and pulled her to him, into a delicious, tongue-tingling kiss that went on and on, and made her stomach do somersaults of desire. She had both her hands high up beneath his shirt now, and was running her palms hungrily across his silky muscle-packed shoulders.

The question burned at the back of her mind; she had to ask, she had to know. 'Did you really mean it,' she breathed, 'about not going back with Chloe that night?'

'I meant it. I was just using her to get some information, and that didn't involve bed. I told you so, didn't I?'

She hesitated. 'Liam, I know that the Docklands apartment you took me to that night belongs to Chloe. I know that she must have given you her keys.'

'She's a generous lady, and a good friend,' he said softly. 'At the time you're talking about, she knew I might need a London base for a few days, so she told me to make use of her place. My friends and I cleared out quickly the morning after Raoni's party, because you might remember that Raoni's men had followed us there, had tried to get in, and I didn't want Chloe carrying any of that sort of trouble. But I was grateful for her help. I took her out for a meal at Les Sauvages, to thank her. Sex wasn't on the menu.'

'But I saw you outside the restaurant, kissing her . . .'

'A consolation prize for her,' he whispered, touching her cheek with his warm lips.

She struggled to resist him. 'You wouldn't win any prizes for modesty.'

He laughed. 'Did you go back with Max? Did you sleep with salesman-suited Max?'

She laughed too, happy. 'No. Oh, no.'

Liam kissed her hard. Then, still kissing her, he eased his thigh round the back of her booted leg and tipped her over, gathering her neatly in his strong arms. He carried her carefully into the sitting room, and laid her down on the big brocade settee.

'Take your dress off,' he said. 'It's wet.'

'Take your shirt off. It's dirty.'

'My mind is dirty.'

'So's mine – take off your shirt, Liam. Oh, God, the fish will be shocked . . .'

'The fish?'

She giggled and pointed to the huge tropical tank set in a cabinet against the wall. 'I told you. I'm supposed to talk to them, every day.'

'Talk to them, then.' Liam had unbuttoned his shirt; the expanse of gloriously tanned, hard male flesh all the way down to the tight leather belt of his jeans was almost too much for Rebecca, whose dress had already slithered to the floor. 'Talk to them,' went on Liam, his eyes dancing as he knelt on the floor beside the settee and let his tongue snake over the delicious curve of her breasts that were revealed by her scanty, expensive bra. 'Tell them what we're doing, and then they won't be traumatised by what they see. No, keep those boots on, Rebecca. I adore your boots . . .'

He was easing her breasts from her lacy bra, drawing their aching fullness into his mouth. Rebecca writhed beneath him on the settee, sighing out her excruciating delight as the warm hard flesh of his torso pressed against her own slender body. She stretched out her booted legs with luxurious enjoyment, drawing his jean-clad hips between them.

'OK, fish,' she breathed. 'Are you listening? Then here goes. There's this gorgeous man here called Liam, and I hope, I really hope he's going to fuck me. Right now, he's kissing my breasts, and he's biting them with his lovely teeth, and his hand's slipping down between my legs, and – oh, my God . . .'

He was smiling down at her, his sun-streaked mane of hair tickling her cheek. His hand was pushing her tiny panties aside to work at the plump, sleek folds of her labia, spreading them like flower-petals; his thick finger started to slide blatantly in and out of her throbbing vagina, filling her with the most delicious shivers of anticipation.

'You're wet,' he murmured with pleasure. 'Your

vagina is so beautifully wet, Rebecca. I can hardly wait to fuck you, but keep talking. I like it.'

Rebecca arched desperately towards him. Her remaining scraps of underwear did nothing at all for her modesty; her breasts thrust towards him from above the scalloped edge of her bra, their crests coral-tipped and burning. Her long supple boots made her feel raunchy, dirty. He was still fingering her, driving her wild. She ached to tear his jeans from his body.

'Tell me,' he said. 'Tell me what you want.'

'What do you think?' she breathed. 'Please, Liam, take your cock out and fuck me with it. I want you inside me, now.'

Dark-eyed, he bent to kiss her. His mouth devoured her, his strong tongue ravished her. She was dimly aware of him unfastening himself, of him spreading her wide, so the cool air kissed her wet yearning vulva; then the blunt head of his cock was sliding between her slick sex folds and driving slowly, deliberately into her, filling all her aching emptiness with bliss. He kissed her mouth, her throat, her breasts, flicking their stiffened nubs to and fro with his tongue until she wanted to scream with pleasure. Then he gathered her in his arms, and eased her face-down on to the floor, on all fours, so her bottom was lifted high and naked.

She felt deliciously wanton, deliciously exposed. She turned round, desperate for a glimpse of his huge, throbbing cock; she moaned aloud when she saw it, her juices flowing freely. 'Please, Liam. I want it so badly. I want you inside me.'

He smiled, but his blue eyes were sleepily hooded. 'In a moment. Let's give the fish something to really listen to. Tell me about your first fuck, Rebecca. Was it with someone like Max?'

He was behind her now, so she couldn't see him. But she could feel the tip of his firm penis rubbing gently at the slick wetness between her thighs.

'Yes. Yes, I suppose he was like Max . . .'

'Rich? Upper class?'

'Yes. Oh, please, Liam. Do it to me.'

'I will,' he murmured. 'Soon, I'm going to drive my big cock right into you again. But only if you'll tell me, Rebecca, about the first time. Were you still at school? Did you enjoy it? Remember, I want to know everything.' He'd leant over her body now, covering her with his warmth, and he was squeezing each of her nipples in turn. She wanted to scream with longing.

'Yes,' she cried out. 'Yes, I was still at school, in my last year. There were some boys, boarders nearby – we went out one night to meet them, for a bet . . .'

'Had you kissed anyone before? Had you felt a boy's cock?'

'I'd kissed, yes. Nothing else. But I wanted to, oh, I wanted to . . .'

She could feel Liam's menacing penis nudging at the entrance to her vagina. Her juices flowed freely, coating its glossy tip. She felt wild with hunger, wild to feel that lovely hard shaft of male flesh filling her to the brim.

'Were you desperate for it then, Rebecca? Did you beg him for it?'

'No! I didn't need to. He knew why I'd come out to meet him. He was good-looking, popular; several of the girls in my year, including Annie, had done it with him, and I was flattered he wanted me. I wanted so much to know what it was like.'

'Tell me what it was like. Did you suck his dick for him?'

She bit her lip, writhing beneath his warm, hard body, struggling to take his tormenting penis inside her silken walls.

'Tell me what it was like, and I'll mount you from behind, and fuck you so that you're crying out in ecstasy. Tell me.'

Half-sobbing with desire, she whispered, 'He played

with my breasts. He licked them. I nearly came then, because the feeling was so strong.'

His hands toyed with her nipples. 'And then? When did you see his cock?'

'He made me take it out of his pants, made me hold it. I was frightened, because it seemed so hard, so hot, so big.'

'And then?' His voice was lazy, gravelly. 'Did he make you wank him?'

'He went all sort of strange, really desperate for it. He pulled up my skirt, and ran his hands over my thighs, and pulled my knickers down, and gazed at me there. I was embarrassed, because I was so wet, my mound was so dark and swollen . . .'

Liam touched her there. 'It's lovely. You're lovely. Soon I'm going to fuck you so hard, you'll scream. What happened next?'

'He – he gripped his penis, and he crouched over me, and he slid it into me. I was shocked, because it felt so huge; it seemed to fill me, to stretch me. It was glorious. I think I started to come straight away; I felt myself shaking, and he was licking my nipples hard, and panting away at me, like a dog I'd once seen. His stiff cock was sort of locked into me.'

Liam's rigid penis was inching its way into her from behind. 'Did he come inside you?'

'No. Oh, no. He pulled his penis out, and jerked it against my stomach; I could feel his hairy balls bouncing against my thighs. Then his seed started to spurt out, and his eyes were all glazed, and I felt wonderful, so wonderful. Oh, Liam. Please . . .'

He was starting to slide into her now from behind, and she gasped as his penis nudged her sex lips wide apart. 'Did you do it with him again?'

'Yes. But it wasn't as good as this. It wasn't anything like this,' she moaned. 'Fuck me. Fuck me hard, Liam. I can't stand it any more.'

He moulded his hard body over her soft one, and cupped her aching breasts, and drove his lengthy penis into her again and again until she was sobbing out his name, rising on a shimmering wave of pleasure until she peaked, and cried out, and hovered on the blissful knife-edge of ecstasy while he continued to ravish her pulsing flesh. Then he drew out quickly, and took her bottom; the feel of his massive cock, driving deep between her buttocks, plundering her secret orifice with dark, powerful demands, sent the aching torment of bliss pounding through her body again.

She lay back sweat-sheened in his arms when he had finished with her, and crooned out her pleasure as his lips continued to caress her burning skin.

'God, Liam, you're wonderful.'

He eased her on to the settee. 'No more wonderful than you. As I'm sure you've been told many times, and in far more refined ways than I've got at my disposal.'

She hesitated, then said, 'It bothers you that I've been with men who are different to you?'

His gaze seemed slightly veiled. 'That you're usually in the company of rich, upper-class guys like Max, you mean? No. After all, is the sex so very different?'

'Yes,' she breathed, reaching to run her tongue across the warm sinewed skin of his shoulder. 'Because with you, it's incredible.'

'Working-class stamina,' he grinned, but she saw that his dark blue eyes weren't smiling. 'Generations of hard physical graft. Plumbing.'

She smiled back, but she said, 'It does bother you, doesn't it? You hate men like Max. Why?'

'Because they don't care,' he said. 'About anything but their bank balances, their expense accounts, their company cars. Basically, they don't care about anything except themselves.'

His eyes were shuttered again. Rebecca was silent, thinking, yes, he's right. But Max is no worse, no better than anyone else I know . . . She said at last, 'When did you begin to care so much about the sort of thing you're involved in now? The environment, and everything?'

'I always cared, I suppose. After all, it's pretty much an essential part of the way we live, isn't it?' Rebecca nodded quickly, ashamed to acknowledge that she'd never even thought much about it. Liam was continuing, 'It wasn't actually until I'd finished my degree – yes, I did manage to bang out some A levels and get to university – that I realised, I suppose, just how badly the rich guys who run most things in this country are screwing up the landscape. And how little time we've got to save it.'

'Are you working on something at the moment? To do with the environment, I mean?'

'Yes. I told you, it's my work. I'm a journalist. It's what I write about. There's this wood, an ancient wood of oak trees that are hundreds of years old. A big business consortium has plans to chop the trees down and build a road.'

Rebecca said, 'Trees grow again, don't they? They can plant some more nearby.'

He smiled and touched her hair. 'You really are a city girl, aren't you, Rebecca? Trees like the ones I'm talking about don't grow again.'

'Then why doesn't someone stop the developers? There are all sorts of agencies, aren't there, and laws to protect the countryside?'

'Most of the laws protect the developers. There is a group of protesters who are trying to stop the scheme going ahead, but the people they're fighting against are powerful. They've got money.'

'Like Hugh Raoni,' she said.

He turned to look at her quickly. 'Exactly like that.'

She'd felt a cold shiver run through her at the thought of Raoni, and the threats he'd made against Liam. 'My friend Annie met Hugh Raoni the other night,' she said suddenly. 'She liked him.'

Liam seemed to go very still for a moment, and then he shrugged. Rebecca was vaguely surprised that he didn't react more strongly. 'He's rich, plausible, handsome,' he said. 'Lots of people like him. I think he's poisonous.'

'You didn't meet up with that news reporter who planned to give you away to him?'

'I still had the meeting. But it was OK. You see, the journalist, Pete Harmsworth, is a good friend of mine. He went along with Raoni's bribe for a little while, and sent Raoni's thugs to a place the other side of London while we met up snugly in a pub in Mile End. I wonder how long they waited for me to turn up.'

She gazed at him, stunned. 'So – you didn't need my warning after all, that night in the restaurant . . .'

He kissed the tip of her nose. 'No, sweetheart. But it was lovely to see you, all the same.'

She was shaking her head. 'The radio station, the one your friend works for. Their receptionist, the one who answered my telephone call, practically clammed up on me, put the telephone down when I asked to speak to someone about you. I thought it was because they were on Raoni's side. But they were protecting you, all the time . . .'

'Exactly. I told you I could look after myself. I've always had to. Even so, it was useful knowing Raoni's plan from another angle. I've got a lot to thank you for.'

She smiled happily up at him. 'I can think of several ways you can repay me. A bit of plumbing work for starters. And then . . .' She reached her hands up to pull his face down to hers, lifting her mouth to meet his. He kissed her with a slow, deliberate passion, and she felt lovely warm stirrings of desire fizz through her body.

'Let's go back to your place, shall we?' said Liam. 'I believe I've got a jacket to collect.'

'Oh, yes,' she breathed as he drew her up from the sofa. 'Yes please.'

As she checked round the flat, and locked it all up carefully, a tiny voice somewhere in her lust-hazed brain was saying, Why now? Why has he come to me now, out of nowhere, when he knew where I lived, when he could have called me any time?

But then he held her close, and kissed her again, and she pushed those faint stirrings of unease to the recesses of her mind.

The evening rain was warm and welcome. Cass revelled in its gentle fall as she made her way around the clearing in the fading summer twilight, checking that all the inhabitants of the little camp knew exactly which phase of the watch they were to cover during the hours of darkness.

If Liam arrived without warning, he would have no cause for complaint about their security arrangements, this time. She longed, more than anything, for him to join them here. In the meantime, she took comfort from the tightly disciplined organisation of the Hegley Wood protest camp, thinking with pride of the carefully constructed shelters, the tidy cleanliness everywhere, the well-organised arrangements for supplies and water and cooking.

And, of course, the watch rota. Liam had been right, as he always was, about the private security battalions that were lining up in the private, mostly forested estates that bordered Hegley Wood itself. She hated their batteries of equipment, their harsh blue uniforms, the stark metal cabins they used as mobile offices; hated the wide scarring of the tracks they'd already ploughed through the adjacent land for the efficient, gleaming four-wheel-drive vehicles they'd brought with them. Ready for the bulldozers, the diggers; and she guessed that iron filings in the diesel wouldn't hold them up for long, this time. She shivered at her helplessness, feeling the pain stab through her as she gazed at the beautiful trees all around.

They were keeping in the background as yet, these faceless security men. So far they contented themselves with checking their equipment, and talking into their mobile phones, and keeping the camp and the public right of way into it under distant but intrusive surveillance.

She was thinking of all this as she checked the arrangements for tonight's watch, wishing as she always did that Liam was here to advise them, when suddenly one of the women who'd taken their supper dishes to wash in the nearby stream came rushing towards her through the gathering dusk. She looked breathless and distraught.

'Cass. You must come. They're cutting the trees down. They've started.'

Stopping only to call for someone to fetch Petro and Stevie, Cass charged after the woman into the woods. She could hear it herself now, could hear the sickening sound of chainsaws against living wood, could smell the obscene stink of petrol fumes despoiling the fresh green scents of the ancient forest. Garish battery-powered arc lights violated the velvety darkness, showing her the way to the scene of desecration. Panting with despair and fury, she almost threw herself on the two big burly men in yellow helmets who were moving on to attack their next victim in a line of marked saplings. Several trees already lay on the ground.

'Stop,' Cass breathed. 'Stop. You have no right . . .'

They paused then to wipe the sweat that had gathered on their foreheads under the rims of their safety helmets. They grinned at her, staring openly at the way the rain had dampened her cotton T-shirt, making it cling to her breasts. Her nipples were stiffening in the sudden chill, and she knew they saw that too. How she hated them.

'We're on private land here,' one of the security men told her dismissively. 'And we've got permission. Best get back to your mud-patch quickly, love, before we get you charged with trespassing.'

'But you need special permission to chop down trees,' she argued heatedly, her body almost shaking with protest. 'You've no right to be doing this.' She gestured despairingly at the felled saplings. 'And what's the point? After all, you've not even got planning permission yet, for the road.'

The man cradling the big chainsaw grinned at her. 'Any day, now, love. Any day. And after that you're all trespassers.'

'You'll never get planning permission, never. This is a protected area. And don't call me love,' hissed Cass, her small fists clenching.

He eyed her with outright scorn. 'All right, then. What do you like to be called, darling, when someone's screwing you? Or do you prefer to do it with other girls? Tell me about it. I'd really like to know more. Come to think of it, I'd really like to watch . . .' He cupped his fist and moved it up and down as if he were masturbating, laughing at her as he did so.

Cass hurled a string of obscenities at him, then turned to run back to the camp, her slight frame shaking with helpless anger. She could hear their laughter following her as she pushed her way through the trees. The rain calmed her; the scent of the verdant leaves soothed her, but only for a moment. She leant despairingly against one of the trees near the edge of the clearing where the protesters were encamped, and tried to steady herself before going back to them all, because if she gave way to defeat, who else was there? Oh, Liam. Come back, please.

She lit a cigarette with shaking hands. Then she saw

Stevie hurrying towards her through the twilight. His eyes were dark with anxiety. 'Is it true, Cass? They've started on the trees?'

'Yes,' she said bitterly. 'Only a few, but they've started. We should have protected them, should have wired them. Oh, God, they can't possibly get planning permission to destroy all this, can they? If only Liam would come.'

Stevie said, 'Liam's just phoned in.'

Her head jerked up. 'When? Why? Why didn't you let me speak to him?'

'He was in a hurry, Cass,' said Stevie gently. 'Said he hadn't got the phone to himself for long, and the signal kept breaking up.'

'When's he coming here? Did he say?'

Stevie hesitated. 'He said he's got to stay in London a little while longer.'

She sat down, a hunched little figure on a tree stump. 'No. He can't. We need him.'

Her fingers trembled round her cigarette, which had gone out. Stevie said quietly, 'Listen, Cass. You'll find out sooner or later, so I might as well tell you what Liam told me. He's getting closer to Raoni, closer to obtaining proof that he's the one behind all this. That's why he's staying in London.'

She was staring at him wide-eyed. 'What do you mean, I'll find out sooner or later?'

He sat down beside her. 'You remember Rebecca? The girl who drove him back to Chloe's place after he'd stolen the papers from Raoni?'

'Yes. What about her?'

'He's with her. She knows a lot of people Raoni knows, so Liam's sticking close.'

Cass's hands were shaking as she tried to relight her cigarette. 'You mean he's screwing her, don't you?'

Stevie held out a light for her. 'Probably. But he'll just be using her, as a way of getting more information on

Raoni. He's got to do something. Things aren't looking too good, as far as Hegley Wood's concerned. This consortium, whether Raoni's behind it or not, might be given planning permission to go ahead within the next few days.'

'They won't get planning permission. They can't.'

'They might. We've got to face up to that. And then there'll be court action against us, as trespassers, and the bailiffs will be sent in to clear us out.'

'No.' Cass squeezed her cigarette so tightly in her hands that it almost burnt her. 'No . . .'

'Yes. Our only chance is for Liam to get as close as he can to Raoni, to prove he really is the one behind all this, and force him to back down. Liam needs to use everyone and everything he can. And he's using Rebecca. That's all.'

'Oh, Stevie.' She gazed up at him, her green eyes wide and haunted. 'Oh, God, I just wish he was here. Everything's going so horribly, horribly wrong.'

He took her in his arms then and cradled her trembling body very close.

'I hate that woman Rebecca,' she whispered against his shoulder. 'I hated her from the moment I saw her. She's rich and beautiful; she must have had everything she ever wanted in life. Why should she have Liam as well?'

Stevie reached with his hands to cradle her tear-stained cheeks. 'Remember that he's using her,' he said steadily. 'And, besides, she's nowhere near as beautiful as you.'

A little tremor ran through her body. Stevie recognised it. He kissed the tears from her dark lashes, and pressed his lips against her mouth, feeling her clinging to him almost desperately as her hands slid around his shoulders.

Silently, as if paying homage, he knelt on the soft grass before her feet and ran his gentle hands up her legs, pulling down her jeans as he did so. Slowly, he parted her thighs and kissed the curling dark bush of her pubic hair, feeling her fingers tense and tighten on his shoulders. With great tenderness, he used his tongue to part the secret folds and whorls of her sex, running its sensitive tip skilfully up and down her moist furrow, dancing against her unfurling clitoris then dropping lower to push and explore at the warmly opening tunnel of her vagina. Every action was performed as if he was supping the most desirable banquet on earth. Cass was making low, husky noises of delight at the back of her throat. Splaying her thighs wider, pushing his head harder against her mound, she pumped her body against him, seizing her pleasure voraciously from the hard, fleshy length of his tongue. 'Ah, Stevie, that's so good,' she muttered. 'So good.'

His tongue was thrusting deeply into her lush furrow now, ravishing her; she clamped herself against him, rubbing the swollen nub of her clitoris greedily against the hard bridge of his nose, almost swooning with delight as his tongue swirled deep within her. Uttering savage little cries of pleasure, her silver earrings tinkling in rhythm, Cass rode to blissful, liquid climax; he continued to thrust steadily with his tongue, sending shivers of ecstasy rippling through to every taut nerve-ending in her body. When she was quite finished, quite limp with joy, he raised himself to her side in the warm darkness and held her close, in silence.

'Oh, Stevie,' she said, smiling rather weakly as she leant her head against his chest. 'That was fantastic. Even Liam couldn't have beaten that. Stevie, you're the one decent thing that's come out of all this.'

'Good,' he said, not even seeming to mind that she was still thinking of the other man. 'Remember it.'

Chapter Seven

'*H*e's gorgeous, Becs. Really gorgeous. You are lucky,' called Annie from the bathroom, where she was vigorously brushing her teeth in preparation for a night out.

She was talking, of course, about Liam. Rebecca, who was in her bedroom trying on clothes, smiled secretly to herself. 'Yes,' she said. 'Yes, he is.'

She would be seeing Liam tonight. She'd seen him almost every night for the last two weeks, ever since he'd turned up on her doorstep like a dream come true. Tonight she was taking him to a friend's house in Hampstead, for supper. He'd been amused and resigned when she told him about it in bed last night.

'Rich society types?' he said, leaning back lazily against the pillows with his hands behind his head. 'The women will love me. The men will hate me.'

She'd curled up to him in her narrow bed, unable to keep her hands off him. 'What do you expect?' she'd said. 'Just try not to shock them too much, will you?'

His face was all innocence. 'Like using the wrong knives and forks, you mean?'

'No.' She pretended to pummel his chest. 'You know

what I mean. Like telling them the other night at Daisy's party that you were brought up in a sink council estate, and were seduced by the rapacious landlady of the local pub when you were only fourteen. And then you told them you worked as a male stripper to get enough money to go to university –'

'They loved it,' he said. 'They absolutely loved it.'

'I know they did. I thought the women would demand a performance there and then. You're a villain, Liam.' She'd kissed him, very tenderly. 'And the other day, at Susie and Jack's, you told them you were a plumber. Didn't you?'

'What's wrong with that?'

She laughed. 'Nothing, I suppose. Susie still fancied you rotten.'

Liam, she considered pleasurably as Annie continued talking to her from the bathroom, was certainly taking her friends by storm. He'd taken her heart by storm, and reduced her body to a molten, quivering mass of longing for him.

Since the evening of the flooded flat, he'd spent most nights with her. She didn't ask him where he lived, and he didn't tell her. 'It's a dump,' he said. 'Shared phone and everything. It's all a bit difficult.'

She wondered then if perhaps he was staying at Chloe's apartment; but she didn't ask him, because she'd decided from the start that she mustn't ask him questions. She knew he wouldn't want her to, that it would drive him away. He was busy, she knew, on the piece of work he was researching about the protesters at the Berkshire road development he'd told her about, Hegley Wood. She'd seen items about it on the news, and tried to take an interest in it, for his sake. But he didn't really seem to want to talk about it anyway. It had to be enough that he was with her most nights, seemingly enjoying the round of social events with her

London friends, and most definitely enjoying the glorious sex they shared together.

What to wear for tonight, for Zoe's party in Hampstead, was the question that occupied her mind at the moment. He was calling for her at eight; she had an hour. After showering, she deliberated long and hard over her clothes, throwing discarded items to the floor in discontent. Finally she decided on a thigh-skimming Chinese-style dress in ivory patterned silk, with a mandarin collar and a leg-revealing slit up the side.

Annie sidled in from the bathroom, smelling of expensive perfume, wearing just a black silk robe over her bra and pants. She looked as delectably wicked as ever, and the glass of wine in one hand and the half-empty bottle in the other indicated her already inebriated state. 'Wow,' she said, gazing as Rebecca slid her feet into some ivory high-heeled mules. 'You look wonderful, Rebecca. Forget the food. He'll want you for starter, main course and dessert.'

'I certainly hope so.' Smiling softly to herself, Rebecca smoothed the creamy silk garment over her hips and scrutinised herself in the mirror. 'Where are you off to tonight, Annie?'

Annie looked a little self-conscious, and drank some more of her wine. 'Didn't I tell you? I'm going out with that guy I told you about. Hugh Raoni. He's picking me up in half an hour.'

Rebecca couldn't believe it. Turning slowly from her mirror, she said, 'Oh, Annie. I know you've met him once or twice, but I didn't know you were seeing him regularly.'

Annie was defensive. 'Why not? He's fun, Rebecca. He makes me feel so good about myself.'

'I've heard things, Annie. His business deals aren't exactly above board, you know. He's got a lot of enemies.'

'Anyone who's rich and successful has a lot of

enemies,' declared Annie. 'What's wrong with you, Rebecca? For heaven's sake, Raoni's a friend of Max's – you went to a party at his house, didn't you? I can't believe you're jealous!'

Rebecca struggled. Anything she said would just sound like stupid, petty jealousy. OK, so she knew Raoni was out for Liam's blood, knew he'd planned to get a gang of toughs together to frighten Liam off. But how could she explain that to Annie, without betraying Liam? She started brushing out her hair, and said quietly, 'I'm not jealous. As long as you're OK, Annie, that's all right by me. Are you sleeping with him?'

'Christ, Becs, you sound like my mother. Lighten up,' muttered Annie, drinking more of her wine. 'Are you taking care, Annie? Are you on the pill, Annie? Are you washing behind your ears?' She flopped down suddenly on to Rebecca's bed, her long blonde hair tumbling all round her shoulders. She grinned suddenly, relenting. 'All right, yes, I am sleeping with him. Not that sleep comes into it much. He's a glorious lay, Becs, darling. There's a slight hint, just a hint of meanness there, you know? So sexy.' She leant back to lounge against the pillows, and just then her robe fell apart, revealing her underwear. Rebecca saw, with a slight frisson of shock, that Annie was wearing a black peephole bra, through which her nipples poked provocatively.

Annie registered her shock, and said defensively, 'Raoni likes me to dress in tacky underwear like this. He likes me to pretend to be his whore. There's nothing wrong with that, is there?'

Rebecca didn't say anything. Annie smiled dreamily, and Rebecca could see how her nipples were already hard and aroused as they poked out of her tight bra, how her face was flushed, her eyes shining.

'He treats me like dirt,' Annie went on softly. 'Then he takes me out for the most fabulous time, to make up for it. I don't think I've ever had so much champagne in my life. He has lots of important, clever friends: businessmen, politicians. He likes me to talk about having it away with them, you know? When we're at a restaurant, he'll whisper to me, "How about that one, over there? Do you think he's got a big dick? Would you like to suck it for him, to feel him spurting away down your throat?" Then when we get back to his place, he likes to watch me fucking myself with a dildo he's got there, while he gets his own penis out, and rubs it till it's really, really hard. Sometimes he takes me from behind, sticking his dick up into my arse, while I've still got the dildo up my vagina; it's glorious, Becs, really glorious. So now you know.' She defiantly finished off the last of her wine, then grinned mischievously. 'I'd swap him for your Liam any time, though.'

Rebecca continued brushing her hair, though her hand was trembling slightly. Her own tender breasts ached with arousal beneath the cream silk dress she was wearing. Between her thighs, where the tight skirt rubbed her bottom cheeks together, she was already wet, longing for Liam's penetration.

She turned and smiled at Annie. 'No,' she said. 'You can't have Liam.'

'Can't we share?' pleaded Annie mischievously. She touched her own breasts lightly, and her dark nipples pushed out through the provocative holes in her bra, obscene in their hardness. 'He's got such a glorious body. I bet he's got enough juice in his dick for both of us.'

Rebecca shrugged, dismissing her words, yet her own body was stirring with forbidden pleasure at the thought. 'You've had far too much wine, Annie. You're drunk.'

'Perhaps I am. But I'd love to see the two of you together, Becs, you and Liam. You've got such a beautiful body.' She stroked her blonde curls dreamily back from her flushed cheeks. 'I've always wanted to see you,

you know, aroused. And the thought of Liam's penis going into you makes me feel quite wild with envy. Is it big, Rebecca? I bet it is. I bet it's really, really big –'

Rebecca laughed and marched towards her friend, taking her arms to raise her from the bed. Her hand brushed Annie's breast, catching the hardness of her exposed nipple, and she felt a shock running through her. Suddenly she wondered what it would be like to touch Annie, to kiss her voluptuous, beautiful mouth.

'Enough,' she said, taking the wine glass from her with mock firmness. 'Don't drink any more wine before you go out, or you won't be able to stand.'

'Doesn't matter,' said Annie airily. 'It's only some boring old art gallery preview.'

'I'm sure it won't be boring, with you around. Go and get ready now for Hugh Raoni.'

'I'd rather be going somewhere with Liam. What does he do when he's not here with you, Becs?'

'I've told you as much as I know. He's some sort of journalist, that's all.'

'Keeping him to yourself, aren't you?' Annie pouted and turned to leave the room, but at the last minute she turned to blow Rebecca a little kiss. 'Love you, Becs. Whatever I might do, you'll always be my friend, won't you?'

'Of course I will. You're drunk. Don't talk such rubbish.'

Half an hour later, Rebecca heard Raoni's sleek car pull up outside and heard Annie clattering down the stairs. She'd worried at first about the possibility of Raoni arriving at the same time as Liam; she had to remind herself that Raoni had no idea of the identity of the man who'd revealed his Green Company as a sham. Though Liam would know Raoni by sight; of that she felt quite sure. She watched out of her window; she couldn't see Raoni within the darkness of the car, but just the thought of Liam's enemy being here, being so near, made her shiver. She wondered again at the strangeness of it all; at the fact that Liam should come so abruptly, so shatteringly back into her life just when Raoni, his enemy, was playing such a large part in Annie's.

She was still wondering an hour later, because there was no sign of Liam. Tired of pacing the small house, tired of waiting for the phone to ring, aware of the growing knot of misery in her stomach, she finally faced the reality that Liam wasn't going to turn up. 'Damn him, damn him,' she muttered. No way was she going to stay in a moment longer, wasting her evening. She rang for a taxi to take her to Hampstead, and tried miserably to think of some way to tell Zoe and all her other friends at the dinner party that Liam had stood her up.

In the dingy bar of a big Victorian pub in Mile End, Liam got up slowly from the table where he'd been sitting with his hardly-touched lager, and turned to face the man who'd just come in. The new arrival looked hot and flustered. His black hair was ruffled and his denim shirt was slightly stained under the armpits with fresh perspiration. Adjusting his horn-rimmed glasses as he looked round the gloomy interior of the dark-panelled pub, he hurried towards Liam.

'Christ, I'm so sorry, Liam. Have you been waiting long?'

'Two hours,' said Liam, beckoning to the barman for drinks for them both.

'I was held up – had to cram news of this afternoon's near-miss at Heathrow into the evening bulletin. Got here as quickly as I could, mate – hope to God I've not messed up your evening for you.'

Liam thought of Rebecca waiting for him, probably going on to her friend's party without him. 'You have, as a matter of fact,' he said quietly. 'I hope that what you've got for me is good.'

'It is. I really think it is.' Pete Harmsworth, fresh from the newsroom of the local radio station he worked for, reached for the pint of bitter Liam had ordered him and drank it down thirstily. 'I've been keeping my ears close to the ground for anything about the Hegley Wood development, just like you asked, mate. And I've heard that the planning application's landed on the desk of one Charles Kerrick. Heard of him?'

'I'm not sure. Should I have done?'

'Not if his friends have anything to do with it, no. Kerrick could be dodgy, Liam. I think he might be open to pay-offs. There was a hint of a fuss two years ago, over plans for an out-of-town shopping centre that he rubber-stamped without going through all the necessary procedures.' Pete lit a cigarette and ran his hand tiredly through his rumpled hair. 'Oh, it was all covered up pretty neatly, passed off as an error of one of his subordinates and so on. But there was still a whiff of something dirty in the air. If it is friend Raoni behind the Hegley Wood consortium, as you seem to think, then it's quite possible that Raoni might attempt to persuade this Kerrick guy to push Hegley Wood through the planning hurdles, by offering money, or other inducements.'

Liam hadn't touched his drink. He said, 'I'll make enquiries. If you can find anything else out about a connection between Raoni and Kerrick, you'll let me know?'

'I certainly will. I'm always on the lookout for anything about Raoni, for the simple reason that I hate his guts. By the way, I did hear that he's been keeping some interesting company lately.'

'Yes?'

'A classy blonde bird, Ann, Annie something. She's figured on the society pages a few times lately. Looks as sweet as an angel and talks as if butter wouldn't melt in her mouth, but really she's as horny as hell, same as a lot of these rich girls once the champagne starts flowing.'

'I know,' said Liam.

'Well, Raoni's screwing her and she's loving it. I'm only telling you about her because she might be a useful source of information about certain of his activities. Think you can track her down? She might even know something about Raoni's relationship with Kerrick –'

Liam was already on his feet. 'Yes,' he said. 'I think I can track her down. Thanks, Pete. I'll see you around.'

He got the tube to Notting Hill Gate, and walked to Kensington Place. By the time he reached the little mews house that Rebecca and Annie shared, it was almost ten o'clock; he knew there'd be a strong possibility no one was in. But, on looking up, he saw that a soft light was flickering from the sitting room, and so he rang the bell.

It was Annie's voice that crackled through the answerphone. 'Yes? Who is that, please?' Her voice sounded slurred; he wondered if she was drunk.

'It's Liam,' he said.

There was a clicking sound; he pushed the door and climbed the stairs. Annie opened the door to the sitting room and let him in, then closed it again and leant back against it. She was wearing a long black silk negligee. Her face was slightly flushed and her huge blue eyes were bright as they roved up and down his body.

'You've missed Rebecca,' she said. 'She went without you.'

She was drunk, he realised. Her skin was heavily scented with expensive perfume. He smiled slightly and took off his jacket. 'I'll wait,' he said. 'I thought you were out as well, Annie.'

She pouted. 'Only at some boring art gallery preview. I was yawning my head off after half an hour.' As she walked slowly towards him, her silk dressing robe fell apart, and he saw that she was wearing a black peephole bra, and tiny panties, and black suspenders and stockings. She saw his eyes fasten on her jutting nipples, and laughed ruefully. 'I put these on for Hugh Raoni,' she said. 'He likes them. But we rowed about staying at that stupid art gallery, so I decided to go home. And Rebecca's mad with you for standing her up, Liam, so she won't be back for ages and ages.'

She draped her arms around his wide shoulders and gazed up at him with her big, innocent blue eyes. Then she pressed her body closer to his and rubbed her crimson nipples slowly against his shirt. The little nubs swelled and stiffened, almost cruelly confined by the tight casing of her black bra. 'God, I feel horny,' she breathed.

Liam put his hands on her shoulders, distancing himself with care from the perfumed softness of her skin. 'You've been seeing quite a lot of Hugh Raoni lately, haven't you, Annie?'

'Yes,' she purred. 'But I'd rather see more of you.'

Rebecca got a taxi home from Hampstead at half eleven. The dinner party was crowded and noisy, and she missed Liam so badly that she felt as if she had a big sign across her forehead telling everyone she'd been stood up that night. Zoe had plenty of spare men; Rebecca saw their eyes lighting up hotly when they saw her in her come-to-bed kimono outfit, and at first she tried drinking and flirting, pretending she just didn't care about Liam. But during the meal she felt more and more lonely; and when the man on her right, a successful graphic designer with roving eyes and clammy hands, clamped one of those hands on her thigh and started to slide it up the slit of her dress, she realised she'd had enough. The meal was, fortunately, almost over bar the coffee and liqueurs, so she was able to make her excuses quietly to Zoe in the kitchen, and ring for a taxi from there.

'So sorry your gorgeous bit of rough couldn't make it tonight, darling,' purred Zoe sympathetically as she piled liqueur glasses on to a tray.

'So was I,' smiled Rebecca. 'But he had something on at work.'

'Bring him again,' said Zoe, lightly kissing her cheek. 'We've all got the hots for him. Bet he's glorious in bed. Sounds like your taxi at the front door. *Ciao*, Rebecca. If I don't see you before, I'll see you at Hortense's in a few weeks, won't I?'

'Hortense's?'

'Yes, you remember. She's invited a crowd of us to her place in Gloucestershire for a long, wine-soaked weekend in September. Her parties are always terrifically rude. You were going to bring Liam, weren't you?'

'Perhaps,' said Rebecca.

She sat silently in the back of the taxi as it sped past the prosperous mansion blocks of St Johns Wood and Bayswater. He'll never come to Hortense's with me. He didn't even turn up tonight, she thought bleakly. I'll probably never see him again.

But as they drew nearer to Kensington, Rebecca's hopes started to lift, just a little. Perhaps there was a really good reason why he was so late tonight. Perhaps there would be a message on the answering machine. He might even be there, at the house; he had her spare key.

The taxi dropped her just outside the house. Her heart jumped as she saw the dim glow of a lamp behind the curtains. Annie would still be out, with Raoni, so it could only be one person – Liam. Her spirits soaring, she let herself in and hurried up the stairs.

She realised then that the soft light she'd seen was coming from Annie's bedroom; the rest of the little house was in darkness. Feeling slightly puzzled, she

191

walked along the carpeted passageway to Annie's door, which was half open. It had to be Annie after all; she must have come back early.

Then she heard soft, strange little noises coming from Annie's room that made her spine tingle in warning. It sounded very much as though Annie had someone in with her. It must be Raoni.

Something, some dark, puzzling instinct, made Rebecca want to go and look. I'm a dirty voyeur, she told herself wryly, and a masochist, seeing as I've no hunk of a man to ease my own frustrations tonight. She edged a little closer, filled with a torment of curiosity.

But what she saw made her blood freeze in her veins, and punched the air from her lungs.

It was Liam, with Annie. He was stretched out on the bed, with her in his arms; he was naked, and Annie was clad in just her underwear, the black erotic underwear she'd bought for Raoni. The peephole bra, the suspender belt and smoke-dark stockings were a shocking contrast to the smooth whiteness of her skin. She was clutching feverishly at Liam, kissing him, clearly beside herself with lust; her stocking-clad thighs were wrapped round his hips, and he was making love to her, driving himself into her with all the cold sexual control of which Rebecca knew he was capable.

Rebecca thought she was going to be sick. She leant back against the wall in the darkness outside Annie's bedroom, fighting for breath. At the same time, she felt a shameful wave of arousal tearing through her, making her loins melt with need, causing her nipples to press hard and hot against the cool silk of her dress; because they looked so glorious together.

Liam had arched himself now above Annie's open body, supporting himself on his arms, and their bodies were still locked at the loins; she saw how the golden muscles of his shoulders and biceps were sinewed with tension. His face too was tense, and his eyes were hooded as he gazed down at Annie's excited face. Annie was moaning softly, moving her hips against him to keep his penis tightly inside her, rubbing her palms across her own lewdly engorged nipples as they pushed through the tight confines of her bra. 'Fuck me harder, Liam,' she was begging through swollen lips. 'Dear God, I'm going to come . . .'

But Liam had other ideas. He often did, thought Rebecca, the numbness of her despair giving way to a kind of wild, consuming envy. She watched, unable to tear her eyes away as Liam slowly withdrew, leaving Annie whimpering, crying out for him, her sex open and wet. His cock was huge, sending a fresh tremor of longing surging through Rebecca: long, thick, and glistening with Annie's copious juices. At the base of his shaft, his balls were full and tight; Annie, with a soft little cry, leant forward to take their bulk in her hands, then she licked them softly with her tongue and took their fullness between her lips.

'Turn over,' Rebecca heard Liam say in the soft gravelly voice he always used when he was in the throes of sexual urgency. 'Turn over, so I can fuck you from behind.'

Annie, half-sobbing with need, hurried to do as he said, lifting her pert bottom cheeks high in the air, rubbing the hard teats of her breasts hungrily against the crumpled bedcover. Liam knelt behind her, his penis throbbing as he ran his hands over her black suspenders and stocking tops and gazed at the dark pink wetness of her cleft.

'Such a beautiful arse, Annie,' he was saying quietly. 'Such a delicious little arse.' And slowly he bent over her, pulling her cheeks apart, and he licked her there, driving his strong, stiffened tongue up and down her cleft, pausing over the puckered brown hole of her anus and driving its fleshy point just inside.

Annie squealed and bucked with joy at the lewd

invasion of her secret place; Rebecca felt the warm flush of her own arousal spreading from her toes to her fingertips, felt her own juices flowing freely. Oh, God. She wanted him too, so badly that it was like a burning ache inside her. She clenched her palms over her breasts, caressing their stiffened nubs through the silk of her dress in an attempt to soothe them that made her need all the greater. She bit back a low cry as she saw Liam's magnificent body preparing to mount Annie from behind. Rubbing the tip of his hugely distended cock purposefully against the saliva-moist ring of her arse-hole, he pulled her bottom cheeks apart as he slowly, surely drove his shaft of stiffened flesh deep inside her. Annie quivered and shook at the forbidden impalement, lifting her bottom even higher. 'Oh, God. Oh, Liam, that's unbelievable. Please don't stop.'

Liam didn't. He ravished her tight, secret place with calm thoroughness that had Annie writhing, shaking with obscene pleasure around his iron-hard penetration. Rebecca watched, stunned, scarcely breathing as he drove between her bottom cheeks again and again, while reaching round to stroke at her soaking vagina with his hand; until Annie, quite beside herself, lifted up her head in exaltation and cried out, 'I'm coming, I'm coming. Oh, Liam, keep your penis inside me. Drive it deep into me – oh, yes . . .'

He soothed her, gentled her with his strong hands as his lengthy penis continued to pleasure her shivering flesh. Rebecca watched, unable to tear her eyes from the sight of his glistening shaft as he withdrew it time after time, only to drive it steadily back in as the slender blonde girl floated blissfully on the shivering edge of pain and pleasure.

Annie's face was flushed and hot, her hair falling about her cheeks like a golden curtain. Her nipples protruded from her bra with dark lewdness as the ecstasy roared through her. At last she collapsed, smiling and happy, nuzzling her cheeks against the crumpled counterpane, her blonde hair spilling over the lace-trimmed pillow; but still Liam wasn't finished. Slowly he withdrew and rubbed his lengthy cock, sliding his hand up and down its thick shaft and caressing Annie's still-trembling buttocks with its velvety purple glans; until at last his release was upon him, and he closed his eyes, his fist pumping hard. His semen started to spurt in milky pools across Annie's white bottom.

Rebecca couldn't bear it. Her own fevered arousal was tearing at her loins, making her vagina throb almost unbearably. With one hand at her nipple, pinching and stroking through her flimsy dress, she drove the other hand into the high slit of her skirt and dug frantically through her panties to rub herself hard with her fingers. Beneath her coppery fleece of pubic hair her flesh-folds were so wet, so slippery, that her fingertips were soon drenched; she gazed hungrily at Liam's still-spurting cock, imagining its fat stiff length driving up into her aching sex, and finally gave a low shudder as the secret conflagration of her release throbbed through her in a mingling of shame and excruciating ecstasy.

She must have been careless. She must have made some sort of noise; because even as she let her dress fall and leant back breathlessly against the wall to recover from her own fiercely snatched pleasure, Liam turned round slowly from where he crouched above Annie on the bed and saw her.

His blue gaze became dark as he gazed into the shadows that surrounded her. At first she thought he hadn't seen her. But then he said, 'Rebecca.'

Was it an acknowledgement, or a warning to Annie? Either way, she realised with cold horror, it didn't really matter now. Annie gave an exclamation of shock, and dived swiftly for her silk dressing robe, which she swiftly belted around her lewdly clad body. Liam, without any apparent hurry, got to his feet and reached for his jeans, which he eased on almost casually.

Annie, biting her lip, said in a trembling voice, 'Oh, Becs. I'm sorry. I had too much to drink. It was my fault, all my fault. Look, I'll leave you two alone together to talk for a while . . .'

'Don't bother,' said Rebecca. She turned to Liam, who was silently starting to pull his white T-shirt on over his naked torso. Dear God, she still wanted him, as badly as ever. 'I think you'd better go now, don't you? Leave me the keys.'

Liam bowed his head in brief acknowledgement, then reached in the pocket of his jeans to hand them over. She couldn't watch as he shrugged on his jacket and walked past her towards the stairs. She tried not to listen as his footsteps echoed into the distance, as the big front door slammed at last behind him.

She pulled herself away from the wall with a little shudder, and said with sharp brightness to Annie, 'He's good, isn't he? Was he worth the wait? I wonder, how long have the two of you been planning that little stunt?'

Annie came towards her, her arms hugging the silk dressing gown across her chest, her eyes bright with self-reproach. 'Oh, Becs, darling Becs, I'm so sorry! Of course I didn't plan it. You know I wanted him – who wouldn't? But I didn't mean this to happen, Christ, I didn't. Even so it was my fault, not Liam's. I got back early from that boring art gallery preview Raoni had insisted on, feeling horny and drunk. I carried on drinking, and when Liam turned up, it seemed like God's gift. I couldn't keep my hands off him. I seduced him, Becs.'

'So you dragged him kicking and screaming into your bed?' said Rebecca bitterly. 'Pull the other one, Annie.' She felt sick now, in the aftermath of shock and lust. She turned to go to her bedroom.

'It's true, it's true!' Annie lunged after her, grabbed

her arm, turned her round. 'At first he only wanted to talk, Becs! It was really boring; he kept asking me questions about Raoni, and this place called Hegley Wood –'

'Raoni and Hegley Wood?' Rebecca had gone very still.

'Yes!' Annie sighed. 'Liam was being quite tedious about it. Hegley Wood – there's some protest there, isn't there, because they want to build a new road?'

'Yes,' she said. 'That's right.'

'Well, anyway, I ended up playing this sort of game with him, wearing him down, telling him I'd only answer his questions if he'd do certain things to me.' She hung her head, blushing, but her blue eyes danced with remembered pleasure. 'God, has he got self-control. He asked me so many things about Raoni before I finally got him in my hot little hands . . .' She turned suddenly desperate eyes on Rebecca. 'Say you'll forgive me, please, Becs, darling? It was my fault completely. What guy wouldn't have succumbed to me dancing around in front of him in this get-up, offering to suck his dick for him? Please forgive me, and then you and Liam can patch things up between you. I don't really think I mean anything to him; but you do, I'm sure of it.'

Rebecca felt cold and clear now, and angry. But not with Annie. 'Tell me,' she said. 'I'm not angry with you, Annie. Just tell me, please, exactly what it was that Liam wanted to know.'

Annie shrugged, looking tired and vulnerable now that the potent mixture of sex and alcohol was wearing off. Her face was very pale, and rings of smudged mascara emphasised her huge eyes. 'Oh, he asked me about Raoni's business friends. I couldn't tell him much, of course; Raoni likes to keep play and work separate. Liam kept asking me about Hegley Wood, and if I'd heard Raoni mention some guy in a government department called Kendrick, no, Kerrick, or something.'

'And had you heard Raoni mention Hegley Wood or a man called Kerrick?'

'No. But I wound Liam up, teased him a bit by hinting I might have heard something, you know? Until I finally managed to get him into bed.' She sighed. 'It was so strange, all those questions he kept asking me. He seemed to be really, really serious.'

He would be, thought Rebecca. Aloud, she said, 'OK, Annie. You go to bed now. I'm too tired to talk any more. I'll see you in the morning, all right? We've got three places on the rota to check up on.'

'I don't know how you can bear to speak to me, Becs.'

Rebecca sighed. 'Look. I'll get over it. I know what Liam's like. And I think the two of us were just about through, anyway.'

Annie got to her feet, running her hands rather distractedly through her hair. Her robe had fallen open, displaying her brazen underwear, her protruding nipples. She was still perfumed with Liam's scent, Liam's sex. 'No. No, you weren't through. You were mad about him, Becs, and I've ruined it all.' She headed almost blindly for her room, and Rebecca huddled back into the chair. She closed her eyes, feeling utterly, totally bereft.

It was all so clear to her now. Liam was still after Raoni, because he suspected him of being involved in the Hegley Wood project. His campaign against Raoni had never stopped; even in his moment of triumph, when those catastrophic revelations about the Green Company had sent Raoni's fortunes into temporary free fall, Liam was already plotting his next move.

And that was where Rebecca came in. Liam had found out somehow that her friend Annie was involved sexually with Hugh Raoni; and he'd realised, with cold, unarguable logic, that the affair between Annie and

Raoni gave him a new way to home in on his old enemy. It couldn't have taken him long after that to work out that his best, most obvious approach was through her, Rebecca, who had already revealed that she had a hopeless obsession with Liam's gorgeous body.

So he'd turned up outside her house, professing interest in her, Rebecca. Not just interest, but glorious sexual passion. All she was to him was a further stepping stone on his path towards his enemy, Hugh Raoni.

Liam wasn't just writing an article about the Hegley Wood protesters; he was directly, passionately involved with them. As soon as he suspected that his old opponent Hugh Raoni might be behind the impending destruction of the ancient woodland, then everything else became incidental to his campaign, even sex. How could anyone care so much about trees? It was fashionable, she supposed numbly; and a kind of class thing, too. Tough eco-warrior Liam gets his own back on rich upper-class people like Raoni. And Max. And Rebecca.

She was almost glad she'd found him with Annie, because it had given her the chance to tell him to get out of her life. An instruction that was really quite superfluous; because it was quite clear now that he'd never had any intention of staying in it.

She jumped to her feet with a start as the door swung slowly open and Annie came in. She was fully dressed, looking fragile but beautiful in a dark brown velvet trouser suit and glossy high-heeled boots. Her face was carefully made up to smooth out the ravages of her violent sex with Liam; and she was carrying a soft leather suitcase.

'I'm going, Becs,' said Annie very quietly. 'God, you must hate the sight of me. I'll be in touch in a week or two, when you've had a chance to decide whether you still want to share the house with me.'

Rebecca was shaken, and aware of a sudden ominous

tightness in her chest. She put her hand to her throat. 'You can't go. Where will you stay?'

'With Raoni, of course. He's away a lot of the time, but this house-sitting business has rather caught his fancy, and I think he likes the idea of me in permanent residence, taking care of his own rather peculiar desires.'

'You can't go,' repeated Rebecca blindly. 'What about the business, the house-sitting? I need you, Annie.'

'You don't, darling,' said Annie rather sadly. 'You do all the work anyway; you're the organised one. I'm just playing at it, like I play at everything. I've already rung for a taxi to take me to Raoni's. Get in touch with Liam, Becs. He'll want you back, I know it.'

'He won't. He's got what he wants out of me, out of both of us,' said Rebecca bitterly. 'Oh, Annie. Don't go.'

But her friend was already closing the door behind her. Rebecca sat back, breathing deeply to calm herself.

She remembered Max, taunting her on the night of Raoni's party. 'Cool it, Rebecca,' he'd said. 'Or you'll get asthma again.'

'Oh, no,' she'd said. 'You're not worth that, Max.'

Neither was Liam.

She stayed there, very still, knowing her inhaler was in her bedroom but trying to will the tightness at her lungs to float away.

At last it did. She was conscious, then, of the overwhelming silence in the house: no music, no TV, no Annie to tease her, no Liam.

She would have to get used to the silence now.

'A two-month contract, starting on the seventeenth of September? Yes, we can manage that.' Rebecca was scribbling fast on a notepad as she spoke into the phone. 'So you want a daily call, with the mail and message checking service. Can I make an appointment to visit? Tomorrow evening at seven would be fine. Yes, I'll look forward to meeting you.'

Rebecca snapped her phone off and leant back in her chair, eyeing the heaps of paperwork on her desk with a mixture of disbelief and something approaching happiness. It was almost a month since Annie had moved out, leaving her in charge of what she'd thought to be a superficial summer diversion, catering for a few friends and acquaintances during the holiday season. But it was early autumn now, and the list of her clients was growing all the time.

She was making a success of it, on her own.

The biggest step had been in bracing herself to take a small room here, in this shared private office suite just off Oxford Street. Rebecca had signed a six-month contract for the room somewhat apprehensively; but she was finding the business address a huge asset, both in terms of impressing her clientèle and in organising all the paperwork and files well away from her rather chaotic house.

And her chaotic personal life. With Liam's betrayal always shadowing the back of her mind, she'd thrown herself into the usual round of parties, finding increasing confidence in rejoining her old circle of friends now that the furore over her father's private life had subsided, and discovering that she was now able to mix with people in her own right, as the manager of her own small but exclusive business. She was even an employer now, in a small way. She'd taken on a bright articulate part-time secretary called Kate, who whizzed around Chelsea and Kensington in her own little car checking on a lot of the properties herself and, together with Kate, Rebecca had interviewed a small team of reliable domestic staff, who ensured that her clients' properties were sparkling clean after their owners' absences.

Rebecca charged a lot for all this, and she had an accountant now, as well, to see to all the ramifications of her business. She even had a direct line to a plumber and an electrician in case of emergencies. 'In House' was a success. Her private life was not.

She leant back in her chair, stretching like a cat as the late summer sunshine sent shafts of light across her cluttered desk. Kate would clear it all in the morning, she thought gratefully. She glanced at her watch: four o'clock, just time to visit a new client's flat off Sloane Street. Its owner, a fading but still glamorous soap star, had flown to Barbados for a month. 'Just take care of everything, darling,' she'd pleaded down the phone. 'And I mean everything.'

Rebecca stood up, smoothing down the micro-skirted charcoal suit she'd treated herself to, checking her sheer stockings for snags and stretching out her slender feet in their high-heeled shoes. She loved the way the narrow ankle straps emphasised the provocative curve of her leg.

You shouldn't wear shoes like that. You'll attract the wrong kind of people . . .

Liam's sexy, sleepy voice echoed through her mind, through her dreams. She was always thinking of him. It was madness; she had to stop. But she couldn't. She was haunted by the memory of that last evening: by the sight of his lean male body arched so passionately over Annie's rapaciously feminine curves. By the obscene yet devastating sight of his proudly virile penis thrusting purposefully into Annie's most secret place, causing her friend to cry out in rapture, while Rebecca watched, in a torment of dark desires, as her world slowly collapsed around her.

She'd rebuilt that world, but at a cost. She'd lost Annie for good, it seemed; her friend had been round in Rebecca's absence to collect all her things, and had left a cheque for her share of six months' rent in advance, but otherwise she hadn't been in touch. Rebecca missed her friend badly. The house seemed empty without her;

and the little blue fantasy pot sat empty on the kitchen shelf.

As for sex, Rebecca took her pleasure where she felt like it, coldly and without commitment. She found that the success of her small but much talked-about business venture gave her a certain cachet, a confidence that attracted the sort of men like Max, who'd once been everything she could ever ask for.

She didn't see Max now. After that night at Les Sauvages, she didn't want to. In fact, she'd heard that Max was abroad on business a lot of the time. But she had plenty of men to dine with, at London's most exclusive restaurants, and men to party with, and go to bed with when it suited her; but always she imagined the man in her arms was Liam.

You've got to get rid of this dangerous obsession with a scruffy, streetwise stud who gets his kicks from allying himself with the latest fashionable cause, she told herself bitterly as she locked up the little office and walked down the street to where her car was parked. You're in danger of making a fetish of him. Grow up, Rebecca.

It was still warm in the late September sunshine, so she let down the roof and drove with panache through the rush-hour traffic towards Knightsbridge, keeping her eyes on the road but enjoying the attention she was attracting as male pedestrians stopped to stare at her and drivers wrenched their heads to gaze. Her stockinged thighs chafed together sensuously within the confines of her tight skirt as she drove. She felt horny; she always did when she thought of Liam. She remembered again that first frightening night when he'd forced himself into her car, his purposeful body emanating sex in spite of the danger they were both in. She longed for him now, to ease up her tight skirt and run his strong hand up between her stockinged legs, to dip himself in her juices and finger-fuck her as she drove.

'Damn.' Rebecca swore as the driver in front of her

stopped suddenly for a crowd of milling pedestrians. She'd slammed on her brakes just in time to avoid sliding into his rear bumper. They were near Hyde Park Corner; there was some sort of demonstration on, people gathering with banners and placards; a few bored-looking policemen. 'Why do they always choose bloody rush hour?' muttered Rebecca, edging her car forward again.

Then a banner caught her eye. 'Save our precious woodland,' it said. 'Hegley Wood is special. It takes hundreds of years for a tree to grow, and one moment of greed to fell it. Save our woods, save out national heritage.'

Hegley Wood. That was Liam's, and his friends', latest obsession, a power trip for people with nothing better to do, and it was attracting national coverage now. Their campaign hadn't been going well, she knew; she'd caught glimpses of it recently in the press, and it seemed as if the all-powerful planning committees were continuing to steamroller through all the environmentalists' objections. She gazed at the protesters in spite of herself, half-expecting to see Cass, and Stevie, and Petro. And Liam.

The traffic was edging slowly past the demonstrators. The car behind Rebecca hooted impatiently; she quickly eased her car into gear and moved forward. Liam was no doubt busy screwing some of his eco-warrior groupies, she thought dismissively, and perhaps a journalist or two, like Chloe Masters, for extra information. Cass would no doubt be in on it all, too. Her heart twisted with bitterness and with a hungry, almost savage sexual desire.

Sex had better be on the menu tonight. She was dating a thirty-year-old stockbroker called Richard, and she could imagine, all too well, how predictably he would seduce her back at his luxurious bachelor apartment in St John's Wood. There would be flowers, champagne, and soft music. Then he would remove her clothes with almost reverential respect, touching her as if she might break, asking her all the time what she liked. Whereas Liam ... She felt her body tingle hotly as she remembered Liam taking her up against the wall in the cloakroom at Les Sauvages, hoisting her hungrily on to his ramrod penis, devouring her with his mouth, his hands, his tongue as he ravished her into a shamefully explosive orgasm.

Heated and aroused, she pressed on through the late afternoon traffic. She was nearly at the flat now. Just as well, or she'd be bringing herself off in the car. Hastily edging into a parking space someone had just left, she grabbed the keys she needed and let herself in through the big front door, swiftly climbing the stairs to the second floor. She rattled the key in the lock, wondering what surprises might lie in wait this time, smiling to herself as she remembered various diversions that came with the job, like the fish, and the champagne in the fridge, and the collection of erotic eighteenth century prints on the walls of one place that she and Annie had giggled over in astonished delight.

'Christ, look at that one,' Annie had breathed. 'Talk about a lusty peasant lad – he's right up her, and there's still six inches of him left. Look at her face – she looks as if she's riding to heaven. God, it will be a vibrator job for me as soon as we get back . . .'

How she missed Annie. She hoped that her friend was all right, and happy with Raoni.

She let herself in and knew, immediately, that someone else was in the place. She froze. There must be some mistake – perhaps she'd got the wrong flat.

Then she heard a voice, a slightly foreign, youthful male voice, saying a little hesitantly, 'Miss Lansdowne? I'm in here.'

She followed the voice to the bathroom; she knew her way round, because of course Mimi had given her a conducted tour. Her heart was beating rather fast now. The bathroom was big, and tiled with gold and white porcelain; the bath was set in the corner, and seemed to fill half the room. In it lounged one of the most glorious creatures Rebecca had ever seen: a young, olive-skinned male, with sleek dark hair and a face that could have been sculpted for a statue of a Greek god. As the water lapped gently around him, she saw that he was rather superbly endowed in other departments too. His torso was padded with sleek muscles, and his dusky genitals moved softly between his thighs as the water lapped around them. He saw her eyes fastening down there and gave a shy smile. 'You are Miss Lansdowne?'

'I'm sorry,' said Rebecca, horrified, 'there must be some mistake. Mimi – Miss Sewell – asked me to look after her flat while she's away –'

'I know,' he said happily, reaching for his thick penis and fondling it with loving fingers as it swelled and stretched like some predatory snake beneath the perfumed water. 'She asked you to look after everything, didn't she? And that includes me. I'm Miss Sewell's special friend, and she didn't want me to be lonely. Didn't she tell you that was why she hired you?'

Rebecca was incredulous. Mimi Sewell's toyboy. Of course she'd read about the actress's lustful propensities in the press. But to expect Rebecca to look after him as well as the flat? This was too much.

He was rubbing more firmly now at his cock. Its swollen red tip was bulging hotly between his fingers; he was gazing at it with pride as it jutted upwards, an eight-inch staff of pleasure. 'Please,' he said earnestly in his husky foreign voice, gazing up at her while his hands worked on his rigid penis. 'You won't leave me all alone, will you? Miss Sewell was sure you would keep me happy. I know no one here in London, you see – she brought me with her from Milan, two months ago.

You will keep me company, please? You look as if you have such a beautiful body.'

Rebecca hovered on the brink of retreat. Then she thought of going back to her empty house, alone. She thought of Richard, and his fumbling ineffectual efforts at seduction so far. Suddenly she grinned back at him. 'Yours is not bad, either,' she told him.

She peeled off her suit slowly, enjoying the look on his handsome young face as he gazed at her pert breasts in their skimpy blue satin bra, at her matching lace-trimmed little panties, and the sheer lace-topped stockings that encased her long legs, made even longer by her decadent high-heeled shoes.

'You are very beautiful,' he said contentedly. 'Miss Sewell told me you were.'

Rebecca looked with equal contentment at his olive-skinned body, glistening like satin with the aromatic oils he'd put in the water; and her eyes fastened on his rigid cock. 'So are you,' she breathed and, with a flourish, she pulled the remnants of her clothes off, peeled off her stockings and slid into the bath with him.

She was hungry for sex, already so aroused that the slipperiness of her stiff nipples against his glossy chest almost brought her to orgasm straight away. Tenderly he eased her astride him in the big bath, kissing her joyously, making love to her mouth with his tongue; then he kissed her breasts, pulling the aching pink nubs into his mouth in turn until she cried out for joy.

'Not yet,' he whispered, 'not yet, my beautiful one.' But already Rebecca's slender legs were twining urgently with his long muscular ones, and the feel of his erect penis, rubbing and swelling against her loins, was so delicious that she wanted all of him inside her, now.

'Take me,' she muttered. 'Please, take me. I want to feel your cock inside me.'

He grinned, nuzzling with his lips against her throat. 'I'm so glad.'

They splashed and laughed together, their bodies slipping against each other deliciously as he reached out for a wrapped condom from the little glass jar at the side of the bath. He kept kissing her as Rebecca, her fingers trembling with desire, carefully eased the sheath over the pulsing rod of his manhood. 'Keep still,' she muttered delightedly, her fingers stroking the hot stiffened flesh of his massive erection. 'Christ, if you grow any more, I won't be able to get you inside me.'

'You will,' he whispered. His hand was already working at her vagina; his thick index finger was slipping up inside her, giving her a sweet foretaste of what was to follow. 'Oh, you will.'

He eased her astride him then, so that the water was lapping sensuously round her waist. He held her tight buttocks, caressing them with his fingertips, while Rebecca used her own fingers to splay her sex wide open and eased herself with little cries of delight on to his massive cock. The perfumed oil in the water had made them both so slippery that his dusky thick shaft slid slowly but surely up into her very heart like a well-oiled machine. As he reached to play with her breasts, she slid herself rapturously up and down his stiffened flesh.

'Your cock is lovely,' she breathed. 'So long, so thick. Yes, squeeze my nipples. Harder, please. Please . . .'

Her voice faded away as the luxurious glow of orgasm started to spread through her pliant body. She saw that his face was dark and tight with lust; he lay back, moaning, as Rebecca drove herself up and down on his massive cock, harder and harder. His lithe young hips pumped in answer, ravishing her furiously, and she started to cry out, short, sharp little animal cries, as the pleasure of their mingled explosion consumed her body.

He continued to caress her breasts softly as she lay sleepily in his arms in the warm water. 'That was so good,' she murmured. 'Tell me, is this on offer every day?'

'Part of the contract,' he grinned. 'Miss Sewell thought you would appreciate my skills. She has some – how would you say it? – tenderness for you herself, and she decided that this would be the next best thing. She told me she would have pleasant dreams about you and me together while she was away.'

'Dream on, Miss Sewell,' murmured Rebecca happily. The man was kissing her, nibbling at her cheek, stroking her thighs; she realised, with incredulous delight, that he would soon be ready for more.

Chapter Eight

*I*t was later, much later, when Rebecca eventually got back home. She showered and changed into a purple velvet jacket and miniscule black leather skirt for her date with Richard, hoping the expensive sluttishness of the skirt would remove his well-bred inhibitions. Then she poured herself a huge glass of chilled white wine. Richard was calling for her at nine. She lay back on the settee, stretching out her long black-stockinged legs. She smiled to herself, wondering if Richard would be able to detect the scent of rampant sex on her freshly showered skin. How shocked he would be if she told him what had happened. Perhaps she would shock him tonight by not wearing panties and letting her legs slide apart. She realised suddenly that for a whole four hours she hadn't thought once of Liam. Things must be improving.

Suddenly the doorbell rang. Too early for Richard. Reluctantly she got up, taking a long sip of wine, and went over to the entryphone. 'Yes?'

A pause. Then a faint, almost hesitant voice. 'Rebecca. It's me, Annie. Can I come up?'

Rebecca was stunned and delighted to hear her

friend's voice. 'Annie! Yes, of course come up; but surely you've still got your key?'

'I wanted to warn you I was here first.' Annie sounded different, tired. Quickly, Rebecca pressed the entry button and waited by the open door as Annie came up the stairs.

Rebecca was shocked by her friend's appearance, though she tried not to show it. Her bright, vivacious friend seemed to be only a shadow of her former self. Her angelic face was pale without its make-up; her long blonde hair had lost its gleam, and her clothes hung loosely, as if she had lost weight from her already slender frame.

Rebecca kissed her cheek silently and led her into the little sitting room. Then she went to fetch a glass of chilled white wine as big as her own and pressed it into Annie's hand. Her friend drank it greedily, then put it down and looked at Rebecca with haunted blue eyes.

'I can hardly expect you to be glad to see me. But I'm glad to see you. I've missed you, Becs, so much.'

Rebecca refilled her own glass and curled into the chair opposite her. 'Of course I'm glad to see you. I've missed you terribly. You should have come back earlier. What's been happening?'

Annie seemed to shake her head a little as if she wasn't ready to talk yet. 'Did you see Liam again?' she asked instead. 'Did you make it up with him?'

'No. But please don't blame yourself, Annie. It was over, anyway. He was using me; he was using both of us. I realised that straight away. I was almost glad that I found you together that night because, in a way, it saved me having to find out for myself.'

Annie nodded sombrely. Then her eyes glinted with some of her old, familiar sparkle, and she said slyly, in her husky drawl, 'God, he was gorgeous, though, wasn't he? Hung like a bloody horse.'

Rebecca smiled. 'Yes. Yes, he was certainly an experience. What about you, Annie? Are you still with Hugh Raoni?'

Annie bit her lip, and her fingers trembled round her glass as she took another long drink. 'No,' she said. 'He was a bastard, just like you said, Becs. I never, ever want to see him again.'

Rebecca found herself tense with apprehension. 'He didn't hurt you, did he?'

'No. Not really. He's just a bastard. Oh, it was fun for a while – he's seriously rich, you know? – and I enjoyed it all: the luxury, the parties, weekends in fabulous places. But then he found out that I really, really wanted to be an actress; and he started playing games with me.'

Rebecca turned on the low lamp that sat on the table by her side, because it was starting to get dark. 'Like what, Annie?'

Annie flinched at the bright light, and Rebecca saw that there were shadows of tiredness under her eyes. 'Oh, you can imagine, I'm sure. We were at this villa just outside Cannes, with lots of Raoni's friends. He told me one of them was a film director, and I was stupid enough to believe him. They were all so wildly flattering, Becs, all telling me how gorgeous I was, how talented. God, I was so stupid.'

'No, you weren't,' said Rebecca quietly. 'You are gorgeous and talented. It's just that, like I said, Raoni is a bastard. Go on.'

'Well, one afternoon, we'd all been drinking round the pool, and Raoni told me that his friend, the so-called film director, Hal, wanted to film me and send it for a screen test, for this great part he'd got in mind for me. He said he knew I could act, knew I was just right for the part, but they needed to test me out for the more intimate scenes.' She drank down some more wine. 'You can probably guess the rest. There was this other guy there, a big black guy from Marseilles. I think he was some kind of bodyguard; he was a real hunk, and I'd been secretly swooning over him for days. Anyway, they told me I had to play the part with him.' She brushed her hair back from her cheeks, and Rebecca saw that her cheeks were slightly flushed with remembering.

'They told me to kiss him first. There was just Raoni watching, and the film director guy, with his camera. The black guy, whose name was Pierre, was just wearing jeans; his body was packed with muscle, and, as I'd said, I'd been secretly fantasising about him all along. I was in my bikini, a tiny little apple-green thing that uplifted my breasts and rode high between my legs, like a thong; Pierre had been watching me too, and I could see that he already had an incredible hard-on beneath those tight jeans of his. I was really wet for him; well, wouldn't you be?

'Pierre kissed me, a real tongues-outside-mouths kiss, for the camera. Then he eased off my bikini top, and ran his big tongue over my breasts, pushing against the nipples until I was wild for him. The director, Hal, was giving him instructions, but I think Pierre had already decided exactly what he was going to do. He pulled off my panties, and spread me out on a sunbed – I was all hazy, with sunshine, and wine, and lust. I did try to protest just a little when I saw the camera zooming in, but Hal said, "I'm going for your face, darling. Your expression, the blatant desire in your beautiful eyes; that's all I want." Then Pierre began to lick me out with his big tongue, driving it right up inside my pussy. And all the time, Hal's camera was whirring. He was saying, "Go for it, Pierre. Go for it." And Raoni was watching, with a little smile on his face . . .

'Then, of course, before I could climax, they got me to kneel up and unfasten Pierre's jeans. God, he had the most enormous penis, Becs; so long and hard and thick, it was like some sort of machine. I wasn't sure I could get it all up me; but you can bet your life I wanted to try. I was so wet from his tongue, and my nipples were sticking out from my bare breasts like stalks. I was close to bursting with wanting that massive black dick pumping away inside me. So you can guess what happened next. A real blue-movie scene: this big French-African guy, stark naked and grunting away, easing his huge penis up between my legs while the camera homed in. God, I was juicy and ready.'

She sighed a little, smiling ruefully at the memory. 'Of course, he was gorgeous, and he clearly thought I was too. He was practically slavering over my tits; his lovely big dick was pounding up inside me while he tongued my nipples. His tongue was incredibly long and powerful, too, just like his penis. I was clawing away at his back, screaming with pleasure because it was all so beautifully dirty. I had a blissful orgasm; I was shouting the place down, clinging to him for dear life as his lovely shaft pumped away inside me. He pulled out before he came, and I saw that his massive cock was all twitching and hungry. He pressed my breasts together and rubbed his shaft between them; it felt delicious, all slick and velvety and hard, while I could feel his huge balls rubbing at the base of my breasts. I had another orgasm when he started to pump his seed out. There was so much, you wouldn't believe it. He rubbed the creamy liquid all over my nipples with the tip of his cock, and I thought I'd died and gone to heaven.

'Afterwards, of course, Hal was all over me, telling me how well I'd done, how his Hollywood friends would love it, and he'd send it to them straight away. Raoni just watched, and smiled.

'A few days later, Raoni had some friends round at the villa, and we were all drinking one night, and talking about sex, and Raoni got the film out and showed it to them. I couldn't believe it. Hal, the bastard, had really homed in close to Pierre's big black penis,

214

showing it pumping away in all its glory right into my pussy; but the close-up that got them all really gasping was Pierre's come spurting out in floods over my nipples, with me moaning in frenzy. Afterwards, I tackled Raoni about it, and said he had no business having a copy made of Hal's film and showing it to his friends like that; but he laughed at me and said, "What copy?" Of course, Hal wasn't really a film director, and he wasn't sending the movie to anyone. That was just Raoni's idea of fun. Can you believe it?'

'You should have left him,' said Rebecca. 'You should have left him then.'

Annie shrugged dazedly, swirling the last of her wine in her glass. 'Oh, I know. But I was kind of hooked, on the sex, and the wine, and the sun. And I still thought Raoni cared about me. I thought the thing with Hal and Pierre was just a joke of his, you know? "I thought you'd enjoy seeing yourself on the end of his big black cock, Annie," he whispered to me as he made love to me that night. He was so wildly excited, he kept coming again and again. Seeing me being fucked by Pierre had really turned him on. He even told me how he'd once enjoyed making love with Pierre himself.

'Anyway, that was really the beginning of the end. We came back to London, and of course I stayed in his house, but he was getting cold to me. A couple of nights ago, he brought another girl back, a beautiful Swedish bitch, and he told me I was to let her tie me up and lick me out while he watched. I refused, and he started to make love to her himself. He told me I was a cheap tart and a hopeless actress, and just left me watching them. He ignored me, they both ignored me as I sat there, sick with misery. That was when I decided to leave. I should have rung you first, but I was afraid you'd be angry with me. I thought I'd stand a better chance of forgiveness if I just turned up here.'

'Forgiveness?' Rebecca had moved quickly to kneel

on the floor at her friend's side. 'You don't have to apologise for anything. Oh, Annie. How do you think I feel? I should have got in touch with you weeks ago, should have begged you to leave him; but I thought you might be happy with him. Oh, Christ, Raoni's even more of a bastard than we thought. If only we could get even with him.'

'I think we can.' Annie's face was pale but determined. 'Raoni thought I was stupid, some brainless bimbo. That rankled, but it meant he talked about a lot of things he shouldn't have mentioned in front of me. Towards the end, when we started to fall out, he always warned me that if I tried talking about him to the press or anyone, he'd make sure that the film of me and Pierre was made public property. But I really think I've got something on him here, something he can't trace back to me.' She reached over for her shoulder bag. 'And the strange thing is it's got something to do with Liam.'

Rebecca froze. 'Liam? What do you mean?' Her heart was thumping slowly at the sound of his name.

'Let me show you these, and I'll try to explain.' Annie was reaching into her bag, and pulling out a big envelope which she handed to Rebecca. Rebecca slipped her hand inside and extracted some glossy A3 sheets. They were photographs, black and white photographs, of a slightly-built half-naked man with glasses and a receding hairline squatting on the floor, his face twisted with rapture as a girl with long blonde hair hiding most of her face – it could only be Annie – sucked with fervour at his surprisingly lengthy cock. There were several more photos, one of them showing the man masturbating himself as he gazed at two half-naked girls who were kissing hungrily, their pert breasts thrusting against each other.

'Me and Karen,' said Annie a little sheepishly. 'God, she was fun. I didn't mind doing things with her.'

Rebecca was staring at the photos, her mind racing. 'But the man, Annie. Who is he?'

'Kerrick. Charles Kerrick. Does it ring a bell, Becs? It should. He's a friend of Raoni's. He's also the man Liam was asking me about so urgently on the night you caught us together. I sat up and took notice when Raoni introduced me to him, because I remembered Liam asking me if I'd met him. Charles Kerrick has been dealing with the planning applications for the Hegley Wood project; I heard the two of them talking quietly about it one night, when I was getting myself a drink and they thought I wasn't listening.'

Rebecca's mind was still racing wildly. 'But the photos. Where were they taken?'

'At Raoni's house, of course. It was about a month ago. The four of us – Karen, Charles Kerrick, Raoni and I – had spent an evening at this incredibly expensive restaurant, where Raoni insisted on picking up the bill. There was lots of champagne; Kerrick got extremely drunk. We went back to Raoni's place, and the rest of the evening was fairly predictable.'

'Sex, you mean?'

Annie coloured slightly. 'Well, yes. We all watched some videos, and this Kerrick guy seemed really excited, you know? He was a bit timid at first, as though he wasn't used to having much fun. When Karen started on him, he was almost beside himself.'

'What happened?'

'Raoni asked him, basically, what he wanted. He said he wanted both of us.' She lifted her blonde head defiantly. 'You can guess the rest, I'm sure. Karen masturbated in front of him till he got a huge hard-on, and his beady eyes were nearly popping out of their sockets. He was rather a strange-looking, skinny little man, but his penis was huge, like a donkey's. He obviously wasn't used to the kind of attention he was getting that night. He sort of moaned to himself when I bent down and sucked his dick for him; he played rather frantically with my breasts, while he watched Karen frigging herself. She was good. She moaned and gasped in front of him, squeezing her nipples, driving her fingers against her clit until I almost came myself. Kerrick thrust his dick frantically into my mouth, and he was finished pretty quickly. As I said, I don't think he's used to that sort of thing.'

Rebecca said quietly, 'I think I'm beginning to understand. Why Liam was interested in Kerrick, I mean.'

'Well, yes. Raoni thinks I'm stupid, but even I could work out that it seems as if Raoni's been encouraging poor little Kerrick to push through the planning procedures for this Hegley Wood business, in return for certain illicit entertainments. I think that Raoni took the photos to guarantee Kerrick's silence. I'm not interested in Kerrick. I'd just like to use them to get back at Raoni.'

Rebecca got up slowly, still holding the photos. 'We've got to get them to Liam, Annie.'

'You think he'll be able to do something with them?'

'You told me yourself that Liam was desperate to get something on Kerrick. He needed evidence that Raoni was backing the development scheme, and evidence of the kind of lengths Raoni would go to get the scheme passed. I think Liam guessed a long time ago that Raoni was using dirty tricks to push his own interests, but he hadn't got proof. Well, these photos should give him all the proof he needs.'

Annie was watching her with big, haunted eyes. 'So you're going to find Liam again,' she said in a small voice. 'Won't you mind? Seeing him, I mean?'

Rebecca drew a deep breath. 'No,' she said. 'I'm well over him, Annie. After all, he wasn't for real, was he? He didn't live in the same world as us.'

Annie was knotting her fingers in her lap. 'He could have been for real,' she said. 'If it hadn't been for me, that night.'

'It wasn't your fault,' said Rebecca with quiet deliberation. 'I keep telling you. He must have been as ready as you were. You didn't exactly have to force him, did you?'

Annie looked at her. 'I told him you were with Max,' she said steadily. 'I was so drunk, so desperate for him, that I told him you'd gone out with Max, and wouldn't be back till the morning. Now do you see why I was so ashamed, why I couldn't expect you to forgive me?'

Oh, God. Rebecca absorbed this with a silent, bewildered numbness. So Liam had assumed she was spending the night with Max. No wonder he'd not even tried to defend himself when she caught him in Annie's bed.

Annie went on sadly, 'That's why I moved out. I knew that what I'd done was unforgivable.'

Rebecca was shaking her head. 'No,' she said tiredly at last. 'No, perhaps it was just as well. If he hadn't been so obsessed with getting evidence about Raoni, Liam wouldn't have bothered with either of us. That was all he wanted us for, to get one step nearer to Raoni. The sex with you and with me meant nothing to him, nothing.'

'So you're still going to find him? To tell him about Raoni and Kerrick?'

'Yes, I am. I hate Raoni, not just because of what he's done to you, but because he once had the arrogance to tell Max to finish with me. I'm going to find Liam, because he's the best person I can think of to deal with all this.'

'But how will you find him?'

Rebecca thought of the grim lines of protesters congregated at Hyde Park Corner. She thought of the news bulletins, the newspaper articles detailing the growing, despairing momentum of the protest at Hegley Wood. 'I think I know where to find him,' she said. 'Or where to find people who'll know where he is. Then it's up to him to decide what to do about Raoni.'

Annie gazed at her. 'Invite him to Hortense's party,' she said. 'You were going to do that anyway, before I fouled things up for you, weren't you? Invite him to Hortense's; because Raoni, the bastard, will be there.'

By the time Rebecca drove into the little village of Hegley, soon after eleven the next day, the rain was pouring down as if it would never stop. She pulled up outside the small half-timbered inn that overlooked Hegley's waterlogged village green. Then she folded up the map that she'd used to find her way there from the M4 and, turning up her coat collar against the downpour, locked her car and ran through the puddles to seek refuge in the lounge of the pub.

It was quite empty, except for a big log fire and a friendly landlord behind the bar. She ordered a coffee, and asked the landlord for directions to the camp where the protesters were.

He nodded. 'You'll be from the press?' he said in his slow rustic drawl. 'Or the TV, perhaps?' He'd already assessed Rebecca's city-smart clothes.

'No,' said Rebecca quickly. 'Nothing like that. It's just that I think a friend of mine might be there, and I need to see him. I've got something important for him.'

The landlord said, 'You'll have to be quick, then, won't you? They're being cleared off the land today.'

Rebecca froze. 'Cleared off?'

'That's right. The court order went through three days ago, so the bailiffs are moving in. They'll start on the road within the next week or two, I reckon: felling those trees, bringing in the heavy diggers.' He put down the glass he was polishing and gazed at Rebecca regretfully. 'It's not right, not right that the trees should go. Us villagers, we've been behind those protesters all of the way. A good bunch, they were. It's not right.'

Eviction. Oh, God. She was too late. Raoni had won.

Rebecca was already on her feet. 'Where will I find them? Are they still there?'

'Yes, I reckon. They won't leave easily.' He pointed to the window. 'Look out there. You can see the track that leads to the woods, just the far side of the green. But I wouldn't go there if I were you. Not today. In fact, I'd stay well clear –'

But Rebecca was already hurrying towards the door.

The rain was sluicing down from leaden skies as she half-walked, half-ran along the track the landlord had pointed out. In parts it was a quagmire, rutted by the wheels of heavy vehicles that had ploughed through it only recently; this morning, perhaps? Her breath caught in her throat as she pressed on through the dense woodland with its gnarled oaks and secret, shadowy glades. The downpour had released all the fresh aromatic scents of the ancient forest, and it seemed to Rebecca for the first time that the cause for which Liam and his friends were fighting was all too real.

The muffled rumble of distant vehicles, of heavy machinery, penetrated the steady drumming of the rain. Rebecca stopped to rub the moisture from her face with the back of her hand, and swept her soaking hair back from her cheeks. Her suede jacket was saturated, and her expensive ankle boots were thick with glutinous mud; but somehow it didn't seem to matter at all because, now she had crested a rise in the path, she could see the bright arc lights set up by the security men in the noonday darkness of the rainswept forest, could see their big, menacing caterpillar-tracked vehicles and their trucks laden with equipment. She could see the garish blue uniforms and yellow helmets of the guards, who were relentlessly putting up big steel fences that they dragged from the back of their trucks, trampling heedlessly in their heavy boots over freshly broken saplings and scarred earth.

Their activities seemed like an obscenity in the depths

of this secretive forest. As if it were having its heart ripped out. Rebecca stood there gasping for breath, the rain and her tears blinding her. She could glimpse some remnants of what must have been the camp: some pitiful kicked-out fires; a few trampled, primitive tents; a tattered banner, like those she'd seen at Hyde Park Corner, trodden into the mud.

There were some protesters gathered in silence behind the fencing, their arms linked to comfort one another as they forced themselves to watch the desecration.

Of Liam there was no sign. Rebecca suddenly realised that her heart was beating painfully as she scanned the proud, silent figures through the bleak curtain of rain. It looked as if she was too late with her news about Raoni. Perhaps Liam had gone back to London, because nothing now could be done.

Then she heard footsteps behind her, and she whipped round. It was Cass. She wasn't wearing a coat, and her cotton top and jeans clung, saturated, to her thin frame; but she didn't look as if she cared. Her close-cropped hair was black with the rain, and her kohl-ringed eyes seemed huge in the whiteness of her face. She said, 'So it's you. Come to gloat, have you?'

Rebecca said, 'No. No, I haven't, Cass. Please listen to me; it's terribly important. Is Liam here?'

Cass's face twisted in scorn. 'Sorry, no. And even if he was, he'd have other things to think about than the likes of you.'

Rebecca caught her breath. 'You've got it wrong. I only want to find him because I've got some information about Raoni and all this.' She turned to look, with sadness in her eyes, at the horrifying scenes of destruction nearby. 'Please. Will you be seeing Liam very soon? Will you tell him to ring me?' The rain drummed down, landing on her face, her lips, making speech difficult.

Cass's expression was still hostile. 'He's not interested. Haven't you realised that, yet? He told us all about you and your friend Annie, how desperate you both were for him. He despises people like you.'

Rebecca flinched. 'Please, Cass,' she said quietly. 'This isn't about me or Annie. I want him to ring me so I can tell him something I've found out about Raoni: some information we've got about the way Raoni got planning permission for all this.'

She thought she saw Cass's face flicker with interest, but her eyes were cold. 'OK,' Cass said tersely. 'I'll tell him when I see him. But don't expect him to come running, will you?'

'No,' said Rebecca tiredly. 'No, I certainly won't. I think I've got that message.'

'You'd better go now,' said Cass. 'Things could get rough here. Officially we're the trespassers, now. Good, isn't it? While those hired thugs there, with their steel fences and brutal chainsaws, have the law of the land on their side. They can destroy all this in days, you know. Days.'

Rebecca looked round at it all: at the rain pouring down on the monstrous machinery, the yellow-helmeted security guards; and the little line of vulnerable protesters, arms still linked, watching their enemy silently advance through the forest. She said, 'Is there anything, anything at all I can do?'

Cass sneered. 'Are you any good at cutting wire fencing? Do you know how to immobilise those earth-moving monsters without killing yourself? Can you drain diesel from the tanks of lorries in the dark, without being seen? Can you?'

Rebecca gazed at her, speechless. Then suddenly she heard shouts from behind her, and the sullen grating of metal; she whirled round again, and saw that the security men were advancing on the protesters, pushing the heavy banks of temporary steel fencing against them like shields. The protesters were shouting, and one woman was screaming at them, but they were helpless.

At one end of the line a scuffle had started; Rebecca saw fists flailing, saw that someone was down, as more of the security guards came from the other end of the clearing to join forces with their companions. Cass's eyes were blazing.

'Go,' she said. 'Just go. 'You're no use to us here.'

Cass began to run, back down towards the clearing where the fighting was still going on, but the gleam of the fencing was spreading inexorably, like a battle line, across the churned-up mud of the forest floor. One woman had laid herself on the ground, but two of the guards picked her up and roughly pushed her to one side. Rebecca watched them, feeling sick; then she realised that two of the yellow-helmeted guards were pointing up at her. 'Another one,' they called out, 'up there.'

She turned and ran, her boots sliding stickily in the mud, her breath catching in her throat, and all the time Cass's words were ringing in her ears. 'You're no use to us here. You're no use to us here.'

There was someone, a man, coming towards her through the rain-soaked canopy of the trees, and she turned again to run; but the man was on her, pinning her by her arms, and she realised that it was Liam.

'Let me go,' she whispered. 'You're hurting me.'

He let her go, and she gazed up at him, her heart thudding in painful recognition of his familiar features. She saw how his hair was streaked dark from the rain, how his wet shirt and jeans clung tightly to his tense, powerful figure.

'What the hell are you doing here?' he said. 'This isn't a game. There are a lot of brutal people out there, Rebecca, who won't let anyone get in their way.'

She was trembling in the aftermath of shock as she gazed up at him. How he despised her; because he thought, of course, that she had deceived him with Max.

And so he had taken his revenge, of a kind, with Annie. There was a familiar, aching tightness at her heart.

'I didn't think it was a nursery outing,' she said bitterly. 'I came to find you, Liam.'

'Why?' His question was coldly discouraging.

'Oh, it's not what you think. Don't worry. Were you thinking that I'd missed you, Liam? No, it's about Raoni. We think – Annie and I think – that Raoni might have bribed someone to get the planning for all this pushed through. I thought you might be interested, that's all. I'm going now. I'm cold, and I'm wet, and I've had enough of all this. You can ring me when you're in a mood to learn more; but looking at all this, I wouldn't have said you've got much time, have you?'

She swung round towards the path, but he was there, barring her way, and she saw that his face had blazed into life. 'Who did he bribe? Do you have any names?'

'Kerrick,' she said tiredly. 'Charles Kerrick.'

He let out a little breath that was almost a sigh. Then he said, 'Names aren't enough. We need evidence, hard evidence, before they start to pull down the trees.'

Rebecca wiped the streaming rain from her face. Trickles of it were running down the back of her collar now, but she hardly noticed. 'Annie has evidence. Raoni's been vile to her. It's yours, if you want it.'

'Why are you telling me this? If you have evidence against Raoni and you want to use it, you could take it yourselves to someone who'd make use of it.'

The rain poured down like a curtain between them. Rebecca felt exhausted. 'I had some misguided idea,' she said, 'that you would know best what to do with it. Raoni's treated Annie like dirt, and I want to pay him back; but I don't want the press involved, or she'll get hurt even more. I thought you would be the best person, because you did such a good job on Raoni before. But Cass has just told me that I'm not wanted here; and you're virtually telling me the same. I think I've made a mistake.'

She turned to go again, but he caught her arm, more gently this time. He said, 'I wouldn't have thought you trusted me enough for something like this.'

She gazed up at him. The familiar planes and angles of his face gleamed with rain. 'I trust you to do whatever suits you and your cause, Liam,' she said at last. 'You'd do anything to save this wood and destroy Raoni, wouldn't you? I'm not even sure which is most important to you; both are good for your ego, I suppose. Annie told me, by the way, that she got you into her bed by informing you that I was still screwing Max.'

He was silent for a moment. 'It wasn't true?'

'No. No, it wasn't. But it hardly matters, does it? You were using both of us, weren't you? To get closer to Raoni, to find out things about him. Well, here's your chance, if you want it. Annie has some evidence, some photographs, of Kerrick. You could give them to that radio friend of yours. Use them, to help Annie; Raoni's really screwed her up.'

He said slowly, 'If I'm doing this, then I want to do it properly.'

'How do you mean?'

'I want to confront Raoni in person,' he said. 'No phone calls to the press, this time, no anonymity. I want to see his face when he realises he's going to have to back out of this thing for good.'

'How can you get near him,' Rebecca asked quickly, 'without him putting his thugs on you?'

He laughed a little bitterly. 'That could be a problem, knowing his fondness for security. I don't suppose he's holding a party again, is he?'

Rebecca gazed up at him. 'Come to Hortense's house party with me, next weekend. I told you about it, remember? You said you'd come. Annie and I are both invited, and we can bring guests. Raoni will be there too and, because it's a private house, miles from anywhere, his defences will be down. You'll have a whole, long weekend to do what you need to do, Liam. You can force him to back out of all this in your own way.' She waved her hand tiredly in the direction of the security forces and their ugly vehicles. 'Just do me a favour, though, will you? If Annie and you should fancy an action replay, then don't let me walk in on it.'

His eyes were dark, unreadable. 'What about Max, blue-chip Max? Won't he be there?'

'I told you. He and I were over, a long time ago. Annie lied.'

'So I'd be going as your guest?' He didn't ask the other question, but of course she knew what it was.

'You'll be my guest,' she acknowledged. 'Separate rooms, no strings, no big deal. Just screw Raoni into the ground, will you?'

For a moment she thought he was going to refuse. But then he nodded. 'I'll ring you,' he said.

He left her then, standing on her own in the pouring rain. She turned back towards the village. Oh, Annie, she thought tiredly. Don't expect me to do anything like this ever again, will you?

'Oh. Oh, my God. That is just so rude . . .' Annie's vibrant voice could be heard quite clearly through the wall that divided her bedroom from Rebecca's.

Rebecca sighed and turned over on her bed, fully dressed and quite alone. It was six in the evening, and she and Annie had come upstairs a little while ago to rest and change before dinner. Only Annie wasn't resting at all, and neither was Christopher, the ardent young admirer whom she'd brought with her to Hortense's house party.

Rebecca would have attempted to get her own back by creating disturbances of her own, only she had no one to create them with. She turned over again, crumpling up the bedcovers in her agitation, and reached to flick on her bedside radio. The music that came out was dire, but at least it blocked out the sound of Annie having yet another breathless orgasm.

Annie had Christopher. Rebecca's partner was supposed to be Liam, but she'd hardly seen him. He'd arrived late last night, during the final stages of the Friday evening dinner which, as the first one of the long weekend, had been a riotous reunion of friends old and new. Rebecca had introduced him quickly to Hortense; and Hortense, a sharply original Frenchwoman married to an industrial magnate who was abroad most of the year, surveyed the new arrival in rapt silence as the rest of her guests continued their partying unabated. Liam grinned back at Hortense, his jeans and white T-shirt making him look almost tangibly beddable compared to the other, more formally attired male guests.

Hortense finished her inspection of Liam with a little sigh, and touched his face lightly. 'Ah,' she said. 'This one I have not met before. You are an actor, perhaps, or a rock musician? No need yet to tell me of your talents. Besides, I can guess, I can easily guess, what you're good at ...'

Liam was still smiling as Rebecca drew him to the seat beside hers, and he seemed relaxed, at ease amidst the noisy jocularity that filled the room. But then Rebecca saw that his expression had changed as his blue eyes casually scrutinised the two dozen or so house guests and she knew that he'd spotted Hugh Raoni. Raoni had brought someone new with him for the weekend, a youthful model called Francesca, whose left hand rested possessively on Raoni's arm most of the time.

Annie had been upset when she'd seen Francesca. 'I knew he'd bring someone,' she said miserably to Rebecca, 'but she didn't have to be so damned beautiful.' Annie and Raoni's first meeting had been awkward, with Raoni, to Rebecca's fury, barely acknowledging Annie. But Christopher, who appeared besotted with her, seemed able and willing to distract her; hence the racket next door.

As for Liam, he was polite towards Rebecca, but kept his distance. She'd had only one chance to speak to him properly, when Hortense had shown him to his room, and left the two of them together. It was then that Rebecca had produced Annie's photos and told him briefly about Annie's evening with Raoni and Kerrick.

Liam had leafed through them quickly. 'So this is Charles Kerrick. And these were taken in Raoni's house?'

He was looking at the photo showing Kerrick masturbating himself while he gazed at the two half-naked girls. Rebecca felt a sudden pang of longing as she gazed at the small man's hotly aroused penis, at his open-mouthed expression of sheer lust as he gazed at the two women. How could Liam study it so dispassionately, when she herself was aching, desperate for sex? God, she'd jump on Kerrick's lusty cock herself if he were here, now.

'That's right. That's Kerrick,' she said flatly.

He nodded and gave them back to her. 'You keep them. They're safer with you.'

She felt her heart give a little leap of fear. 'Raoni doesn't suspect anything, does he, Liam? He doesn't know who you are? Perhaps I should never have told you about all this. Perhaps you should have done it all through your friends, like you did last time –'

He gave her a reassuring smile. 'I wanted to do it this way, remember? Relax. Raoni doesn't know me. He will, soon, but by then I'll be on my way.'

She nodded, determined to remain equally cool. On his way. Out of her life, naturally.

She'd gone to bed early last night, by herself; and today she'd hardly seen him at all, since most of the men, including Liam, had gone out shooting after a late breakfast. As far as she knew, they weren't back yet.

Just as you expected, Rebecca reminded herself. Just as you wanted, surely? But it was going to be hard enduring Liam's coolness; especially as it had occurred to her, as she watched Hortense and her friends run their eyes acquisitively over Liam's all-too-virile body, that he was very unlikely to remain celibate all weekend.

Annie was whimpering with sexual pleasure next door. Rebecca had a sudden graphic vision of Christopher's aroused penis driving into her friend's lust-hazed body, and she shivered with longing. Oh, God, any more of this and she'd be begging Annie for the loan of her vibrator. Sad.

She got up impatiently from her bed, pulled off her clothes and stormed into the shower cubicle, vigorously soaping herself under the stinging needles of water. When she emerged, dripping and a little breathless, she saw that Annie was there, busily opening the bottle of white wine she'd just discovered in the little fridge by Rebecca's bed.

'Chris is fantastic, Becs,' she sighed, pouring out two big glasses of the chilled Chardonnay. 'Thought I'd come to tell you about it.'

Rebecca smiled as she wrapped herself up in a thick white towelling robe and rubbed with a hand towel at her wet hair. 'I take it you mean thick, long and strong?'

'Yes. Oh, yes.' Annie sprawled on her bed. 'But he's so sweet as well, so kind. He might be young, but he's certainly keen to learn.' She took a deep swallow of her wine and suddenly leant forward. 'Rebecca, has Liam said anything to you yet about, you know, what he's going to do to Raoni?'

Rebecca realised that her friend was still tense, still strung up about Hugh Raoni. 'No,' she said as she eased a comb through her wet hair. 'But I trust him to know what to do, Annie. And he won't take long – he can't afford to. Liam told me last night that work's due to start on the road next week, now that all the protesters have been cleared out.'

Annie was playing restlessly with her empty wine glass. She reached jerkily for the wine bottle to refill it. 'I hate Raoni,' she said suddenly, 'for what he did to me, the things he said to me. Of course I'm over him and everything. But turning up like this, with that beautiful cow of a model in tow, and looking at me as if I were dirt . . .' She was picking anxiously at the label on the wine bottle now, without really noticing what she was doing. 'God, I hate him. I really want to see him brought to his knees, Becs.'

Rebecca saw to her dismay that her friend had tears sparkling in her eyes. She went over quickly and dropped to her knees beside the bed, resting her hand lightly on Annie's arm.

'You shouldn't have come,' she said. 'It was too much to expect of you, Annie. Look, get Chris to drive you back to London – or I will, if you like. You don't have to spend another hour under the same roof as that bastard Raoni.'

Annie brushed her hand quickly across her glittering lashes and smiled. 'What, and miss the moment when Liam dishes the dirt on him? You're joking,' she declared. 'After all, what else are we here for?'

Rebecca pretended to ponder this. 'Sex?' she offered.

Annie grinned delightedly and hauled herself up from Rebecca's bed. 'Yes! Sex with the delicious Christopher, of course, and with others by way of diversion. After all, isn't that why Hortense invites us on these weekends? I should think that all the corridors between the bedrooms were rather well-trodden last night, don't you? What about you, Becs? Surely, surely this is the weekend to make up with Liam, isn't it? You still want him. You must want him. Who wouldn't?'

Rebecca said, 'I told you. There's nothing between us any more.'

'But you've told him, haven't you, that I lied about you and Max? I'll tell him myself, if you want.'

Rebecca got to her feet and repeated, 'Sex isn't on the agenda between Liam and me, Annie. That was one of the agreements about this weekend. I think Liam decided it would only complicate things. And so did I.'

Annie looked crestfallen. 'But you can't let someone like that go to waste.'

'Somehow,' said Rebecca, 'I don't think he'll go to waste. Do you?'

'Oh, no,' said Annie, clearly relieved by her friend's apparent indifference to Liam's activities. 'And it's just as well that you don't really fancy Liam any more, because I've heard that Hortense is intent on shagging him. Probably already has done, as a matter of fact — you know what a man-eater she is, especially for a bit of rough.' She swung herself gracefully off Rebecca's bed. 'Better go and dress for dinner. Re-fuelling stop, as Hortense would say in her sexy accent. Isn't she delightful?' Suddenly she paused and reached in her pocket for something, a flimsy scrap of black material. 'Here you are. A little present.' She grinned mischievously. 'Wear this tonight. You'll feel so aroused, you'll be quite irresistible to anyone. The men will be able to feel the heat rising from your body, Becs.'

Rebecca picked the garment up dubiously, guessing already what it was — a pair of split-crotch knickers in firmly-stitched black satin. The sort of thing Annie loved. She let them drop again on to the bed and smiled. 'Thanks, Annie. But I'm not at all sure that I want to be that irresistible.'

When Annie had gone, Rebecca drank her own glass of wine, then went to lean her hot forehead against the window that overlooked the grounds surrounding

Hortense's spacious mansion. She was shocked at how badly the news that Hortense was after Liam affected her. What else had she expected? Within the next twenty-four hours, Liam would be confronting Raoni about his crooked planning deal; her vulnerable friend Annie would be revenged in full; and Rebecca would be able to return to London, never to see Liam again.

She felt a crushing sense of depression at the thought. Sex, she told herself fiercely, that's all you're deprived of at the moment. That's why Liam's haunting you so. You just need some good, raunchy sex. She poured herself more wine and drank it defiantly.

Just then, there was a knock at her door. Flustered, she pulled her towelling robe more tightly across her body and hurried to answer it.

It was one of the local men Hortense had hired for the weekend, in order to help round the house generally, and serve the evening meals. The man was in a tight short-jacketed black suit, of the kind that all Hortense's male servants wore. 'Shows off their arses so well, don't you think?' she would breathe as she gazed after them. And this one was certainly one of Hortense's best. He was not tall, but he was broad-shouldered and sturdy, with short fair hair. He couldn't have been more than twenty-one or twenty-two, and his fresh smooth face was flushed with admiration as he gaped at Rebecca.

'For you,' he said with an effort, holding out a small satin-lined box in which lay an exquisite rose corsage. Rebecca took it, realising it must be a gift from Hortense for all her female guests. She put it to one side, then turned her attention back to the young man, who was really far more interesting. Taking her glass of wine, drinking slowly and deeply, she went to lean back against the heavy mahogany dressing table.

Realising she was feeling pleasantly drunk, she let her gaze slide down to the man's groin, where his tight trousers stretched appetisingly over the bulge of his genitals. Why not? she thought. Why not? After all, there was little else on her entertainments programme this weekend. Slowly she let her towelling robe fall back over her slim thighs, revealing the furred mound of her sex. The young man's eyes were riveted there, and she saw him swallow.

'Shut the door,' said Rebecca softly, letting one naked thigh slide sinuously against the other so that her swollen labia chafed pleasurably. 'What's your name?'

'Mark. My name is Mark.' He spoke with a pleasant country burr.

'Listen, Mark. You're on hire to this household for the weekend, aren't you? And Hortense has told you, hasn't she, that you must do anything that her guests order you to do?'

'Yes. Yes, she has . . .'

'Well.' Rebecca's voice was a sensuous purr. 'I want you to fuck me, Mark. I'll give you money; fifty pounds. Would you like that?' She reached lazily over her shoulder so that her dressing robe fell still further apart, and felt in her bag for the crisp notes. It made her feel beautifully dirty, the thought of paying him.

'Oh, God,' he muttered, his eyes greedily drinking in her rosy-tipped breasts, her tiny waist, her long shapely legs. 'I'd do it for nothing, you're so beautiful.'

She laughed, not unkindly. 'I want to pay you. At least, I will if you're worth it. Let me see if you're worth it, Mark. I've heard that you country boys have got good strong cocks. Let me see if it's true.'

With a little gasp, he tussled with his zip. Within seconds his thick penis was rearing out. His balls were plump, almost hairless; she reached out, fascinated, to touch them. He groaned at her touch and lunged towards her so she could feel the blunt tip of his cock trembling wildly against her abdomen. He kissed her hungrily, his tongue delving between her lips, while his big hands rubbed over her breasts, nudging the distended nipples to and fro until Rebecca felt the delicious shafts of lust spearing her body. The ache at her loins was intense now. She could feel the swollen silky folds of her labia throbbing with need, could feel the silvery moisture of her arousal anointing her passage, preparing for penetration.

He was already hoisting her with his strongly muscled arms so her bottom was resting on the dressing table, and her legs were wrapped round his hips, revealing her sex to him. He gazed down at its pink, whorled secrets and gasped, his cock throbbing anew. 'God, you're so beautiful.'

He thrust one thick finger into her, rubbing and stroking; she shuddered almost violently. He slid it up into her vagina, rasping against the tightness of her flesh; she spasmed with pleasure, and he kissed her again, harder. She ground herself against the sturdy digit that impaled her.

'Do it to me, Mark,' she whispered. 'Fuck me. Please fuck me with your lovely cock.'

He was more than ready. With a groan, he shoved his penis between her legs, prodding blindly at her soaking cleft until at last he found his way and thrust the whole length of his shaft all the way up inside her, almost lifting her from her perch.

Rebecca started to shake with delight as he held himself like that, filling her, stretching her.

'There, my fine lady,' said Mark breathlessly as he rubbed his calloused hands over her nipples. 'Isn't that good, now? Isn't it true, what they say about us country boys and our cocks?'

Rebecca almost laughed with happiness. 'Oh, it is, Mark,' she whispered. 'How about a bit of action now? Make me really, really happy.'

His face blazed as he steadied her on the dressing table. He pulled her legs even wider apart, and gazed down hungrily at the place where his thick cock disappeared between the lips of her swollen vagina. Then he drew himself out, so she could see his rigid shaft, all glossy with her juices, and his tight smooth balls; then he began to pound into her, again and again, holding her close to him, dipping his head at the same time to lash her exquisitely erect nipples with his tongue.

Rebecca clung to his powerful shoulders, loving the sheer animality of his vigorous thrusts as his trousers sagged around his brawny thighs. He pleasured her relentlessly, grinding the root of his cock against her soaking clitoris; his teeth fastened round one nipple, driving her up and up into realms of physical pleasure that were almost pain. She clenched herself around him, almost dancing with desire as her inner muscles rippled up and down his iron-hard shaft, and then she was over the edge, filled with wave after wave of ecstasy that wrenched the breath from her body. She felt his penis throbbing violently deep inside her. She loved his out-of-control spasming movements as he, too, reached his climax.

He slumped against her, hot and sticky and breathless, smelling of male musk. Slowly Rebecca extricated herself and drew her towelling robe across her body.

'That was good, Mark,' she said coolly, picking up ten five-pound notes from her bag and wafting them in front of his dazed eyes. 'But not a word to anyone, you understand? Or I'll tell Hortense that you hid in my room and were spying on me.'

He nodded, still bemused by his good fortune. With clumsy fingers, he pushed the dwindling length of his penis back into his pants and zipped himself up. 'Will you want me again?' he said eagerly.

'No. I don't think so.' She saw the crushing disappointment in his eyes; but he silently nodded and made his way out of the room, closing the door behind him.

The room reeked of sex. Rebecca sighed and ran her

hands with lingering pleasure over her softening nipples. Oh, God, that had been surprisingly good, and given her a welcome respite from the sexual tension that enveloped her.

But it was still Liam that she wanted.

She showered again, and dressed in a long dress of dark emerald that she'd bought specially for the weekend. It was sensuous and sleek, with narrow straps and a low draped neckline, into which she inserted the rose corsage; she studied herself in the mirror, feeling opulently sensuous herself, like the flower. She wanted Liam's hands on her, Liam's tongue plundering her mouth, Liam's cock driving sweetly up between her legs, opening up the petals of her sex to reveal rich, dark secrets like the heart of the rose.

She gazed at her reflection scornfully, despising herself for her dreams, because it seemed, from what Annie had let slip, that he was willing to bed anyone except her.

Suddenly she glimpsed the knickers Annie had brought for her, still fresh from their wrapping. The colour rose in her cheeks as she picked them up and fingered the cool satin. Impulsively she pulled them on; they were tight, almost like a firm harness around her still-swollen sex. She was silently shocked at the way the open crotch enclosed and thrust out the pink, lightly furred flesh of her sex, still wet with juices from Mark's cock. She felt hotly aroused again.

Swiftly she pulled down her dress, feeling the lewd black panties chafing like a delicious secret at her very heart.

She was making her way down the wide, curving staircase to meet the others for drinks before dinner when Liam joined her and put his hand lightly on her arm. The black dinner jacket he wore took her by surprise, made her pulse unsteady as if he were some

237

stranger, a stranger from a dream. 'It's going to have to be tonight,' he said quietly. At first, confused, she thought that he was talking about sex; but she quickly realised her mistake. 'Raoni's getting suspicious,' he went on. 'He's been asking questions about me, making calls. Tonight I'll have to confront him, and then I'll get the hell out. You don't mind? You won't be afraid of him when I've gone?'

She shook her head casually, even though her heart was still hammering at his nearness, at his touch. 'I'll say I don't know a thing about you,' she said. 'Which is pretty well true. I'll say I picked you up in a wine bar. I'll say that all I know about you is your first name. No, Liam, I won't be afraid of Raoni. But he could turn on you, before you can get away. You say you'll get the hell out, but how? Do you want me to drive you somewhere?'

She knew he'd arrived last night by taxi, from the station, because he didn't have a car. He said, 'No. The less involved you are, the better. Petro and Stevie are arriving for me at midnight. They'll provide back-up as well, in case things don't turn out.'

They'd been proceeding down the staircase, slowly; now Liam tightened his hold on her arm and said, 'Rebecca. In case I don't get the chance to say it again, thank you.'

'You're sure you'll be able to stop Raoni? You're sure it's worth the risk, confronting him in person?'

'I'm sure. After what I'm going to say to him tonight, he'll have his company backing out of the Hegley Wood development plan as fast as he can.'

'Send me a photo of the celebrations when all this is over,' she said.

'I've already given you a flower.' He lightly touched the rose at her breast.

So the flower was from Liam. Rebecca's skin burned as his hand, brown against the immaculate white cuff of his shirt, brushed against her skin. She realised how his face was very close to hers, how his eyes were shadowed with something she couldn't understand. She thought for one moment that he might be going to kiss her. But then a large group of Hortense's guests burst noisily into the hallway that spread out below them, and some more were coming down the stairs behind them.

It was time to move on, for dinner, and for the last moves of the game.

Chapter Nine

'So,' Hugh Raoni was saying in his smooth public-school drawl, 'we finished shooting when it started to get dark, and found some entertainment at the local pub instead.'

It was late in the evening. Hortense's house guests were gathered in various states of inebriation around the long mahogany table in the dining hall. Branched candelabra filled the room with flickering light, which was reflected in the gilt mirrors that lined the oak-panelled walls. The savoury scents of roast pheasant and beef braised in wine still lingered in the high-ceilinged room, though the main course was long since over. Quite a few of the less stalwart guests had already departed for bed, and all the servants had been dismissed, except for Hortense's little French butler Jacques and his one assistant, who kept reappearing with a wine decanter to replenish the guests' glasses.

They were all, without exception, hanging on Hugh Raoni's every word. 'Go on, then, Hugh,' said one of his friends. 'Tell us.' Francesca, the slender young model at Raoni's side, looked flushed with excitement. The candlelight burned at the heart of the exquisite diamond earrings she wore.

'There was a girl in the pub,' said Raoni, toying idly with his crystal wine glass. 'One of the beaters' daughters; she serves behind the bar. She was serving us with drinks, in the private room we'd booked. A plain, plump little thing: pasty face, appalling clothes.'

Francesca whispered, 'Hugh. Don't be cruel.'

'I'm not being cruel. It's true – she was wearing appalling clothes. Anyway, this girl obviously thought that James here was the most exciting creature on two legs she'd ever seen.' James, a distant relative of Hortense's who'd come without a partner, blushed. 'So,' went on Raoni, 'we plied this girl, Emma, with cheap cider, her favourite drink, and asked her if she wanted to shag James. Of course, she was quite speechless with excitement; and we got a pot together and bet James he wouldn't do it for a thousand pounds. James was drunk by now, as well –'

'Come on, Raoni,' said James, aggrieved. 'No worse than the rest of you.'

'So he said he would, for the money, but only if he could take her from behind, so he wouldn't have to see her ugly face.'

Some of the dinner guests roared. Hortense listened delightedly. This, Rebecca knew, was just the kind of thing she adored at her house parties. 'James, how cruel of you,' Hortense said in her husky French accent. 'So did you take her from behind? Did you ravish her little bottom?'

James grinned. 'That would be telling.'

'Then I'll tell,' said Raoni. 'For an extra five hundred, James said he'd do it so we all could watch. And he did. Remarkably well, in fact. Hortense, you would have loved the sight of his rampant cock diving in and out of the excited girl's plump arse. We could hear it, even, she was so damned wet for him.'

241

'Hugh,' said Francesca, 'enough.' But her exquisitely made-up eyes sparkled with excitement, and she nestled closer to Raoni's side.

Hugh Raoni held out his crystal goblet to the butler for more wine. 'Hortense doesn't mind,' he said. 'It's why she invites me. Your guests are expected to earn their keep, aren't they, Hortense?'

Rebecca toyed tensely with the remnants of cheese on her plate, and wondered if she and Annie next to her were the only people in the room to find Hugh Raoni, the man who'd told Max to finish with her, an intolerable bully. She wished Liam was at her side. He'd sat between her and Hortense for the main part of the meal and been a pleasant, if slightly distant companion. But he'd left a while ago, as if sated by the rich fare and increasingly decadent talk, to join some of the other men in the billiard room, and Rebecca had watched him go rather hopelessly, the ache in her heart echoed by the empty seat beside her.

She found herself more than once wishing that she hadn't invited him here at all. Soon, he would be dealing in his own way with Raoni, and the fear ran ice-cold through her veins at the thought, because Liam was on his own. His choice: but she was frightened for him.

With an effort, she dragged herself back to the conversation that Raoni had initiated. The avid talk was now of the afternoon's entertainment; of how James had pleasured the excited girl as she leant over the table of the private room at the back of the pub, her buttocks widespread to reveal her glistening sex while they all watched and drunkenly encouraged him. Afterwards, it emerged, the girl had willingly performed oral sex on several of the men in turn, happily taking their cocks in her mouth while she freed her plump breasts from her straining blouse and allowed them all to gaze their fill. Raoni was sitting back now in silence, letting them

242

relive every detail, while Francesca, who was obviously new to this kind of entertainment, listened with horrified delight.

'No,' she repeated, 'no, I don't believe it.' But Rebecca saw the gleam of excitement in her eyes. And Rebecca, too, was disturbed, for she could feel the tight encasement of her lewd satin panties ringing her sex, pressing the swollen petals of flesh together, chafing her. She shifted in her seat, suddenly hot and uncomfortable, and a little spasm of excitement, a warning, rippled lingeringly through her abdomen. Oh, God. She was as aroused, as shameless as the rest of them.

Hortense, their hostess, was lapping up the salacious details with open glee. 'So this girl, this girl from the pub, she had one man's cock in her mouth, while she pleasured another with her hand and let his semen spurt over her breasts?' she breathed in her smoky French accent. 'No, my friends. That is too wicked...' She snapped her jewel-laden fingers suddenly at her stony-faced little butler. 'More wine, Jacques. Bring us champagne as well. And I want to hear lots, lots more about your naughty games. But leave the innocent little Francesca alone, Raoni. See her blush. She is not very bright, is she? You make her shy.'

'She loves all this,' said Raoni calmly. 'Don't you, Francesca?'

The girl was silent, wide-eyed, her exquisite breasts rising and falling within the brief confines of her low-cut evening gown.

'Don't you?' he repeated.

'Yes,' she whispered. 'Oh, yes.'

'Francesca,' Raoni said. 'I want you to go to Hortense's butler, now, and suck his penis for him.'

The room was suddenly filled with a hot, delighted silence. Francesca coloured. 'I can't.'

'If you don't,' Raoni went on in the same steely voice, 'you might as well go home now. Run off back to

Mummy and Daddy. I'll spend the night with Annie instead. Annie will do whatever I say. Won't you?'

His dark eyes snapped across the room at Annie; Rebecca saw her friend go white, and saw Christopher at her side look as if he was about to leap to his feet. No, Rebecca pleaded silently, no, can't you see, Christopher, that's just what he wants? Oh, Annie, stay calm, please. Ignore him.

But there was no ignoring the way that Francesca, pale now and almost ethereally slender in her long black gown, had got up from her seat and was making her way across the room towards the butler Jacques, who stood as if transfixed.

He let out a soft groan when Francesca's exquisite fingers reached for his zip and pulled out the pale, snaking length of his cock. And when she sank to her knees in front of him and wrapped her lips round its rapidly thickening bulk, he began to tremble, and his eyes closed, as if in prayer. Francesca closed her long-lashed eyes and parted her beautiful mouth and began to suck, with long, engulfing strokes, up and down the hardening shaft, cradling his balls tenderly as she did so. The men round the table watched in restless envy, while the women gazed in disbelief as the beautiful Francesca, toast of the catwalks, obediently pleasured the transfixed little butler.

Rebecca felt her own lust reawakening treacherously at the sight of Francesca so willingly humiliating herself at Raoni's drawled command. The butler's penis was angry and red now; he was gripping Francesca's naked shoulders and starting to thrust dementedly as if he was on the verge of coming. Rebecca's nipples tightened with lust, and the juices of her vagina, already so well-lubricated by Mark's vigorous thrusting, began to run anew. The cunningly shaped open-crotch panties she was wearing seemed to have tightened almost cruelly round her sex, forcing her labia to protrude obscenely.

Her vulva throbbed with a secret pleasure that was almost painful. She leant forward to try to find some escape; but the movement sparked a renewal of liquid heat through her belly, almost sending her into orgasm. She gripped the edge of the table with her fingers, unable to drag her eyes from the sight of Jacques' lewdly pounding penis.

Then Raoni's oily voice was cutting into the silence once more. 'Let him come over your breasts,' he ordered Francesca. 'Like the slut this afternoon in the pub. Over your breasts. You hear me, Francesca?'

The girl's face was pale now, pale with humiliation. The butler, hearing every word, had pulled his rearing cock from her lips, and was watching eagerly as Francesca pulled down the flimsy straps of her evening gown. Her breasts, small and perfect, pouted upward; a low growl of appreciation seemed to run round the room at the sight. And then the butler was pushing his angry penis against her nipples, rubbing ferociously at his own shaft as the glossy purple tip swelled and burnt against the creamy flesh of Francesca's breasts, until he gave a low cry and his semen spurted, again and again, over the girl's rose-tipped crests. She moaned too, her cheeks flushing with excitement as his cock continued to ferociously assail her; she clutched his buttocks to her, engulfing his pulsing manhood with her breasts.

Annie, at Rebecca's side, gave a little sigh, and seemed to shift restlessly in her seat. Rebecca, turning, realised that her friend was caressing Christopher beneath the tablecloth; Rebecca could just glimpse the hot stem of his cock protruding from his trousers, could see Annie's fingers working busily, sliding the foreskin up and down, caressing the hot purple glans. Christopher's eyes were almost closed; he was in an agony of delight and shame. His penis was slim, but long and firm; Rebecca imagined it sliding up into her own moist sex, and her longing for release became almost unbearable.

Across the room, Jacques continued to rub his own penis tenderly against Francesca as the last of his seed was spent. Silence, the hot silence of desire, filled the candlelit room. James was leaning forwards, gazing at Francesca as if he would like to ravish her in front of all of them. It was Hortense who was the first to break that silence.

'Pour the wine,' she said softly to the pleasure-dazed butler. 'And I want you to tell me more stories of your adventures, my friends. Who will begin?'

Just then the door opened, setting the multitude of candles flickering in the sudden draught, and Liam stood there, outlined in the doorway, devastating in the dark formality of his dinner jacket. Rebecca almost felt the little shock waves of desire that ran through the female guests gathered around the table. Francesca, who was still on her knees with her head bowed, stirred at last and began to pull her sticky gown over her flushed bosom. The little butler slid back into the shadows, fastening himself up hastily before starting to pour the wine.

'Liam, my dear,' breathed Hortense. 'Why have you left us for so long?'

Liam smiled his lazy smile. 'I've been playing billiards.'

'But you have left poor little Rebecca looking quite desolate.'

'It's OK,' said Rebecca. 'I'm used to it, Hortense.' Which was true.

'Not good enough,' scolded Hortense. 'You must come and sit here, Liam, between me and Rebecca. And you must have more to eat. You left us before the meal was properly over.'

'Thanks, but I had enough to eat earlier.'

'Then you must drink, my dear.' She snapped her

fingers at the waiter, who'd been hurriedly sent by the butler for four bottles of champagne and some fresh glasses. 'Champagne, for Liam.'

'Thanks, but I don't drink.'

Raoni's voice cut into the silence. 'All in all, you're rather boring, aren't you, my working-class friend? You don't ride. You don't gamble. You left the shooting party early because you don't enjoy shooting. You don't pay much attention to Rebecca. You don't even drink. I wonder, why did Hortense invite you?'

Someone else, Rebecca thought it was James, brayed drunkenly and said, 'Well, the women don't seem to have any complaints about his appearance, Raoni. Can't take their eyes off him. Hadn't you noticed? Perhaps Hortense has brought him here as a stud, a working-class stud.' He grinned at his own jest and twisted round towards Liam, who had taken his place at Hortense's side. 'Am I right, my friend? How much does a woman have to pay you for a shag? Fifty? A hundred pounds?'

Liam sat back calmly in his chair with Rebecca on his left. She could feel the heat of his body. She longed for him. 'I don't know,' he said. 'You all seem to be the experts at money. What did they pay you for the performance this afternoon? A thousand pounds? Rather over-priced, I'd say.'

James looked suddenly angry, but some of the others were laughing. Then Liam swung round slowly: firstly to stare at Raoni, then to gaze at the flushed Francesca who was now seated again at his side. 'And how much does Raoni pay you, Francesca?' he said. 'How many diamond earrings does it take for a man to be able to humiliate you in public like that? What's your price, Francesca?'

Raoni was on his feet, and the mood changed to something dangerous. Rebecca suddenly felt the fear slicing through her, fear for Liam. She remembered Max saying casually, 'Raoni has his way of dealing with people who displease him.' And it was still only eleven: far too early for Petro and Stevie to be here, to help him.

Yet Liam, quite unfazed, was leaning forward with his elbows on the table, gazing round at them all, linking his strong hands together on the pristine table-cloth. 'It's a game, this money thing,' he said. 'Just a game, but an interesting one. My point, with which I think you'll all have to agree, is that we all have our price. You remember the film, where a woman is offered a million dollars to spend the night with a man she's never met before? Just one night? Well, I want you all to consider very carefully how much it would take to tempt each one of you to do something really, really dirty. And then I want you to tell us all about it.'

He grinned that sleepy grin that turned Rebecca's heart over. It would take nothing, nothing at all to let Liam take her here and now. But he didn't want her.

Raoni, forgotten by everyone else, sank back into his seat, but Rebecca noticed that his eyes still glittered with anger. Hortense, meanwhile, was enraptured. She gazed at Liam as if he were the answer to all her prayers.

'You start us off, Liam, darling,' she breathed huskily. 'You tell us what you would do for money.'

He smiled. 'No. You start, Hortense. I'm sure you've got plenty of ideas.'

Hortense drank a deep mouthful of freshly poured champagne and shivered with pleasure. 'You mean – if a man came up to me on the street, and asked me for sex, how much would he have to pay me? Oh, darling, I don't know. If he was as handsome as you, I'd do it for nothing. But if he was ugly – a fat businessman, for instance, oily and lecherous – then perhaps I would ask for five hundred pounds. It would make me feel exceedingly dirty, to know I was being paid. Would I take him to a hotel room, this man?'

'No,' said Liam. 'He's desperate for it, sweetheart.

And you're desperate, because you're so excited by the fact that he wants you so much. He wants to do it with you now, Hortense.'

Her eyes glittered. 'Then we would find a dark little street, a doorway, yes?'

'Yes. And then what would you do?'

She considered dreamily. 'I would let him run his hands up under my clothes. I would be wearing a tight, short little skirt, stockings and no knickers. I would let his stubby fat hands play with my sex, so his fingers were coated in my juices. Then I would feel for his cock, and I would bend to lick it; it would taste hot and musky, of male sweat. He would be kissing me desperately, jabbing at my mouth with his fat tongue; and then he would push me back against the wall, and ram his penis up me with huge, shuddering strokes, and I would come. How I would come, as he spent himself inside me . . .' Her face was rapt, her eyes shining. 'Then I would pull my skirt down, collect my five hundred pounds and walk away, with my juices still trickling down my legs.'

Rebecca could hardly bear it. Every time she moved, the tight bands of her panties chafed her melting sex. Her nipples pressed stiffly against the lace of her bra, longing for a man's hand, a man's mouth.

And then suddenly she felt Liam's warm strong hand sliding across her lap, beneath the heavily draped table-cloth. She almost jumped from her seat as his finger curled itself slowly into the cleft at the joining of her thighs and began to scratch lightly through the fabric of her dress at the pad of flesh just above her clitoris. A hot, liquid heat churned through her belly. She could feel the flush rising in her cheeks. Oh, God. If he carried on like this, she would come, in front of them all.

He turned to smile at her, a knowing private smile. He relaxed his stimulation to the merest touch, to the point where she simmered, aching with lust, desperate for penetration. His hand was still lightly caressing her as he turned, apparently all attention, to where another of Hortense's guests, a needle-thin, face-lifted woman called Marcia, held out her glass imperiously to the waiter for more champagne. 'I'd want more money than that,' she announced. 'I'd want a lot more. And if we were doing it like that, up some shabby alleyway, I'd want him to stick his cock up my arse; more appropriate, don't you think?'

'Uncomfortable,' shuddered another woman, excitement making her voice hoarse.

'Not if I moistened his lovely penis with my mouth until it was all slick and wet,' Marcia said quickly. Rebecca realised that she was rather drunk. Weren't they all – wasn't she – for this to be going on? 'After that, I'd let him bend me over, in this dark little side street, so he could lick my bottom with his fleshy tongue – delicious, Hortense! – and then he'd pull my bottom cheeks apart, and ease his throbbing cock up into my arse – long, slender, hard as iron – and I'd cry out in delight as he penetrated me, out there in the street.'

'What if someone came along and saw you?'

'I'd let him join in,' she breathed. 'A young sailor, perhaps. He could take me from the front. I'd crouch over him, and he could pump his vigorous prick into my vagina, while the other man ravished my arse. Oh, I would scream with joy.'

'How much?' said Liam. His hand still worked slowly, deliciously between Rebecca's legs. Each time she thought she could bear no more and was about to topple over the edge, he stopped, only to begin again, with more finesse than ever, until her molten nerve-ends were screaming for release. She was trembling, feverish; her hands shook on the table. She couldn't understand how no one could notice.

Marcia was pondering Liam's question, stroking her sharp chin with one scarlet-taloned finger. 'The fat businessman would have to pay me a thousand pounds. The young sailor, if he's handsome and strong, will also get a thousand pounds; because afterwards, while I watch, the businessman will fuck him as well. He'll bend the young sailor over on all fours and pull his tight bottom cheeks apart while he slides his stiff cock right up his arsehole. Then he'll pound away at him, loving the tight, clenching embrace of the young sailor's arse; and just before the end, he'll pull out, his face red with excitement, and cream all over him.'

There was a shocked silence, then low murmurs of appreciation. Liam's palm still firmly cupped Rebecca's heated sex, and Rebecca was beside herself. Just his finger would be enough, or his calloused thumb, ramming down into her soaking cleft, driving her over the edge. But, as if he knew, he kept his hand still.

Hortense was sighing with happiness. 'Extinguish the candles,' she ordered Jacques. 'The light from the fire, surely, is enough for a night such as this.' Then she turned a little, to assess who was left in the darkened room, and her eyes alighted on Annie.

'Annie, darling,' she breathed. 'You and your friend Rebecca usually have such wicked, wicked fantasies. Tell me one of them, do, and then tell me how much you would charge.'

Annie blushed hotly. Rebecca guessed it was probably because her hand was still on Christopher's turgid cock.

It was Hugh Raoni who broke the silence. 'Oh, Annie will do anything for free,' he said in his slow, drawling voice. 'All you've got to do is tell her you might be able to get her a part in a film, and she'll shag anything that moves, in any combination; although her preference is for the outsize and the exotic.'

Rebecca saw Annie tremble. Christopher was gripping the table, his youthful face tense with anger. But before he could do or say anything, Liam calmly poured wine for himself and Rebecca; and then he said clearly,

'And what about you, Raoni? What will you do for money? Shall I guess? Does anyone else want to guess?'

Rebecca felt cold, her arousal draining from her body. She looked at the clock. Half eleven. Half an hour till his friends arrived. Too early. Oh, too early.

Raoni was gazing at Liam speculatively, but the anger glittered in his dark eyes. 'Listen, my friend,' he said. 'I don't know who you are, or why you're here. You say you've come with her –' he nodded at Rebecca '– but I don't believe you. You don't speak to her, you don't sleep with her. You disappear at all hours of the day to make phone calls. I think you're spying on us. Or on me.'

Rebecca said quickly, 'It's not true; he is with me. I invited him.'

'Then why isn't he screwing you?' said Raoni softly.

Oh, I wish he would, thought Rebecca desperately. Beneath her gown, her sex gaped wide open within the confines of the tight crotchless panties she wore. She shut her eyes briefly, imagining Liam's lovely strong penis driving up between her silken walls, easing away the agony of longing, sliding in her slippery juices while she climaxed blissfully around him.

'Why isn't he screwing you?' repeated Raoni. He turned back to Liam. 'Listen, my friend. I'd like you to prove you're here for the party and nothing else. You come here laughing at us all with your barrow-boy manners. You insult us, try to make out that we're somehow for sale –'

'Well, aren't you?' said Liam.

Raoni said softly, 'I have friends within call, yob. Friends who'll make you sorry you ever started this little game of yours. Unless – and I'm giving you this one and only chance – unless you finish it.'

Their hostess Hortense was watching wide-eyed with excitement, hanging on to every word. 'Finish the game? What do you mean, Raoni?'

Raoni leant back in his chair. 'You came with her,' he said, pointing at Rebecca. 'You say you're with her, but I don't believe you.'

Rebecca said steadily, 'He is with me. I invited him. What more proof do you want?'

Raoni smiled. 'I want you to let him make love to you,' he said. 'Here, in front of us all. A fitting end to the game, don't you think? Afterwards I'll pay your working-class stud whatever we decide, as a group, that he's worth.'

A frisson of shock ran around the room. Hortense leant forward, rapt. Liam said, 'And if she refuses?'

'I told you, friend. I'll know then that you're lying, about being here as her lover. I'll know that you're a troublemaker of some kind, perhaps even some cheap journalist from the gutter press. I've got friends close by, friends who can be here to deal with you within minutes. I'll make you sorry.'

Liam said steadily, 'The girl's not for sale. I'll do whatever you want, but not with the girl.'

'Then I'll consider your bluff called.' Raoni was already getting out his phone.

Rebecca put her hand swiftly on Liam's arm. 'I'll do it,' she whispered. 'You need time. You must let me do it.'

Liam made no reply. Instead he gazed at Francesca, lolling at Raoni's side, her wide eyes dazed with champagne and excitement. 'I'll tell you what, Raoni,' said Liam. 'I've a proposition for you. Let Francesca have the butler; she was clearly longing for him earlier.'

Francesca looked excited. Raoni sat up sharply. 'What, here? Now?'

'Yes, why not? I don't think Francesca would object. Let's make it an evening to remember. Then, perhaps, Rebecca and I might decide to show you exactly why we're here together.'

Rebecca felt a spasm of excitement so strong that it

made her unsteady. To do it here, with Liam, in front of them all. Oh, yes. She could think of nothing more delicious. She turned to him, her eyes shining, every part of her body a gesture of assent. Liam smiled back at her.

And Raoni said, 'Very well. Francesca is very rapidly turning out to be a slut. Francesca, go ahead.'

Francesca looked very pale, but her eyes were shining. She got up slowly from her chair, and the little butler Jacques hurried towards her. He was much shorter than the girl, but the memory of his outsize cock was what everyone remembered; Francesca was already shivering beneath his eager fingers as he slipped her dress from her shoulders again and guzzled greedily at her rose-tipped breasts. Suddenly Francesca's eyes opened wide, as if she was realising, for the first time, what was going to happen.

'I can't, Hugh,' she cried out. 'I can't, in front of them all . . .'

But then Marcia, Hortense's thin-lipped avaricious friend, had moved quickly to Francesca's side. 'Of course you can,' she said sharply. 'You have an exquisite body, child. Enjoy it. Let us all enjoy it.'

And swiftly, with rapacious fingers, she undid Jacques's fly and drew out his member, rubbing it with her thin fingers until it reared almost grotesquely from his trousers. Then she took Francesca's trembling hand and drew up the girl's long skirt, so they could see her stocking-clad legs, her tiny knickers. While Jacques rubbed steadily at his own cock, gazing at the revealed treasures greedily, Marcia pulled down Francesca's panties. 'Naughty girl,' she said with disapproval. 'You're soaking wet already.' Then she dropped to her knees, caressing the girl's firm thighs all the while, and began to lick her sex.

Francesca was silent with shock. Then she cried out, leaning back against the wall for support, her hands clenching and unclenching. 'Oh,' she cried. 'Oh, my God.'

Raoni watched, a harsh smile of approval on his face as the older woman ravished the girl with her flickering long tongue. Marcia was clearly loving every minute; so was everyone else as they watched. Francesca seemed to shake with pleasure as Marcia's greedy mouth sucked at her pudenda and the tip of Marcia's tongue lashed wickedly in and out of her cleft. Jacques stood patiently waiting, rubbing his huge cock; his balls trembled tightly at the base of his shaft.

'Not too much, *madame*,' he murmured warningly. 'Not too much. Save some of her sweetness for me.'

The lewdness of the scene seemed to have sent everyone else in the room over the edge of restraint. Annie was gazing at them hot-faced; but her own gratification was imminent as Christopher's hand rucked up her dress and worked its way between her thighs, rubbing hungrily at her slick wetness. Hortense had pulled James down beside her, and had let him slip his hands inside her gown, so he could squeeze her erect nipples; she was starting to fumble rather desperately for his cock. But the main attraction was Francesca. Rebecca watched in an agony of lust as Marcia finally drew her face, wet with female juices, from between the girl's thighs. She held open the girl's dark pink labia, spreading them wide. Francesca was panting, moving her head from side to side, playing frantically with her breasts. 'Do it,' she begged Jacques. 'Do it, for God's sake.'

The little butler strutted towards her, his distended cock at the ready. He was just the right height. Marcia moved out of his way, and with a triumphant cry he drove his thick penis right up into Francesca's open vagina, gripping her buttocks tightly as he did so. His face was a picture of delight.

Francesca cried out, clasping him to her, gasping with

pleasure. 'More,' she gasped. 'Harder. Oh, do it to me, please.'

The butler huffed and puffed, drawing out his cock so they could all see its stiff, juicy length. Then he rammed it back into her; and Marcia, watching the girl's tormented face, bent to take her rose-tipped breasts in her mouth, licking and biting as Francesca moaned out her pleasure. Rebecca watched transfixed as the butler's lusty penis rammed into her again and again. She watched as Francesca cried out wildly, then went very still and began to whimper with pleasure, her cries going on and on as the butler and Marcia lovingly tended her.

Hortense was on her knees now, eagerly licking James' cock. Annie was trembling into orgasm as Christopher rammed his fingers up inside her vagina. Some of the others had slid away into the shadows around the room, to slake their own lust; the room reeked of arousal, of sex.

Only Raoni and Liam seemed immune. Raoni was watching Francesca with scorn etched on his face. After a while he turned to Liam. 'Well?' he said. 'I hope you've not forgotten our bargain, friend.'

Rebecca turned quickly towards Liam, her pulse racing, her body an agony of need. Liam looked down at her. He said quietly, 'It's all right. We don't have to. It's all right.'

She shook her head fiercely, half-laughing, half-crying. 'Oh, God, Liam. Don't turn me down now. Do it to me. Do it, please.' She saw that his eyes, as he looked at her, were blazing with desire. She felt suddenly, dizzily happy.

'Let's give Raoni something to remember us by, shall we?' he said.

She reached for her full glass of champagne and drank it down. 'A game.' She smiled up at him. 'The best game ever.'

Then Liam's powerful kiss as he took her in his arms shut out everything else for her. He slid his tongue hard inside her mouth and she clung to him, feeling the needlepoints of desire assaulting her breasts, her loins. He released her from the kiss at last, but his arms were still round her, and his gaze still held her, so that she felt drowned by his sleepy blue eyes. His warm hands slipped to her waist, cradling her close.

'I want you,' he said. 'I want you to give yourself to me.'

Slowly Rebecca pulled down the straps of her dress and offered her breasts to him. The rose fell to the floor. Tenderly, with one hand, he released her breasts from her bra's little half-cups of satin and lace. Her rosy nipples puckered in delight at his sure touch, and a low sigh of arousal ran around the darkened room, exciting Rebecca still further. The butler had finished now with Francesca, and they were all watching her, all breathless, greedy with silent lust. Their jealousy turned her on more than she could ever have dreamt.

'Take my breasts, Liam. Take them in your mouth,' she whispered.

He bent his head to suck at her breasts, drawing the jutting crests into his mouth, lengthening them and swirling at them with his hot wet tongue until the shafts of pleasure darted almost unbearably throughout her body. Her sex was wet and wanton within the tightness of her lewd panties; her labia tingled with arousal, and a slow insistent pulse beat in her womb, desperately hungry for penetration. Rebecca threw her head back, closing her eyes as she offered her breasts to Liam, knowing that every man in the room wanted her, and loving the feeling of power. Every man in the room would be gazing at Liam's tongue on her hard coral nubs, and every woman would be envying her.

Slowly she hooked one long leg over a chair. 'I'm ready for you to fuck me, Liam,' she said quietly.

He drew back just for a moment to prepare himself, but his eyes never left her face. Oh, God, she wanted him so badly. Quickly she pulled up her skirt and heard a low collective gasp as everyone saw the obscenity of her knickers, which thrust out her swollen pudenda for everyone to see, to delight in. Then, with one leg still hoisted over the chair so that her sex was spread wide, she began to fondle the juicy folds of her vulva, caressing them, parting them, feeling their sweet honey flowing freely over her fingertips. She pressed her forefinger hard against her wide-open vagina, shivering with delight at the knowledge of the penetration to come. The rose. Ah, the dark heart of the rose.

Liam was ready for her. From the dark discretion of his formal clothing, his penis reared up, shocking yet magnificent in its strength. As if from a great distance away, Rebecca heard the other women sighing with longing. She thought, too, that she heard Hortense give a lascivious little moan, and she saw that Marcia, still standing next to the naked Francesca, was masturbating openly; but none of them mattered. Liam was hers. All hers.

Still rubbing slowly at the throbbing pearl of her clitoris, spreading her legs wide so he could see how ready she was for him, she reached out her hand to his shoulder to draw him nearer, and lifted her face for his kiss again. This time his mouth on hers was openly demanding; she shuddered at the assault of his tongue, and heard herself cry out at another onslaught as the blunt head of his cock rested briefly at the entrance to her vagina then slid strongly and deeply in. The stimulation of her panties, and of his fingers earlier, had already raised her to a plateau of lust that made the force of his hard flesh within her so exquisite that she almost came.

'Oh, God,' muttered Rebecca, clenching herself

around the impalement. 'That is so beautiful. Just keep doing it to me, Liam. Please.'

He held her strongly, steadying her as she shook with desire. His powerful penis drove up into her again and again as she moaned his name. Her vagina felt impossibly tight and wicked within the confines of her panties. She arched her head back, offering her breasts to him; he suckled them with fierce tenderness, sending shafts of pleasure-pain down to join the growing furnace of heat at her loins. She braced herself against the pounding of his cock, almost delirious with pleasure as she felt its steely strength filling her, stretching her silken walls. Once, as he paused to steady her with his firm hands, she glanced down and saw the thick dark root gliding in her nectared flesh, which protruded obscenely from the tight black satin; she smiled, catching her breath with delight.

Liam whispered in her ear, 'You like seeing that, Rebecca? You like seeing my cock driving into you, driving you wild? You feel so good, Rebecca. Tight, and sweet, and trembling with pleasure. This is just for you, sweetheart, just for you. Hold on to me.'

Already almost faint with the tingling pleasure that flooded her veins, she clasped her arms round his wide shoulders, feeling the faint stubble of his lean jaw deliciously rasping her cheek. Then she felt him withdraw his penis almost to its tip, so that she cried out, missing him desperately. But then he was sliding into her forcefully again, filling her with blissfully hard male flesh, and his fingers were down there too, wickedly stroking the side of her swollen clitoris, and she was over the edge, spasming without control around his steel-hard shaft, feeling the contractions of lust shake her entire body as the most excruciating orgasm she had ever known tore through her. She cried out again and again as Liam's thick penis thudded into her; she felt every tremor of his powerful body as he too climbed towards his climax. And then it was over, except for the little after-shocks of pleasure that still shook her helpless body as he continued to caress her. Then he was holding her tenderly, stroking her hair as he pressed her cheek against his shoulder. She felt glad to have given him this, to have shared this with him. Glad, defiant and proud.

In the distance, as if in some hazy dream, Rebecca heard the grandfather clock in the hallway strike twelve. She pulled herself away from him and smiled up into his eyes.

'Perfect timing, Liam,' she whispered.

He lifted her hand and kissed it, and his eyes blazed down at her.

Slowly the other guests intruded on her consciousness. It was as if they'd all, every one of them, been holding their breath for the final act; as if they'd been waiting for that moment of release. And now she could almost hear them relaxing, concealing the evidence of their lust, sighing a little as if they were regretting that they hadn't been a part of what Liam and Rebecca had shared.

Hortense was already offering rapturous praise to Liam, her eyes fastened greedily on him as he gently released Rebecca and proceeded, with the utmost casualness, to rearrange his clothes. Rebecca, who had already eased her dress back over her bosom and smoothed her skirt down again over her hips and her thighs, sank serenely back in her chair. She was still warm from Liam's embrace.

It was Annie who put her feelings into words as she poured a glass of champagne and pushed it towards her friend. 'Well done, Becs,' she whispered. 'The ultimate fantasy, perhaps?'

Hortense, whose clothing was neatly rearranged but whose mouth was still red from caressing James' cock, was saying in a rather breathless voice, 'Well. We know

now, I think, why Rebecca invited this young man to our party, don't we?'

Only Raoni's face was cold. He said, 'Capably done, my friend. You could clearly make money out of that sort of thing. Perhaps you already do. A working-class gigolo.' He reached inside his jacket for his wallet. 'How much? What's your price, I wonder, for a floor show like that? Five hundred? A thousand?'

Rebecca was suddenly aware that Liam was gazing at Raoni, confronting him with open scorn. A renewal of fear trickled down her spine, driving away the warmth of sated lust.

Now must be the time.

Liam said, 'I thought I told you. I'm not for sale. How about you, Raoni?'

Hugh Raoni laughed, but his teeth showed, as if he was snarling. 'I've no need, I think, to sell myself.'

'No?' said Liam softly. 'Then I must have made a mistake. Because I was under the impression that you would sell your soul to the devil himself. For money, naturally; or, even better, for a good, thick slice of woodland, with planning permission for a road, houses, shops –'

Raoni was already moving towards him, an expression of absolute fury on his face.

Liam stood very still. 'You really want everyone to hear this?' Liam said. 'All of it?'

Raoni stopped in his tracks. 'Outside,' he muttered at last. His skin was drawn very tightly over the bridge of his nose, over his sharp cheekbones. 'You will talk to me outside, my friend, and tell me what all this stupid nonsense is about.'

Liam lifted his shoulders in a shrug, casual as ever. 'Whatever you say.' He followed Raoni out of the room, turning only once, to smile at Rebecca.

The room erupted noisily. Francesca was distraught, thinking that they would fight. Hortense was bubbling with excitement, and all the other guests were busy with their own kinds of conjecture. Except for Annie and Rebecca. Annie was unusually quiet, and looked anxious. Rebecca sat motionless, scarcely able to breathe. Please, let Petro and Stevie be here by now, to take him safely away. Please.

'What's going on?' James was protesting drunkenly. 'Dear God, the man was on about trees and roads. At a time like this. Can't we change to another topic? The one we were on earlier, preferably?'

Hortense gurgled with delight. 'Of course. More champagne for everyone, I think. And we need more entertainment, more games, to keep us all happy while Raoni and Liam settle their business outside.'

There were quick nods, and murmurs of agreement. Glasses chinked as they were lifted for more champagne, and faces turned greedily in search of more lascivious matters. Rebecca shook her head as the bottle came round; she twisted her glass nervously in her hands, her ears straining for any sounds from outside the room.

Annie leant forward suddenly, a little smile playing at the corners of her mouth. 'Let's play the fantasy game,' she said. 'You know my fantasy game, Hortense? I'll start. It's past midnight, and I'm all alone, in a little cottage by the sea, miles from anywhere. There's been a storm, but now all is quiet. Except for a knock at the door . . .'

But Rebecca wasn't even listening. Because she'd heard the faint thud of the big front door closing, and the sound of a car's tyres crunching on gravel as it made its way slowly down Hortense's long drive towards the road. A moment later Raoni came in alone, looking angry, shaken and defeated. Rebecca knew then that Liam had done what he had come to do, and had gone out of her life for ever.

Goodbye, Liam, she said silently to herself.

* * *

262

The love duet faded at last, and the curtains glided across the stage, none too soon for Rebecca. She shifted uncomfortably in her seat as the applause exploded around her. Another act to go. How could she bear it?

Max stood up beside her, stretching his legs in the confines of their private box. 'Puccini,' he said. 'No one to beat him. Divine.'

Rebecca guessed he'd actually been thinking stock market prices all the way through, but she said nothing.

'Drinks,' he said, rubbing his hands. 'I'll fetch the champagne; it's already ordered. Fifteen minutes to go before the last act. It will give us a chance to talk about your little business. You really should make sure all your employees are fidelity-bonded, you know. And there are a few points about employment law I'd like to flag up . . .'

'Yes, Max,' said Rebecca. 'Champagne, you said?'

He strode purposefully to the door, closing it behind him, and Rebecca was left alone in the warm privacy of the box. She wished she hadn't come. When Max had rung her the other day out of the blue, to tell her he'd heard how well her business was doing, and ask if he would like some financial advice, she'd been at a low ebb. So she'd foolishly agreed; and Max, magnanimously suggesting an evening at the opera, moved in on her again like a bailiff on a dispossessed house.

Except Rebecca didn't want him in her life.

That was the trouble with any sort of vacuum, she thought. People were always trying to fill it. And there had been a massive vacuum, a black hole even, in the region of her heart since that night a month ago when Liam had made glorious love to her, then confronted Raoni and disappeared into the night.

After Liam's departure, she'd been scared, briefly, of Raoni, and scared for Annie – surely Raoni would connect what Liam knew about Charles Kerrick with Annie? – but when Raoni moved in on her to ask her questions about Liam, she'd been able to reply truthfully, sadly, 'I hardly know anything about him. And I shouldn't think I'll ever see him again.'

Well, she'd been right about that as well.

For a few days, the newspapers and TV bulletins had carried the news that the anonymous business consortium had withdrawn abruptly from the Hegley Wood project, saying that it wasn't really a profitable proposition after all.

She'd kept the rose Liam had given her until it disintegrated before her eyes. Max had given her a flower to wear tonight: a garish orchid without scent, without soul. Typical of Max. She sighed, running her fingers through her hair, remembering.

Suddenly she realised that the lights were dimming and the musicians were poised for action. Strange: no Max, no champagne.

Feeling piqued, she leant forward in her chair and tried to concentrate as the curtains glided back for the final act. She heard the door to the box open very quietly, heard footsteps, but she didn't turn. A hand touched her shoulder; she shook her head, still gazing at the stage. 'I don't want champagne, Max. You have it.'

And then a voice, not Max's, said, 'It's not champagne. I don't like champagne. Remember?'

She whirled round, almost knocking over her chair. It was Liam. He was lowering himself on to Max's empty seat, casually balancing two just-opened bottles of beer. He was dressed in a dark formal suit; but the effect was rivetingly counterbalanced by the fact that his tie was slung loosely round his unbuttoned collar; and his hair, though shining clean, looked as if he'd just got out of bed.

She couldn't do anything but smile. 'Beer would be fine. Just fine,' she whispered. 'Liam, I didn't think I'd ever see you again.'

He handed her the beer, his eyes never leaving her face. 'Raoni. He left you alone? You and Annie?'

'Yes. Oh, yes.' The sheer gladness of seeing him was bubbling inside her. 'He didn't seem to connect what you knew, what you told him, with me and Annie.'

'How do you know what I told him?'

She was puzzled. 'Why, you told him, of course, about Kerrick and those photos . . .'

'No, I didn't,' he said.

'No? But I thought – that was why you came to Hortense's –'

'I had plenty of stuff, eventually, to frighten him, to make him back off. But it wasn't what you and Annie gave me. No – it was information I was getting from a dizzy but enthusiastic little secretary who works for a road-building firm. Her name's Charlotte, and we've a lot to be grateful to her for.'

She gazed at him numbly. 'Then – why did you come to Hortense's?'

'Firstly,' he said, 'because it offered me the best chance I was likely to have, to get Raoni on his own, in a relatively vulnerable position.'

She hung her head. 'I thought we were helping. But you were just using us.'

He put his warm strong hand quickly on hers. 'You haven't heard me out yet. Reason number two: I needed to see you again. I needed to talk to you again.'

'Why?' Her heart was beating painfully as his fingers tightened over her hand.

'I wanted to see if I could compete with bloody Max.'

She turned rather wildly, not quite absorbing what he'd said. 'Max. Where is Max?'

He shrugged, and she saw the familiar glint in his eye. 'God knows. I got a message taken to him at the bar, to say his car had been broken into at the underground car park; so he rushed over there straightaway. Priorities.'

Rebecca suppressed a giggle. 'Liam. Oh, I've missed you.'

'And I you,' he said simply.

People from neighbouring boxes were turning to glare at them; Rebecca hung her head, feeling that everyone would see the overwhelming, almost embarrassing elation that filled her. She wanted him so badly. She wanted this to be over, wanted to get outside with him, laugh with him, touch him, see if he was real.

'Christ, I hate opera,' said Liam, finishing off his beer.

She nodded. 'So do I.'

'Let's go.'

'We can't. We'll disturb everyone.'

'Then we'll have to pass the time a little more pleasantly, won't we?'

'How?' she whispered.

'This,' he said, putting down his bottle, and cupping her face in his hands, and kissing her with a deep, toe-curling kiss that had her heart thumping with joy.

And then, just as she was drawing breath, trying to calm her racing pulse, she felt his lovely strong hand on her thigh, sliding up over her lace-topped stocking, gently stroking the bare smooth skin beneath her skirt. 'Liam. No . . .'

'Why not?' he whispered. 'No one can see.'

It was true. The darkness of the box, the barrier around them, ensured waist-high privacy at least. Rebecca still tried, half-heartedly, to protest; but then his purposeful fingers had found their way under the gusset of her panties, and his thumb was exploring the plump flesh-folds of her sex, sliding deliciously into her cleft until she was jumping on the edge of her seat.

'Liam. Don't –'

But as usual, he took no notice whatsoever of her. Instead, with his free hand, he drew her into a kiss that melted the last of her resistance; then his forefinger started stabbing deliciously at her vagina, and her thighs slid apart wantonly as her juices flowed over his hand.

'I want you,' he whispered. 'I want to fuck you so badly. But for the moment, this will have to do.'

Her body flushed and tensed with the heat of her arousal. Her breasts grew heavy, her nipples hard. All the time his fingers probed her: two, now, driving up and down into her nectared love-passage. She clamped herself around them, on a sweet knife-edge of approaching pleasure, half-lifting her clenched bottom from her chair. And then he was stimulating the bud of her clitoris with the fleshy pad of his thumb, still fucking her with his fingers, wriggling them deep inside; and she was arching in delight, clinging to his wide shoulders as her orgasm wrenched through her. 'Oh, God, Liam. Oh, God . . .'

With a crash of brass and woodwind, the orchestra erupted into the heroine's death-scene. Rebecca writhed greedily on the penetration of Liam's fingers, her breath coming in noisy, sighing sobs. He held her, kissed her, pleasured her until it was over. She lay, wanton and wide open, like a slut in his powerful arms, and she adored it. She could smell the scent of her own sex-juices on his hand. She knew that Liam wouldn't mind, that he would adore her shamelessness too.

'Just a few minutes to go,' murmured Liam in her ear. 'What were you and blue-chip Max going to do after the performance?'

She blushed. 'Les Sauvages. But I don't want to go there, Liam, not tonight.'

'You're hungry, though, aren't you?'

'Starving. Absolutely starving.'

'I know a wonderful greasy spoon in Clerkenwell. Eggs. Sausages. Beans. Tomatoes.'

'Chips?' Rebecca's eyes had lit up. 'Real chips?'

'Oh, yes. The best. We'll have everything.'

'And then,' she whispered, 'you'll come back to my place?'

'Most definitely yes,' he said softly.

The music was fading, the curtain slowly falling.

He kissed her again, and the applause exploded wildly around them.